BEFORE THE STORM

a novel

MARIA RIGOU

ISBN 9798988205715

Developmental Editor: Katie Wolf, www.thekatiewolf.com

Editor: Bobbi Maclaren, www.authorbobbimaclaren.com/editing

Cover art & design: Eri Ikuno, @ilustraeris

AUTHOR'S NOTE

Before the Storm is a story that takes place in the fictional town of Tres Fuegos, in the province of Córdoba, Argentina. Although this town does not exist in real life, it was inspired by a real place. Many of the cultural and societal aspects depicted in this novel are unique to this country.

Please be aware that this novel contains topics that could be uncomfortable for some readers. These include but are not limited to mentions of death of a relative (although not explicitly on page), toxic familial relationships, mentions of grief, fears and mental health issues, vulgar language, and consensual sexually explicit content.

Read with care.

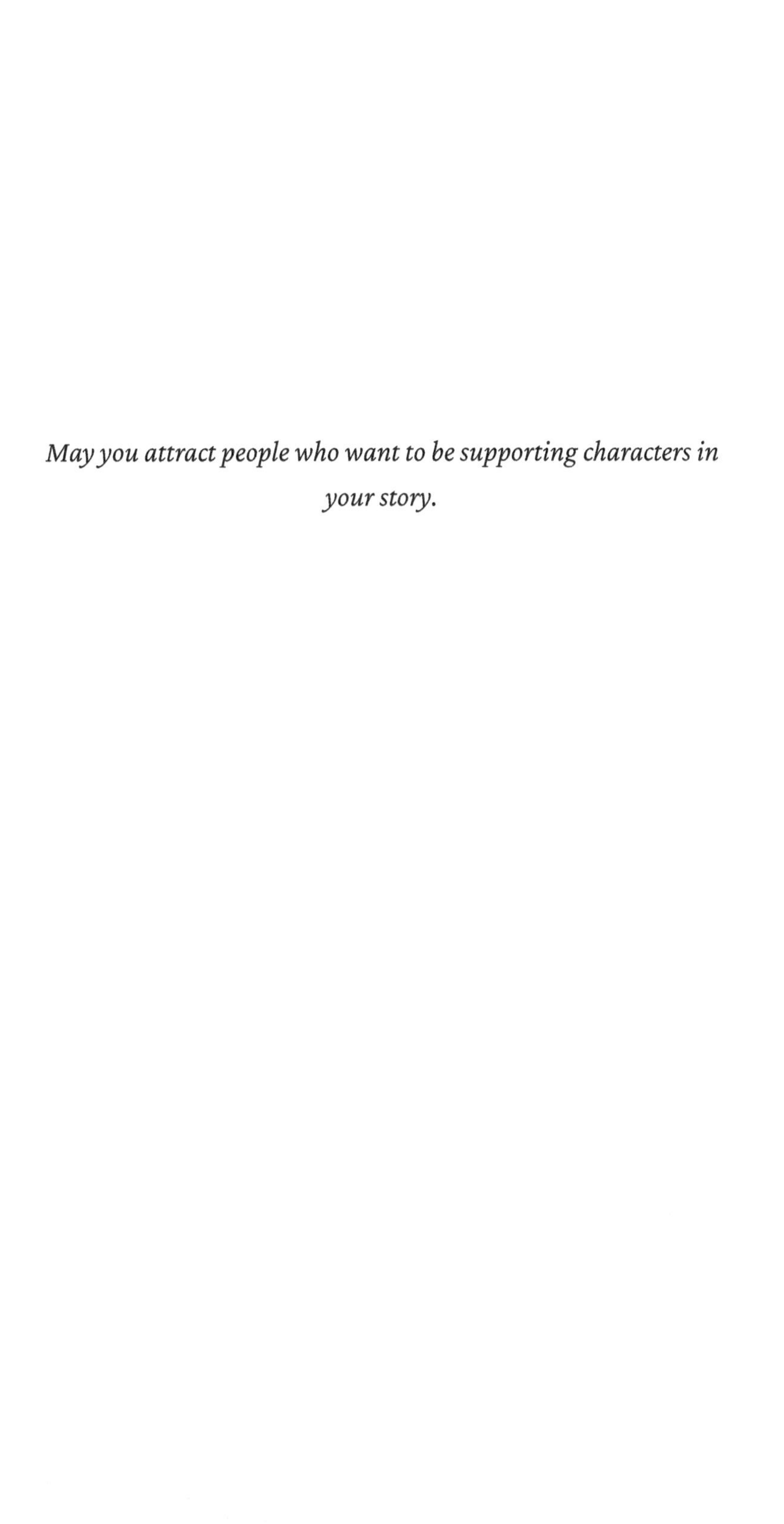

May you attract people who want to be supporting characters in your story.

1

LUCÍA

Not a question. A bold statement. And it was coming from somewhere behind my head, so far that I had to squint my eyes to see if I was hearing correctly. Not that the sense of hearing would be enhanced by narrowing my sight at the wall in front of me, but... yeah. I thought I was making sense. At least in my head, I did.

"Huh?" I turned around, completely confused by whatever was going on in my own office. Valentina was leaning against the door frame, chewing her gum loudly and twirling a lock of auburn hair that had fallen out of her messy bun between her fingers.

"I've been talking to you for, like, five minutes, Lu," she said, moving into the office and immediately jumping on the exam table. She was wearing bright pink scrubs, a specific set that she usually reserved for gloomy days because they made her feel happy. "What's going on?"

It was like time froze. As if we were in the eye of a storm, and everything was moving in slow motion. I was hyper-aware of my surroundings: the door to the cabinet where we stored our gloves and masks sitting a little askew, the paint chipping around the hardware where it had been pulled day after day in our practice.

"Lucía," she repeated, her brown eyes wide.

I blinked a few times to try and focus on her. I coughed quietly and swallowed. The only thing I could distinctly hear was the beating of my heart, comparable to how it felt when I used to go for runs back in the day. "Sorry, spaced out for a minute." I gave her a weak smile, but she didn't return it. She was on to me, because these things, these blips, were happening more and more in recent weeks. And this time, it was a patient file that had the same last name. That was all it took.

Flatline.

The constant beep had been singed into my brain since that night many moons ago. Despite the fact that years had passed since that moment. Despite the fact that I moved back to my hometown to get away from it all. Despite the fact that my direction changed, my ambitions reduced. Which was fine. Absolutely fine.

But every December, as we inched closer to the date, I went back to her. To the time when she died alone in her room, with unfamiliar faces around her.

I took a deep breath and walked towards my desk, wincing at the amount of stuff covering the tabletop. It was almost the end of the year, and the practice would soon close so that the staff of two—Valentina and I—could take some time off for the summer.

We had a handful of regular patients, but the practice was growing, and some families from the neighboring towns started coming over with their children, and what was once a dull and *normal*—in every sense of the word— office was now a colorful and cheerful place. The previous summer, Valentina and I had done a sloppy job painting the walls, adorning them with mediocre drawings of animals that our patients seemed to love. The corner of the waiting room featured an assortment of colorful children's books and toys, and for some reason, the collection kept growing, despite us not investing a single cent in new stuff during the year.

"Okay," she said, her eyes squinting in my direction, apparently not believing a single word that was coming out of my mouth.

I started hanging out with Valentina when I first moved back to Tres Fuegos three years before, after finishing my pediatrics residency at a big hospital in Buenos Aires. I heard through the rumor mill—fine, my parents—that Dr. Martín was getting ready to retire, so I took it as a sign from the universe that I needed to go back to my hometown. I blamed it on the sounds and smells of the big city. I claimed a bad breakup, a boyfriend who couldn't deal with the rhythms of my career, and so he bailed. But that wasn't entirely true.

Although I *would* tell anyone who would listen that there was nothing like the smell of this town after a rainstorm passed by in the middle of the summer. The rain in the city never hit the same, and it made me homesick. So I returned and slowly but surely made a name for myself.

The town was small, still, despite new people and the younger crowds returning to make a life here after they were away for college. Like Lourdes, one of my close friends from high school, who was moving back next spring and was going to work for my brother Santiago at the inn. Or, for example, in Valentina's case, ending up here because of her family issues.

I looked up and saw her studying my face. I was clutching the tablet in my hand, my knuckles going white at the effort. Nowadays, closer to that date, it didn't take much to make me remember. It happened every year like clockwork.

"What?" I said abruptly. I pinched my eyelids tightly and rubbed them with my hand, taking long, deep breaths to calm myself down. *Five, four, three, two, one.* Deep breath.

I could feel my hand holding on to that tablet for dear life, and I could hear my friend's consistent breathing in front of me. I opened my mouth to say something, then thought better of it. For a flash of a second, I felt like screaming at her for no apparent reason. Maybe just in irritation. "Sorry," I mumbled.

Valentina shook her head and scowled. She wasn't used to my irritability. Because outwardly, I was bubbly, like most of my brothers. But today, my patience was thin. As a matter of fact, this month, it was nonexistent. This year needed to end, fast.

"*Nada.* Calm down, crazy," she said with a freaking tone. I knew exactly which one because that was how she talked to some of the more *extra* parents at the practice. Those who felt that their children should be the priority over others.

I rolled my eyes and took a big breath, letting it all go quickly. "Fine. How can I help you, dear?"

"*Bueno, tampoco para tanto,*" she replied with a big smile on her face. She had the eerie ability to let things go immediately, not holding on to anything that really didn't matter. She never got angry, and it was incredibly annoying. She reminded me so much of my youngest brother, who just existed on vibes alone, and the guy got shit done. Exhausting. "Your mom called." She looked at her nails, then looked up at me, blinking a few times like she was expecting a response from me.

I blinked.

She blinked back. "She wanted me to remind you that—"

I furrowed my brows. "Why would I need reminding? I live there." I turned and dropped the device on the desk and moved some things around so that it was buried under the largest pile of paperwork the tabletop could handle.

"*No sé,*" she added, her legs moving in a specific rhythm

that was starting to increase my heart rate. She jumped off the table and stood straight, her nose going up in the air as she spoke. "Anyway, you have three more patients today, and then you are free to go. Your mom said that Victoria was getting ready at the big house, and she was walking there from work at around four if you wanted to join them."

I looked at her with my most impatient look. She knew it well, so she immediately raised her hands and said, "What? I'm just giving you your messages!"

"Whatever," I huffed. I couldn't help but smile at her as she walked back to her desk, her fingers tucking that loose strand of hair into her bun.

"Valen?" I muttered as I stood, gathering my things into my purse. I walked outside my office, and she was sprawled on her desk, scrolling mindlessly on her phone. It was one of her most annoying habits, but I shrugged it off because she did a good job. "Ready?"

She looked up at me. "Yep," she said. "I'll see you tonight."

I stepped out of the office and squinted at the bright sunlight, adjusting to the change in lighting. It was hot and humid, the kind of weather that made everything feel sticky all over. I squared my shoulders and started walking towards my parents' home a few blocks away from my office.

I was supposed to only stay with my parents for a few months after I moved back and then move into Santiago's newly purchased home, until he decided to move back from the city and settle in our town. He had been smart about the whole house thing and prepared for when he would eventually move back, taking a role at our family's law firm. And I would "house-sit" until the time came. But Victoria—his now fiancée—suddenly showing up in Tres Fuegos put a wrench in his plans, and mine. So I was stuck with them. It wasn't bad, but it wasn't ideal. Nothing in my life really was —nothing was as I planned, but it still worked out. I had a job, a stable career, and a place to live. What else would I want?

The streets were busy with people resuming their activities after stopping everything for the sacred *siesta*. That was the issue with small towns—things never changed. And this was one thing that hadn't changed at all in decades, even as the population got younger. It was a weird phenomenon, how we all ended up back at home despite moving away for college to the big city and getting to experience that for a few years.

I turned the corner onto my parents' street, and I saw people moving from that far out. Their house sat at the end of a cul-de-sac, the yard extending hundreds of meters and ending where the hillside started. My hometown was certainly something out of a movie, the rolling hills changing colors with the seasons. But this season was by far my favorite, not only because of what was going on, but because it just felt... different. Magical. Not in the literal sense, but in the more whimsical way.

My brother's wedding was going to be an intimate affair in the backyard of our parents' home, with close family members and some friends in attendance. This meant upwards of one hundred people because our close family members were too many to count. And Victoria had gone all out, with the festivities extending for about a week and different things to do around town in the lead-up to the actual wedding.

"Ma?" I yelled as soon as I stepped into the foyer, closing the door behind me with a loud bang and dropping my things on the floor. "*¿Dónde están?*"

I could hear noises coming from the kitchen, where they were setting up for food. The welcome dinner was tonight, intended for a few out-of-town guests to mingle with the bride and groom and their families.

"*¿Mamá?*" I called again. There was a lot of movement around the house, and I could hear sounds coming from every corner. Our mom had had the interior of the house repainted a few months ago, the moment Victoria even hinted at having the wedding here. She loved her future daughter-in-law—and she made my brother so happy that it was inevitable to bend over backwards for her. "Are you upstairs?"

I headed up the stairs, straight into my bedroom. The room was filled with nostalgia and a sense of familiarity, and it looked almost identical to the day I'd left for medical school. The walls were painted in a soothing shade of pale blue, complemented by white furniture and delicate lace curtains that fluttered gently in the summer breeze. The only thing that had changed was the bed—swapped kindly by my mother for a bigger size when I moved back home. The last rays of sun filtered through the window, casting a warm glow on the room. And the smell of jasmine that I loved so much—but was bittersweet during this time of year—wafted in, reminding me of other times.

I sank onto the bed, the comfort enveloping me like a warm embrace, but exhaustion finally hit me hard. The end of the year was rough on my body. Parents came into the office to bring their kids like it was the end of the world. Friends wanted to have dinner and nights out, as if the first day of the new year were a future that was so unknown that *we better see each other!* just in case. It was chaotic, normally. And this year, a little bit more so because of the wedding. But that didn't matter because we were all very happy for them anyway, and no one could be bitter about it.

Least of all me, the blonde, upbeat girl who knew all the town's secrets. I almost felt like I wanted to roll my eyes at myself. Maybe even growl in frustration—who knew. I couldn't put a finger on it, but there was an underlying sense of annoyance at myself. Perhaps it was because as the years went by, I couldn't shake off the feeling of being stuck. Despite the exciting things happening to everyone around me, I was just not there, instead stuck in a cycle of grief and routine. I was annoyed at that because I was starting to feel that I couldn't keep myself afloat amidst this storm that was brewing. And I was drowning.

2

LUCÍA

Just as I was about to fall asleep, a knock on the door startled me. "Come in," I called out, my voice carrying a touch of weariness. I had been looking forward to the wedding for months, but I was exhausted, and I needed to stop or otherwise I would burn out. It had happened once before.

"Lucía," my father, Carlos, said. He walked into the room, carrying my purse in his hands and moving slowly to the far end, then depositing the heavy bag on the corner chair. His tone was stern, reminding me of when we were teenagers and he would walk into the house after work and trip over all our things. "You need to remember to bring your things to your room."

I nodded tightly at him instead of screaming. I was an adult, but this man kept treating me like a child in his house.

I understood where he was coming from, but not even my youngest brother was receiving this treatment.

"Did you wash your hands?"

I closed my eyes and took a big breath. "I'm headed to the shower now," I said quickly, hoping he would get off my back with the childish concerns. Like I didn't wash my hands multiple times a day, sometimes more than ten times an hour when we were busy. I stood from the bed and moved towards the bathroom.

"Did you see the driveway?" he questioned while motioning to the bedroom window that overlooked the front of the house. "Mom planted all new jasmine bushes so that guests associate the smell of the flowers with the wedding." It was true, the smell was strong, and it seemed to cover every single molecule of air both inside and outside the house. And that was what made this season so special in this small town—the smell, the storms, the light, and the darkness. All combined into infinite moments of peace. "Don't look at me that way."

"What way?" I feigned innocence. I stopped by the closet door on my way to the bathroom. "I mean, the smell is good. It's a great idea." I grabbed the hanger from the top of the door and pulled the short emerald-green dress out, draping it on the edge of the bed. I needed a shower to wash the day away before heading down to dinner because it had been long and hot.

"Did you see Santiago yet?"

"Not yet," I said curtly.

"Okay then." He knocked on the closet door. "I'll leave you to it."

He closed the door behind him with a small click, and I could hear his steps receding in the direction of Santiago's childhood bedroom, where Santiago and Victoria were probably getting ready. The noises from downstairs started getting louder and louder, signaling the arrival of the guests. The house was transformed—it was already a large home, happily worn after years of use and abuse by our many cousins and friends. Our home had always been the hangout spot. For all of us siblings, our friends had gathered here consistently. When we were in our teens, the house was a revolving door of hormones, and my parents welcomed it.

There was a loud knock on the front door, followed by the sound of the doorbell, which got me moving straight to the bathroom for that overdue shower.

———

I made my way to the back of the house, where the tent for the actual wedding was already set up. For the welcome event, Victoria had organized a cocktail reception with a more casual feel, so we were all mingling around in the yard. She had set a few lounge areas around small tables for the older people, but no one was sitting yet. There was a lot of movement for this early into the night; mostly finger foods and cocktails were being passed around by an army of teenagers—local students who were probably working a catering job for the summer to make a few *pesos.*

"*Ey.*" I heard a whisper right behind me.

"No, Jacinto," I replied. Because this could only mean one thing, and it was not the time.

"You don't even know what I'm going to say," he whined. Martina, his best friend, was standing right beside him wearing a bright pink dress. Her dirty blonde hair was pulled up into a loose braid that draped over one of her shoulders. She was smiling into her drink. They both had mischief in their looks, and I immediately knew he was up to something. "*Por favor.*"

"*No,* mamá *te va a matar,*" I whisper-hissed. "This is not the night for any of your shenanigans."

"Uh-huh, because her *golden boy* is getting married." He rolled his eyes, and Martina giggled in response. Those two were inseparable and had been for years now. Even more since he returned to Tres Fuegos after law school. "Finally, if you ask me."

"No one asked. And don't get into any messes today of all days, *te lo pido por favor,*" I begged. I turned to face him and fixed his tie for him, like I'd done so many times in the past. "Martina, *es en serio.*"

She sobered at my warning, but I knew that the moment I turned my back to them, she would immediately acqui-esce. Because this town had a soft spot for the Williams brothers, apparently. I eyed them both. Then Jacinto turned around dramatically and walked towards the house, huffing and puffing and talking animatedly at Martina.

Victoria was standing with Santiago towards the edge of the lawn, their fingers threaded together. She was leaning against his side, looking relaxed and entertained with the conversation going on around her. She was wearing an off-white bodysuit, the wide pant legs hitting the grass under her feet. Her brown hair was styled in loose, long curls, and her makeup was "on point," as the youths would say, probably courtesy of Martina, the only hair and makeup person in our small town. She looked stunning. And happy. Both of them did.

But I digressed. The whimsy was everywhere tonight. There were string lights draping over the grass from the house to the tall trees in the back, and the larger ones had paper lanterns hanging from their branches, all lit up with candles on the inside. There was a long table immediately below it with two benches on either side. The top was covered in different floral arrangements of wildflowers, the reds and oranges and yellows burning in the night. If you looked closely, you could see what looked like hundreds of lightning bugs contributing to the setup.

Magic.

And the smell of flowers and rain was everywhere.

Granny was sitting at the table, laughing quietly at something my father was telling her. He was hovering over her, standing by the bench right next to her. Her gaze wasn't on him, but rather on my grandfather laughing loudly by the pool, chatting with my aunt Julia and her oldest daughter. My cousin was doubled over in laughter at something he had said, and she was holding on to her mother for dear life. My grandfather's eyes were shining with mirth, so much like Jacinto's that it was disturbing.

I walked towards the table and sat to Granny's side, tucking my long legs under the table. She turned to face me and smiled one of her soft smiles, so like the many she'd given us all our lives. She was a patient woman, made infinitely more so after she had grandchildren and we turned into a wild pack of hyenas when we were all together.

"What do you think Grandpa is telling them?" I asked her, and she chuckled.

"He's probably telling them the story of how on the day of our wedding, it was raining so hard that as soon as he stepped out of the car, his shoe sank into a giant puddle of mud." She took a deep breath and kept going. "And was covered in dark brown sludge so thick, he couldn't get it out. He had to call the priest to help them."

We'd heard this story multiple times throughout the years. Always at someone's wedding. And every time they told it, it got more embellished. Wilder, just like our family as the years went by. I laughed with them and absorbed the scene—my brother finally marrying the woman he had loved silently for years, my parents seeing their home packed to the brim with people who loved them and their children, my closest friends thriving in their own lives.

Everyone looked happy. Even my oldest brother Charlie, who was in the corner, contentment on his face, deep in conversation with Agustín and Catalina, Victoria's brother and sister-in-law, who also happened to be her best friend.

Probably talking about work.

Definitely talking about work.

"*¿Y Jacinto?*" she asked, her face softening for her actual golden boy. He had Granny wrapped around his finger. "I haven't seen him yet."

"He's inside with Martina," I said, immediately turning towards the door that led to the inside of the house, expecting him to come bursting out any minute. But the only movement was the catering staff and some of the guests lazily moving around and mingling on the back patio.

"Probably up to something, that boy." She shook her head, and the corners of her mouth tipped up. Her hair was styled neatly in a short bob that she'd been sporting for a few years now, ever since she decided to let her grays grow in. She said it was because she was a *cool* grandma. Not because she was old. But her eyes still shone with so much appreciation for life and love, it was enviable. "So much like your grandfather when we were kids."

From the corner of my eye, I noticed one of my brothers making his way through the small crowd towards where we were sitting. The soft glow of the lanterns and the twinkling string lights seemed to reflect on every surface of his clothes, closely matching Victoria's outfit. It was casual, a white shirt tucked into khaki pants, boat shoes on his feet. He looked like a lawyer on vacation.

"*Hola, Lu,*" Santiago said as he kissed the top of my head. He sat next to me, draping one of his long arms over my shoulder and pulling me towards his body, so warm on this summer evening. It was late December, and the heat was usually unbearable, but, as luck would have it, it was a perfect evening.

I looked up at him, smiling widely. He looked relaxed, happy. Finally.

"You look good," I said, scanning the crowd as we chatted. "She looks amazing."

"Yeah," he replied, his eyes immediately finding his soon-to-be wife and softening at the image. "Yeah."

"It's been a long time coming, no?"

"Thank you," he said while looking at me, a soft smile on his lips. He was my closest brother in age. We were only eleven months apart, so from the start, we were treated almost like twins. We went to the city for college almost at the same time, sharing an apartment during his law school years. Jacinto replaced Santiago after he started law school a few years later, but Santiago and I remained close, sharing our daily lives and some of our adventures.

"For what?" I said, crossing my eyes and poking my tongue out at him. I heard his deep chuckle in my body, the vibrations extending from his arm to my shoulders. This was, indeed, a long time coming. More than ten years in the making.

"For this." He waved his free hand in the air, first towards Victoria, then in a circular motion all around us. "Thank you."

I reached up to squeeze his hand, holding on to it for a few seconds longer than I would normally do. I suspected Santiago was the only one in my family who thought that my abrupt departure from my hospital job had nothing to do with me being homesick or with that bad breakup. But he never asked any questions and instead lingered around me in silence, waiting patiently to see when I would talk to him. I surmised this had been his strategy with Victoria too.

She had cracked. But I was still holding out for a little longer.

"She's amazing."

"I know," he responded.

3

FRANCISCO

I was running late, like usual. This *new normal* thing that had happened naturally. My job had kept me busy, and in the past few years, I had been distancing myself from who my family was. That meant working hard to make a name for myself as a family law attorney, away from the spotlight of my father and his long political career.

"That's what I'm saying," the voice on the other end of the line said.

"So we are aligned then." It was a question, but I made it sound like a statement. I needed to get going, but I was stuck in the office on the last working day of the year, my bags packed neatly by the front door of my apartment. It was quiet in the hallways at the firm. Only one of the partners was in, finishing up the last details of his work before our leave.

Our firm technically closed right before Christmas,

giving associates a few extra days of vacation for the holidays. And then a month-long adjournment period started, where the courts rested and we did work, but at a different pace. This year, I would take the month off and disappear, hiding in a small mountain town and taking it easy. Make it easier on my mental health.

"Do you have any inkling who the judge might be?" I asked. I rubbed at my chest, trying to get rid of that heavy feeling lingering there constantly.

Someone on the call sucked in a breath and paused for a second, then said, "They have been favoring Black recently, but a clerk on her team told us she's overloaded with cases. So we might get lucky and get Álvarez instead."

"Shit," I replied. Judge Black was ruthless in these divorce cases and usually favored the party that had originally filed since it tended to be women and after many years of discontent. We were representing a B-list actor, and the fight for custody of their children had gotten bad. "Álvarez isn't any better, though."

"No, but I think he's more open to looking at some of the supporting documents we bring."

"Alright, well..." I looked outside the window. The streets were busy with people and cars, all moving quickly in the heat of the summer. It had been stifling the previous week, but a big storm the night before had helped with the temperature. "Let's talk in a few weeks and make sure the summer interns are briefed for discovery, please."

"Okay," someone else said. My team was already away,

the bulk of them choosing to take the first few weeks of January off. There were three associates on call every month, and they would take over in case of any urgency or issue we had with our open cases. This call was the last one on my schedule, and I was counting down the minutes to close my laptop and then go meet Pilar for drinks.

"Okay, everyone, good work," I said. My inner politician was coming out, despite me trying to control it. It was how I'd been raised—being able to talk to anyone and everyone about anything at all: the weather, the news, sports. Whatever. But now that I'd been separated from my family's legacy for a while, I noticed that being personable and charming worked great to motivate my team. "Have a happy New Year. I'll see you in a few weeks."

"Bye, boss," someone uttered, and then the line went dead.

I closed my laptop and shoved it in my backpack as I walked around my desk and started turning off the lights. This would be the last time I did this for the year, a new one starting soon. A new countdown to that dreaded date that kept me up at night.

"Francisco," the partner that was in the office said, startling me out of my thoughts. I walked in the direction of his office right in the corner of the building, the floor to ceiling windows spanning two of the walls. He was leaning back in his chair, feet crossed at the ankles on his desk and hands linked behind his back.

"Jaime." I nodded, standing at the doorway. All his lights

were off, but his computer screen was highlighting his features, if ever so slightly.

"Have a good break, man," he said. "Don't work too hard."

He was one of the founding partners at the firm, and he had hired me after I decided to leave politics and switch over to family law. I had worked with my father's campaign early on while in law school, and then immediately after graduating, I had transitioned to an aide position for one of his friends. But after a few years, I'd realized that politics was not for me, despite everything my father had ever tried to impress on me. This was a better fit for me.

"Never," I said with a laugh. He had aged a significant amount since I'd met him maybe half a decade back. We'd had an abnormally large number of high-profile cases in the past two years, and that had taken a toll on a lot of the staff. Santiago Williams, one of my closest friends at the firm, had taken a leave of absence after a particularly nasty and media-driven case. He then had never returned to work, instead switching careers and staying in his hometown. "I'm going to Williams's wedding in his town and staying for a few weeks. See what that mountain life is all about."

Jaime chuckled and dropped his legs to the floor, moving his computer mouse a few times to wake it up. "Don't get any ideas."

I laughed in response, shaking my head at the older man. "Nah, I'm good. *Feliz año*. Send my regards to your wife."

I walked a few blocks to the small, cozy bar close to the office. It was the second time I was seeing Pilar; I'd first met her at a colleague's birthday party a few weeks back. The conversation was nice, and she asked to go out for drinks. To explore this. But I wasn't feeling it, not really. My mind was occupied with thoughts of my sister, hoping that tucking myself away in the hills of Tres Fuegos would help me heal, even if a little.

PILAR

I'm here.

Where are you?

Sitting in the back by the window.

The dimly lit bar was abuzz with laughter, clinking glasses, and the low hum of conversations. There was faint background music, some sort of *rock nacional* that I couldn't quite put my finger on. I scanned the crowded room until I saw Pilar, her phone in her hand, typing away at something. Her nose was scrunched in concentration. She was sitting with her back against the window, the soft glow from the streetlights casting a warm halo around her. She looked up as I approached, a bright grin lighting up her face. Her green eyes shone even in the dim setting.

"Pili," I greeted with a smile, kissing her cheek and then

pulling out the chair across from her. "Sorry about that. Work stuff."

"Oh, no worries. I just got here," she replied, gesturing with her hand. She flipped her phone over on the table, sliding it slightly inwards towards the center. I scanned the room while I settled on the seat, placing my backpack on the floor by my feet.

"*Chicos*," the waitress said from right next to us. "What can I get you?"

"I think we'll have beers, yes?" Pilar said, glancing at me and then smiling back to the waitress.

"You got it." She rapped her knuckles on the table and took off in the direction of the bar, then loaded up her tray with a few drinks that were resting by the register.

"So," Pilar said, her forearms resting on the table and her upper body leaning towards me. She had a big smile on her face, and her cheeks were slightly flushed. Even in the soft light of the bar, the smattering of freckles across her nose was visible. "Any big plans for New Year's?"

My chest tightened for a second, releasing after I rubbed it with my right hand. I closed my eyes, hoping I could blink away the memories and the pain that were brought on by what she had just said.

"I'm heading to Córdoba for a friend's wedding, then staying for a few weeks," I said awkwardly. What was I thinking when I agreed to drinks with this woman? I was going to be gone for at least a month, if not more. This was stupid. "To a small town up in the mountains. I'm excited."

"Oh," she said. A look of confusion flashed on her face for a moment, and then she chuckled lightly, shaking her head. "Well, that sounds like an adventure."

"Yeah, it should be interesting," I replied, taking a sip of the cold beer that had just arrived at our table. The condensation on the glass felt cool against my fingertips. Pilar took a sip of her own beer, her gaze never leaving mine.

For the next hour, our conversation flowed easily, drifting from work to personal interests to plans for the summer. Pilar had a contagious laugh, and her easygoing nature made it surprisingly easy to forget the weight that had been pressing on me.

"You want to head to my house?" she asked, the tips of her ears turning red. She looked away for a moment, then laughed at herself, almost like she was surprised by her own question. I checked my watch, realizing that I needed to wrap things up, even though I knew I was going to decline her invitation. Maybe this was the polite thing to do, to shut her down gently.

"Ah," I said, running a hand through my hair and squeezing the back of my neck. "I have to leave early tomorrow. So, a rain check?"

"Oh. No problem," Pilar replied, smiling. She took out her wallet and dropped a few bills on the table, and I matched what she did. She stood, grabbing her purse from where it was hanging on the chair and shoving her phone haphazardly inside. I followed her to the front of the bar, the night air refreshing after the time we'd spent inside. "Maybe we can catch up when you're back in town."

My heart sank. Not because this was particularly heart-wrenching. But because I felt a little guilty. That maybe I had led her on, made her believe this was more than just friendly drinks. I was just not into this whole dating thing. Hadn't been for more than three years now.

"I—" I started to say, but she interrupted me.

"I get it. That's okay." She smiled a little and shifted her weight from foot to foot. She leaned her body towards me and gave me a friendly hug. "*Igual me divertí.*"

"Yeah," I agreed. It had been fun. A momentary distraction.

But as soon as the distraction was over, my mind hovered around the anniversary of my sister's death.

4

LUCÍA

I BLINKED, and the first thing I noticed was the strong smell. The window was open, and the cool breeze of the early morning was sweeping in, hitting my arms and giving me goosebumps all over. The sun wasn't out yet, and the color of the sky was a deep blue with a few twinges of gold. I tucked my arms inside the covers and tried to muffle the sounds from outside with my pillow, but my brain was already wired and going straight to my to-do list.

"What is that noise?" I said out loud, hoping someone would hear me call out. I wasn't ready to get out of bed, especially since I didn't have to be in the office that morning.

Valentina and I had decided, as soon as Dr. Martín retired, that it didn't make sense to open the practice early every morning during the week since we had to accommodate a few patients that could only come in the evenings. So twice a week, we had the morning off but stayed late in the office. And on those days, I usually stayed in bed for as long as I could. Some days, I was successful in going back to sleep. But others, like today, the thoughts started consuming me early.

The date was slowly creeping up on me. It was all-dominating. And the closer we got, the harder it was to breathe through the blips and the memories.

I remembered her like it was yesterday. Her brown hair was still growing back after the previous round of chemo she had had a year earlier. I was hoping to specialize in pediatric oncology after residency, so Dr. Varela, the head of the pediatrics service, had assigned me a few patients as a way of getting my feet wet. I wasn't necessarily tasked with anything cancer-related, but I did look at her regularly, analyzing her chart and checking her stats consistently to make sure she was on the right track with her treatment.

I knocked softly on the door and let myself in. There was a crucifix hanging smack dab in the middle of the wall, immediately across from the bed. It was impossible to ignore it, and it was by design. A little hope for the patients to hold on to, even though some of them were too young to know what it represented.

Her petite body was in the middle of the bed, her chest rising and falling in a steady pattern. The heart rate monitor threw back uniform stats. Her color was improving, which was a wonderful thing because she had gone through a lot in recent months. In and out of the hospital for chemotherapy. A chaotic family life. It was all the nurses talked about.

I could hear voices right outside the door, probably some of the staff catching up on a slow evening. It was my least favorite time of day, when everything was still and quiet and there was not much to do, too early still for my body to go to sleep in the on-call rooms.

The room was small and sterile, with only the patient's bed, a reclining chair in the corner, and a small table that was littered with things. Jazmín was still in school, and because of her health issues, she did a lot of her schooling online. I had lost count of how many times she'd been here. It was probably her ninth or tenth, her initial diagnosis well before I was a resident at this hospital. She had been in remission for a few years, but it had since come back. It was looking good for her despite the very real possibility of another round of chemo in the next few months.

"Hey, you," I said, and Jazmín's lids fluttered open. She smiled at me, her silver braces glinting in the dim light. Her drapes were open, and the moonlight was shining into the room.

"Oh my god," she said, placing one of her hands over her heart. "You scared me to death."

I rolled my eyes and bit my cheek to avoid laughing. She was one of the more dramatic patients. She loved the attention and thrived on being social, so the long hours just sitting by herself were hard.

"Okay, let's check you out, yeah?"

"Lucía," she croaked, her voice still laced with sleep, but she pushed her body against the headboard and moved the covers away from her body. "I thought it was your day off today."

I cocked my head and looked at her, lips tilting up slightly, slyly. "I'm covering for Dr. David today. His son is sick, and his wife had to be in surgery until late." I grabbed my stethoscope from around my neck and placed it in my ears, rubbing the chest piece a few times to warm it up before placing it on her bare skin. She unsnapped the sides of her hospital gown, the stiff fabric falling down towards her lap.

"But also, you are so nosy," I drawled, my eyes going wide for dramatic effect.

She hooted a laugh, the sound reverberating in the room above the sounds of the machines near her bed.

"What? It's my brand." She lifted one shoulder and then dropped it immediately, cocking her head in response. "I thought it was your boyfriend's birthday today."

Damn her and her good memory.

"Ah," I said, then looked away from her, focusing instead on the sounds I could hear through the earpieces that were tight in my ears. "Right."

She gasped. "Oh no. What happened?"

What happened was that he thought my career took up too much time, too many nights away from him. The classic reason why I couldn't make anyone stay. He was impressed at first, oohing and aahing at the stories I told.

But then the novelty wore off, and I wasn't enough to make him stay.

"Whatever." I shrugged nonchalantly. "Grown-up things."

She frowned, then reached out and squeezed my bicep. Once, twice, then dropped her hand back towards her body.

A grin sprang across her face. It was full of mischief, and it almost made me stay and tell her all the details. "Oh my god, call Sonia in, and we can stalk him on social media and comment nasty things on his photos."

I barked out a laugh at the absurdity of the scene. A teenage patient acting like a sister, immediately on my side, no questions asked. I shook my head and draped the stethoscope back around my neck. She slumped back into the bed and dragged the covers up to her chin, relaxing into the pillows and closing her eyes.

"Tomorrow," she said, visibly worn out. "Let's do it tomorrow."

And then I was out the door of that room, the nurses back at their station and everything around me back to normal.

Back to normal.

The knock on my door startled me, and I sat up on the bed, the covers pooling around my waist. The sun was now creeping in, the shadows on the floor much darker. I blinked a few times, trying to clear my brain from that fog. It was a day away, her anniversary. A date that was so close, yet so far. And there was still no reason for me to hang on to her so tightly. But I couldn't let it go. With all my might, I tried, but I just couldn't.

"Lu?"

It was Charlie outside my room, waiting for me to reply. Either of my other two brothers would have knocked and then walked right in, but Charlie was the one who had the most decorum. He was grumpy as all hell, who knew why, but the most respectful. He didn't want anyone up in his business, so he stayed in his lane, only asking questions when needed. It was a relief, really, because I didn't have to pretend around him.

"*Aha*," I answered. It was the fifth word I had uttered that day, more than I had planned. I enjoyed my quiet mornings off, leaving my room once the house was quiet and no one was around. But with the wedding so close, it was impossible to get that time alone. "Come in, Charlie."

"Hey, did I wake you?" he asked, looking around the room and zoning in on the open window. He frowned and walked right in, making a beeline to close it. "Keep the windows closed. It's going to be hot outside today."

I was always amused by his practicality—always quietly looking out for others. "What's up?" I said as I got out of bed and grabbed my phone off the nightstand where it was charging. I immediately looked and saw that I had twenty-seven new text messages, all from unknown numbers. I would have normally loved it, having people rely on me to care for their sick loved ones. I scowled.

"Nothing." He shrugged. "I need to hide for a second."

I bit my lips to avoid laughing at him. "Who's downstairs?" I whispered to him, widening my eyes to create a more dramatic effect. "Should I stay in hiding too?"

"Not funny."

"A little funny if you think about it." I lifted one shoulder nonchalantly, then walked towards my closet to grab clean clothes. "You can stay, but I'm taking a shower."

"Okay," he said, taking off his shoes and lying on the bed, propping his torso against the headboard. He took his phone out of his pocket and started scrolling through it, his thumbs moving quickly over the screen. He glared for a moment, then looked at me impatiently. "Go shower, and then we can go downstairs together."

"Who even is downstairs that you are so scared of?" I laughed, walking to the attached bathroom and closing the door behind me. "You are a grown man!" I yelled through the closed door and heard his grunt in reply.

Once I was showered and dressed, I went back to my room to find Charlie lying on his side, head propped on his hand and scrolling on his phone. His expression was neutral, but every few seconds I could see how his jaw hardened. It was either something that he was looking at—which I doubted—or he was already in his head about something that had happened. All my bets were on the latter.

"What has you so stressed?" I asked as I put on my sandals. He was right; it was going to be a hot day. I looked out the window, and I could see the stillness in the trees.

Those were the worst days, when there was not a single drop of breeze to cut down on the heat. "How can I help?"

"No one," he said too quickly. He shook his head. "I mean, nothing."

I turned towards the door and hid my grin. He had been extra grumpy for the past few years, but especially so since I had become head doctor at the practice. I never asked him if it was me, but I had a small inkling that he hated that people took advantage of my position in town, sending me texts at all hours of the night to help diagnose their kids. Because again, he respected everyone's personal space and wanted his respected as well.

He followed me downstairs quietly. The hum of the kitchen was obvious from the landing. We walked all the way to the back of the house and found Jacinto and my father sitting at the kitchen table, having their morning coffee and chatting over each other. Valentina sat quietly to one side, listening in on the conversations.

I smiled as I walked to her. "What are you doing here?" I asked, taking a seat next to her. Charlie stood by the door, casting a furtive look in my friend's direction.

"Coffee." She shrugged, lifting her mug full of the hot liquid. "I was bored at home."

"Maybe we should open the practice early again," I said. She rolled her eyes in response, but the edges of her lips moved. I nudged her with my elbow. "I get bored too, you know?"

"Where is your brother?" my mother asked as she

walked into the room, her hair up in a messy bun. She was wearing leggings and a sleeveless shirt because it was easier for her to run errands in her athleisure, she said. She repeated over and over that it made her feel productive, like she was working out. "He didn't want to come over for coffee?"

"His friend is coming from out of town today," Jacinto replied, looking at his phone screen and smirking. "And Victoria was doing something at The Inn." He shrugged, then stood up and walked to our mother. "I'm leaving anyway," he said to her and kissed her cheek, then hooked his arm around her neck and hugged her tightly.

"Jacinto," she said, slapping his arm but smiling nonetheless.

"See you later." He waved at everyone and took off, the front door closing loudly behind him.

"Yeah, I'm out too," Charlie said, leaving his dirty mug in the sink. He kissed our mom, then turned and walked out of the kitchen, his departure a little quieter than our youngest sibling's. Valentina's eyes followed his body, trailing his movements to the front door.

"Ready?" I said, looking back at her with a blank expression. "The sooner we go in, the faster we'll take care of everything."

"Yeah," she said, her face back towards the kitchen. "I'm ready for our time off."

5

FRANCISCO

Three fires indeed.

More like a fucking fire on top of a heaping pile of garbage tucked inside a smelly dumpster.

I gripped the steering wheel, my knuckles turning white as I navigated the last of the winding road leading to the small town in the hills of Córdoba that was now the home of Santiago, my former colleague and good friend. The drive had been long, made even longer by the unpredictable weather of the summer, with its heavy rains and loud thunderstorms and the unease that settled in my stomach every year around this time.

It wasn't the town's fault, my foul mood. It was just life. And the freaking looming date.

Tres Fuegos was picturesque, I would give it that. The sun was dipping lower in the sky, casting a glow over the landscape and giving a golden tinge to the dark green leaves on the trees. The heat was obvious even to the naked eye. There was a permanent clear haze ahead of me, radiating from the hot asphalt of the road.

I parked outside a small, single level home. The views from my parking spot were stunning, peaks and valleys stretching all around me. It was obvious this town was inside the mountain, a part of it. Nestled would be the right word. And the house didn't look out of place at all, despite its striking white color. It belonged.

Fuck. I got out of the car, my arms shaking from the exhaustion. I was running on fumes by now in between getting everything ready for the year ahead and prepping for my extended leave. I would take a week off for Santiago's wedding, and then during our month-long adjournment period from the courts, I would stay in Tres Fuegos and house-sit for them. A welcome respite.

With my suitcase in hand, I walked up the steps and rang the doorbell. It was a large home at the end of the cul-de-sac, and the mountain started immediately behind it. It was quiet, save for the sound of a few birds and the wind in the leaves. Victoria opened the door, a bright smile on her face. She was wearing loose jeans and a half-tucked striped shirt, her feet bare. She was different than the woman I remembered back when we moved in the same professional circuits. She was known for being ruthless. Stoic. But she had changed, apparently, and it looked good on her.

"You made it!" she squealed, running down the steps

and giving me a big hug. She took my suitcase from my hand and moved to the side, clearing a path towards the house. I could see Santiago inside, coming to the door to greet me. There was a tea towel on his shoulder, and his hands were dark with charcoal dust.

"Hope you are hungry," he said with one of his characteristic grins. "Food is almost ready."

"Hey, man," I said with a smile on my face. The inside of the house was pristine, and it reminded me of the old Victoria, polished and clean, but there were a few signs of life here and there. Plants lined the living room windowsill, and shoes littered the small entryway. There was a crooked picture hanging above the entry table. "Thanks for having me."

Santiago grabbed the tea towel and wiped his hands, then threw his arms around me in a welcoming gesture. He laughed a deep laugh, then let me go. "You look like shit."

I grunted. "I'm aware. So much for a welcome."

"Fran, do you want to go unpack? I can show you to your room." Victoria looked over to Santiago, who nodded and then smiled. Victoria led the way through a long hallway tucked on the right side of the home, where a few doors opened on either side. It looked lived in. Frames hung on both sides of the hall, filled with images of their lives: their friends and families, and themselves. And it was refreshing to see how these two loved each other and the people around them. "Bathroom is the door right across. And whenever you are ready, we'll be out back. You'll be able to find us." She closed the door behind her, her steps heading back in the direction we'd come from just a minute earlier.

I took a deep breath.

One more day.

And then the timer reset itself, and the countdown started all over again. One day at a time, inching closer to the date.

Hopefully the mountain air would clear my thoughts, lessen the pain, make time go faster.

I shook my head, then stopped by the bathroom for a minute to freshen up. I followed the sound of female laughter coming from the patio and joined Santiago and Victoria, who were cuddling on the love seat, facing away from the house and looking out to the big yard. I opened the sliding door, and both of them turned their faces in unison, large, lovey grins plastered on their faces.

I couldn't relate, but I smiled in return because it was contagious, even if for a fleeting second.

"How's the city?" Santiago asked. He sat a little taller, draping an arm around Victoria's shoulder and squeezing for a moment. I walked around them and sat in the lone chair arranged across from them, my back to the yard.

"You know, same." I shrugged. He knew of my family's quoteunquote fame, and he was asking, but not in as many words, about them. The things I couldn't get away from because of my last name. "Eugenio is running again," I mentioned but didn't elaborate. My father had had a seat in

Congress for years but had decided to run for governor in a hopeful step towards a potential presidency.

Santiago raised his eyebrows, and Victoria nodded, both understanding the political process and what it meant to take steps to become the highest elected official in the country. I didn't give any more details, not wanting to dampen the mood with my family's antics and, for lack of a better word, politics.

"Anyway, everything ready?" I asked, making it obvious I was ready to change the subject. "Are you all packed?"

"Not even close." Victoria scoffed but then followed it up with an eyeroll. "This one here"—she motioned with her hand towards Santiago—"won't even start packing until the day we leave." She shook her head and looked over to her fiancé, giving him a wide, intimate smile.

"Oh, I meant to tell you, my sister will probably stop by to water the plants," he said, looking around at the potted plants covering a large amount of the patio. I followed his gaze and turned my body to face the large yard lined on either side with flowering bushes, all different kinds of flowers of various sizes and colors. The grass was pristine, freshly cut, and a deep, deep green. The yard extended all the way to a line of trees, and that ended at the mountainside.

There were no fences between neighbors, but Santiago had mentioned that his family lived all on the same block in this town, so I assumed that they would cross into each other's yards when they needed to get to their homes. It sounded like living in a planned community, where everyone greeted each other in the morning. Such a big contrast to the city, where it was rare that you ran into someone you knew.

"She has a really green thumb," he continued, "so she'll also water the plants inside."

I nodded as I followed his eyes inside the house, looking at the plants in small pots by the window and beyond, into the living room.

"*Genial*," I muttered. "It's too much responsibility for me." *Right now.* I could barely care for myself. I couldn't even imagine caring for another living thing.

Santiago barked out a laugh, and Victoria looked at him in awe, like she'd never heard such a magnificent sound in her life. And the only thing I could do was smile in return because it really sounded ridiculous. But it was true.

He stood by the grill and asked a thousand questions, using the time until the steaks were ready to catch up on our lives. Victoria kept going back and forth into the house, bringing out a few things from inside to set the table for our meal.

After dinner we went back inside and sat in the living area.

"When did you move into this house?" I asked Santiago. Victoria was already in their room, giving us some space to chat between us both. "It's very different from your other place."

The last time I'd seen him, he was still with Clara, his

former girlfriend. They had just moved in together, and their shared apartment was nothing like this house. This looked more like a home, like both Santiago and Victoria had poured part of their personalities into it. It was cozy but unexpected.

"I bought it when I took that sabbatical, remember?"

I nodded, remembering how he'd worked a highly publicized case a few years back that had drained all his energy. He was a different man after that case, and judging by what had happened afterwards, it really did change him. "It was an impulse buy, believe it or not."

I chuckled at his tone, relaxing into the large sofa by the fireplace. It was full of candles, some of them melted on the bottom of the firebox, like they had been lit over and over again.

"Does it never get cold enough that you need to light a fire?" I asked, curious what the melted wax meant.

"Oh, it does. The candles are just because we get blackouts during the summer," he said nonchalantly. "We keep a box of matches right there." He pointed at a deep bowl on a side table.

I stretched my body to look into it, acknowledging what he said.

"Nothing too bad," he continued. "A few hours here and there."

A few hours? My body froze, but Santiago didn't notice. He kept talking, motioning with his hand towards the back of the house and saying something about his sister that I couldn't quite make out. Then he took his phone out and looked at the screen, and his mouth quirked on one side. He rolled his eyes and set the phone down on the coffee table.

I blinked, emerging from my stupor.

"And hopefully," he added, "it won't happen at all. Fingers crossed."

Shit.

6

LUCÍA

I STEPPED OUTSIDE of my office and started my regular walk back to my parents' house. It had been the same commute for some time now. The only difference was that I was now the person who took care of closing the practice and setting everything up for the next day. Valentina was walking with me, heading to the big house for a quick meal. It had quickly become like a ritual for us, once a week when we closed the office late to have dinner together. Sometimes we would go to the restaurant at The Inn; other times we would go to her place. But this time, we walked to my parents' house together.

The scent of the summer jasmines hit me like a wall. It was strong, almost overpowering, and filled my nose completely. I took a deep breath—the smell never stopped reminding me of the endless summer evenings in town when we had nothing to do and nowhere to go. It was a heady, almost intoxicating fragrance, full of promise and potential. I closed my eyes and breathed deeply, letting the fragrance wash over me, the memory of my grandparents' home filled with the flowers taking over my brain.

I knew what it meant, the strong smell. These flowers only bloomed in the summer here, and the scent was at its strongest right before a heavy rainfall. They were like nature's barometer, warning of an impending storm. The air was heavy with moisture, and the sky was darkening by the minute. One of my favorite things about the summers in this town was how late it turned into night, and once it was dark, the stars shone like nowhere else I'd ever seen. But now, in the early evening, the sky was dark. I could feel the electricity in the air, the sense of anticipation that always came before a thunderstorm.

"I love the smell," Valentina said, like she was reading my mind. "I don't think it gets that strong back home." She was from a suburb of Buenos Aires, where there was more space in between houses and people had big yards. She had mentioned once that the small town felt like the country club where she had lived with her parents, but that Tres Fuegos was much nicer, especially because the people were so kind.

I turned the corner onto my parents' street. There was a rumble of thunder, and the inevitable flash of lightning followed after. There was something so majestic about storms in this town. And they looked so different than what storms looked like back in the city. Storms in our small mountain town made lightning dance across the sky, and the drops of water pounded against the soil, making it smell fresh and clean and alive. It was a weird thing, how storms took over here. How you were enveloped by their strength. It felt almost like they took over you, even though the large parts of the storm were weathered inside in the comfort of our homes.

Another flash of lightning startled us, hurrying our steps towards the front door. I could hear the rustling of the leaves around me as the wind picked up speed, and the storm clouds rolled in, dark and menacing, warning us of what was to come. The house was dark and lonely, the cars parked in the circular driveway at the front of the lot. It wasn't normal for it to be so quiet, especially during this time of year, but with the wedding and the out-of-town guests, I guessed everyone was gone on one of the activities Victoria had planned. It was a welcome silence on the eve of the anniversary. It would give me a moment to be alone with my thoughts once Valentina left. Get it together so I could go to bed and *pretend* to sleep and instead toss and turn all night thinking of them.

I walked up the paver driveway to the front door, my shoes squeaking against the hard surface. I fumbled with the keys in my hand for a second, trying to find the right one among all the options on the key ring. I inserted it into the lock and twisted the door open as big, fat raindrops started to fall.

The rain hit the pavement, creating small splashes as it

made contact and immediately cooling the hot, dense air. The sound of the rain was soothing, a steady drumming that joined me as we walked to the back of the house towards the family room. It was getting heavier, a classic summer thunderstorm, one that could soak a person to the bone in seconds.

I dropped my bag on the kitchen table and walked to the fridge.

"Drink?" I asked as Valentina settled on the couch and looked out the large windows. It was a beautiful sight, the way the droplets danced on the glass and the way the trees swayed in the wind. The sky was completely dark, and the only things illuminating it were the downward streaks of light that would occasionally rumble. She turned to me and nodded, then stood up and walked towards me.

Our nights together were usually quiet. We didn't need to say much to each other to understand what the other was thinking. I knew Valentina had a small inkling of what really brought me home. Not the homesickness I claimed or the bad breakup. But the *real* reason.

She never said anything. She was just *there,* a steady presence when I needed it the most. Just like my brother.

There was a loud knock on the front door, followed by the sound of the doorbell and more pounding.

"Jesus." I sighed, bringing my hand to my racing heart. It wasn't rare to have people over in the evenings—this house was a home to so many people in town beyond our large family. I looked at Valentina, and she made a face, then headed to the front of the house. I could still hear the heavy drops on the tiled roof, the sound amplified in the large entryway.

"Hey, Dr. L," the woman standing outside the door said. She was waiting below the steps that led to the covered porch, a large umbrella covering her and stopping the large amounts of water from soaking into her. Her car was at the edge of the driveway, the lights still on and the windshield wipers going at full speed. There was someone in the driver's seat looking our way. "Can you tell me what this says?"

She took a step forward and held up a white piece of paper: a prescription from my pad. It had my signature and my seal. I squinted and moved closer, the door closing behind me with a large, startling sound. Gladys jumped in her spot and let go of a big, surprised laugh, then shoved the small note in my face.

I smiled politely and took it from her hand, looking over it carefully and chuckling quietly at the words that were written on there. I heard the door open behind me, and a small sigh came from Valentina, who was now quietly standing next to me as the scene unfolded.

"Ibuprofen," I said. It was hard to give this woman an attitude. She was kind and clearly went above and beyond for her customers at the pharmacy.

"Oh, silly me." Gladys laughed and rolled her eyes at herself. "I left my glasses at home today, so everything has been extra hard." She took the paper from my hand and turned towards the car. The person in the driver's seat waved at us, the windows foggy from the temperature difference between both spaces. "Thanks, doc. I'll see you tomorrow," she said over the rumbling of thunder, then made her way quickly to the car. In a matter of seconds, they were gone.

"What the fuck?" Valentina said right next to me. I turned to face her. Her arms were crossed at her chest, her face hardened with anger. "Does this happen often?"

She had never witnessed one of these moments. It was usually a text or a call. Sometimes I would run into people at the hotel's restaurant or out on a hike and they would ask me for medical advice, but I'd never told her.

"Calm down, crazy," I said, uttering the words she had used on me a few days earlier. "It's fine."

"How is this fine?" she asked. She cocked her hip and started tapping her foot on the porch floor, her movements getting more impatient. "She could have called the office tomorrow! And also, ugh." She took a deep breath, then let her arms fall to her side. Her jaw clenched. "Ibuprofen? Really?" She rolled her eyes, then turned to walk into the house, not giving me time to even react to her rare outburst.

I laughed at my friend's display and followed her back to the kitchen. She had poured two glasses of wine and took out some of the leftovers we still had in the fridge from dinner the other night. She sat at the counter and took a long gulp of her drink, then took a deep breath.

She did this thing where she wouldn't let anything

simmer. She was normally the quiet one in our group, taking in everything that happened around her, then making her own decisions about the events. If she had something to say, she would say it and then immediately let it go. Like it was old news, and she was moving on to better, more positive things. She never stewed.

"It's not a big deal, Valen," I said as I sat down to eat some of the appetizers she had set up for us. "I'm happy to help."

I tried to give her a big grin, but she wasn't having it. She rolled her eyes at me again, then turned to look out the windows, where the rain had stopped, but the trees were still moving with the wind. The tent for the wedding was still up, but the side walls had been rolled down to avoid it getting wet in case of rain.

"Victoria really does think of everything," she said, moving on from the topic at hand.

"Mm-hmm," I agreed, taking a sip of the wine. "It's like she's always a step ahead of everyone."

"Are you ready for tomorrow?"

No. I wanted to scream it at her. *Of course not.* "Yeah, I think so." I smiled at her, then turned to look out the window, my gaze focusing on the tent. "They brought in the remaining tables and chairs at, like, noon today."

She stood from her seat at the island, then walked to the back door. She cocked her head and squinted, looking towards the tent. Maybe trying to see inside the thick plastic sides to figure out what was in there.

"Are they setting up in the morning, then?"

I nodded, then went back to my food, grabbing a soggy bruschetta from the plate in front of me. "Martina comes in at ten in the morning. I go first, and then she does my mom, Catalina, then Victoria last."

She was quiet for a moment, then sighed. I went back to my food, and Valentina stood quietly by the door, looking intently at me. She opened her mouth, then slightly shook her head, maybe changing her mind about saying what she wanted to say. I tried to ignore it, but her eyes were burning a hole through my head. If I didn't shut it down immediately, she would read my mind, and then the questions would come. She would say it once and then be done with it, as she did. But I wasn't even ready to talk about it once. *Nope, not happening.*

The sound of the front door closing startled me. Valentina brought her hand to her chest, then walked to me, a wide-eyed expression in question.

"What is wrong with people today?" I said under my breath. She chuckled, taking the intensity of the moment down a notch. We heard a few heavy steps, then a squeak like someone had turned on their heel. The steps receded and headed up the stairs instead.

"Lucía," my brother Charlie yelled.

Valentina blushed, then hurried to the couch to grab her purse. I smiled at her, then winked and yelled, "In the kitchen!"

The steps turned louder as he approached the threshold.

Valentina fumbled with her purse as a reaction to hearing my brother come into the house. She blushed again the moment he stepped in the doorway, his large frame blocking the path out the kitchen and into the entry.

"Oh," they both said at the same time. Charlie cleared his throat.

"Good evening," he said, then walked into the kitchen towards me. He kissed my cheek, walked to the fridge, and opened the door. "What are you up to?" he asked into the refrigerator nonchalantly.

"I'm just leaving," she said quickly, her voice sounding raspy. "See you tomorrow."

She turned to leave, and then Charlie's face snapped to me. "I'll walk her home."

"Sure." I shrugged. He followed her out of the house, the front door closing loudly behind them.

And then I was alone, in that big house, with all those thoughts.

7

LUCÍA

What a clusterfuck, right?

What I meant to say was: how was one supposed to tell their brother not to get married to the fucking love of his life, literally, on that date because they were still grieving a patient that they shouldn't have gotten attached to? And her brother. Her freaking brother, who wreaked havoc on my heart.

A mouthful, for sure, but also not justifiable.

So I went along with the motions, helping them plan and figuring things out with them as time passed.

And now I was paralyzed. Standing in the middle of the kitchen, people moving around me and asking a million questions I had no answers to. Because how would I know if the flowers were supposed to be bigger or smaller or if the tall candles went inside the glass containers or not? Should I have had answers to those questions?

The only thing I wanted to do was to curl up in bed and hide from the world. Force my brain to shut down and take a moment to waddle through the mud. Maybe break down and cry. But everything was moving fast around us, with the ceremony and the party and the crises that we needed to get to.

———

"Lu."

Motherfu— "No, please, no."

"You need to stop it with that, Lucía," Jacinto whisper-hissed at me. "I just need to tell you something."

"Can it wait? Like, maybe in eight hours once the ceremony is over?" I begged. We were standing in the kitchen, a flurry of movement all around us as the minutes ticked on. The nervous energy was palpable. "Please, *Mamá* is going insane, and it's freaking everyone out."

"Fine. Goodbye."

"Drama king!" He turned on his heel and bowed at me, making a little flourish with his hand that had me cracking a smile on this difficult day. Everything was ready. Victoria was hyperventilating upstairs, but in a good way, she had said. So excited to marry Santiago that she couldn't contain herself. But I knew that deep down, she was still a little hurt from all her family drama from a couple of years ago. Her family was going to be at the wedding. Her grandmother would not, and it was painful for her. For everyone, really.

I ran up the stairs in my bare feet, still wearing the old T-shirt and shorts from the night before. Victoria and Catalina were getting ready in Charlie's old room. The door was ajar, and I could hear them cackling inside at something unhinged one of them had said. By the snorts coming from inside, it had probably been Catalina. She had an extra level of energy that even my family couldn't match.

"Lu." I heard a soft voice coming from my left. I wanted to scream, even though I knew it was Martina, and I also knew it was my turn for hair and makeup. But I just wanted a moment alone after cleaning up messes and putting out fires downstairs and stressing about Jacinto's shenanigans. The man was a child. A man-child. Clearly the youngest of us all because he literally did whatever he wanted and got away with it. He could probably get away with murder too.

I sighed and turned. "Yep." I popped the *p*. "Ready," I lied.

I followed her to my room, where she had set up a chair in front of the large mirror that was hanging from the closet door. I sat and took a deep breath. From the reflection in front of me, I could see the sun up high in the sky out my bedroom window. The tall trees were stiff and unmoving, a sign that it was stiflingly hot outside. By the time the ceremony came around, it would be nicer, hopefully. These early summer days were traitorous like that; it was either suffocatingly hot in the evening or nice and cool. The latter would be preferred.

Time ticked incredibly slow for me that day. I could feel

Martina moving fast around me, working in choreographed movements like the pro she was. But it was like time was still for me. Everything was buzzing with energy, but I was dragging my feet along, trying to catch up to those around me. In a matter of hours, Santiago and Victoria would be married, and everything we had worked up to during the year would be virtually over. It felt like in the blink of an eye, they were moving on, and I was being left behind. And then in the blink of an eye, it would be a new day, counting down again.

There was a knock at the door that startled me from my thoughts. I looked up, and Valentina was standing there, all ready in her flowy dress, her hair cascading down her back.

"Hey," she whispered. "Did you know Jacinto is hiding a cat in his room?"

What. The...

I lifted my head to look at Martina in the reflection, and her eyes were round. She licked her lips and swallowed audibly.

"Martina," I snapped. I heard Valentina chuckling by the door and wanted to snap at her too. "I can't." I sighed.

"What? It's all him, I swear!" she squeaked, her voice rising guiltily with the last syllables of the sentence. I groaned at her response because it was probably true.

Valentina walked into the room and sat on the bed, looking around the space. It hadn't changed at all since the last time she was here a few months ago, when she'd had a small fight with her great uncle and stayed the night.

"Where is everyone?" she asked, focusing on my reflection.

"Vee and Cata are in Charlie's room. Santiago is in his house with Charlie, Victoria's brother, and, hopefully, Jacinto. My parents are in their room, I guess."

She nodded along to what I was saying, probably not paying any attention to the actual words but instead searching my face for something I couldn't quite place. Martina started moving again, finishing up with hair spray all around my head.

"Okay," she said. "You're all set. Just come find me once you are in your dress so we can get those pins out of your hair and touch up your lips." She smiled at me and immediately turned around to collect her things, avoiding my eyes like the guilty friend she was.

I blinked a few times, trying to ground myself. It had already been a busy morning, and we still had a few more hours to go, so I tried to center myself and enjoy whatever else was coming. Valentina would stick close to me all night, which was a welcome reprieve because I wasn't ready to deal with dozens of people asking me to diagnose their kids —or themselves—via a blurry photo on their phone. Especially not the day of my brother's wedding.

A couple of hours later, we were all at the back of the house under the big tree that had been adorned with lanterns the night of the welcome reception. The sun was slowly setting behind the tops of the trees, casting a warm, golden glow over the backyard, and guests began to take their seats on the neatly arranged chairs set up for the quick, casual ceremony. It was all a blur in between saying hi to the guests, checking that everything was ready, and posing for photos as a family. From the corner of my eye, I could see Jacinto and Martina whispering in the corner. Valentina was lingering a few meters away from them, looking casually disinterested but probably eavesdropping in on their conversation.

"Excuse me," I said to the couple of locals that were chitchatting away at me. They had arrived a few minutes prior and came straight to say hi to me, wanting to talk about the practice and the patients and how old Dr. Martín was doing. Tres Fuegos wasn't overly gossipy—it had its rumor mill, as any small town did—but its inhabitants insisted on pretending they didn't snoop in on every single conversation. Case in point: Valentina.

"You are unbelievable," I whispered loudly enough so that both Martina and Jacinto would hear what I had to say. Martina took a quick look at me and turned the other way, heading straight into Valentina. "I can't believe you are hiding a cat in your room!"

Jacinto rolled his eyes at me and smiled, one of those shit-eating grins that came out in full display only on certain occasions and only with a few, select people. "It's not a cat," he added, rubbing his palms together in a sign of mischief. He was partially dressed—his shirt sleeves were rolled up his arms, and he wasn't wearing the tie he had only moments ago for our family photos. Martina was holding on to his suit jacket, draped over her tan arm. "It's kittens," he whisper-yelled, cupping his hand towards my ear like he was trying to tell me a secret.

"More than one?" I croaked. It felt like my eyes bulged out of my skull, and the only one laughing at my reaction was Jacinto, giddy with excitement. Martina cowered a few meters away behind us. "We'll deal with it later." I took a deep, dramatic breath just for the sake of it. "Please go get dressed and come to the front to take our seats because we are about to start."

Jacinto nodded eagerly and turned towards the house, Martina following closely behind. Valentina scanned the backyard for a second, then nodded at me. We walked together to the front of the set-up. We would be sitting in the front row. The plan was to have a quick and casual ceremony. Agustín, Victoria's brother, would fake-marry them and pronounce them husband and wife. In reality, they had already had their legal marriage at the registry the day before, with only a handful of people attending for logistical purposes. This was all about them, and the scene really did reflect that.

By the time we made it to our seats, Santiago was already standing at the front with my parents and Agustín. Victoria's father was a little bit away from them, chasing his granddaughter around the large tree. They were both laughing and giggling and having the time of their lives. She was cute.

The ceremony was short and sweet. Santiago bawled his

eyes out, of course. And I didn't think I had ever seen Victoria smile so much and so hard consistently. They had come a long way. She looked radiant in a floor-length satin gown. It was the complete opposite of what I would have expected of her, but again, she was a different woman than the one I met a few years ago. Much more carefree, like my brother.

"Hey, honey," I heard my mother say from behind me. She was wearing a blue dress that brightened her face and made the color of her hair pop. She looked happy, and none of the stress from the previous days was evident. "Did you eat?"

I rolled my eyes while still looking ahead of me at Victoria and Santiago dancing in the middle of the dance floor. They had their closest friends around them, all amping them up and creating a fun and loud atmosphere. "Mm-hmm," I said loudly enough for her to hear over the music. Ever since I'd moved back, both my parents had been constantly on me. Which was okay, I was their daughter, but it was like they treated me with kid gloves, and I couldn't get away from it. The moment I would step into the house after coming back from the office, they were on me. Especially my dad, who wanted every single detail about my day. "It was good."

I turned to look at her, and her gaze was fixed on the newlyweds. Who would blame her, really? They were breathtaking together. I followed her gaze and took a moment to look around. All eyes were on them and their love, which was evident by how they were looking at each other.

The tent was set up in a similar way to how the welcome reception had been, twinkle lights draped over the ceiling and hundreds of candles illuminating the tables. It was still casual. There was no assigned seating but different options for people to choose from: low seating areas, large tables with matching chairs around them, and tall cocktail tables for people to stand around. There was a large open bar towards the back of the tent, the glass top lit up with different colored lights that moved to the beat of the music.

I took a moment to scan the room, take in my bearings, and center myself to my surroundings. But that feeling of dread kept tugging at me. Of course the date was important to me, and despite my festive surroundings, I just... couldn't get rid of it. But then, my gaze stopped cold.

Because there, standing by the bar, was *Francisco*.

8

LUCÍA

No.

Impossible.

Or maybe I was seeing ghosts.

I wouldn't put it past me, really. Between the date and the stress of the wedding and the end of year, it could be possible, right? That I was seeing ghosts, I meant. Visibly conjuring a person from my past who was so closely associated with that thing from said past I couldn't get over.

She was haunting me. Jazmín was playing a cruel joke on me. On this date, no less.

"Let's go dance," a voice behind me said, pulling on my elbow in the direction of the dance floor. I turned to look at who was dragging me, but everything was a blur. I couldn't focus on a single face or sound. My heart beat wildly out of control in my chest, the sound echoing inside my head despite the music around us. I shook my head to clear my thoughts, but the only thing that did was manage to make me dizzier than I was, my knees weakening with every step I took. "Are you drunk?" the voice said over the loud music. I knew this person was right next to me, speaking into my ear, but I couldn't focus and figure out who it was. I squinted, but nothing happened. My body was moving in slow motion, but my heart rate was accelerating, pumping faster than it had ever done before.

I turned my body slightly back to the bar, the arm on my elbow still tugging me in the opposite direction. But he was no longer there.

"Lu, *dale*," Jacinto whined in my ear. "Let's go dance."

It couldn't be. He wouldn't be here because why would he be? I scanned the room once more, trying to find even a glimpse of those brown eyes that used to be focused intently on me during that time. The long nights, the adrenaline of sneaking around, the bonding over everything and nothing at the same time. And then, the silence that was absolutely deafening in my grief.

But I didn't blame him at all. I was also my own form of wreck, spiraling down so fast and so hard, I had to move back to my parents' home, claiming homesickness and a bad breakup.

Jacinto dragged us to the center of the dance floor, where Valentina and Martina were dancing together with a few other locals in a little circle. He shoved me inside and started moving along with the music, lifting his hands up and moving his pointer fingers to the beat. I laughed, trying hard to hide my mood. I looked at my friends, who were each in their own element. Valentina was silently scanning the room, probably trying to sneak a peek at Charlie. Martina, doubled in laughter at whatever shenanigans Jacinto was up to, sneaking smiles and glances and secrets in between dramatic dance moves. And Victoria and Santiago, very much the center of attention, of course, in their own little love bubble.

"You should get a cat," Martina yelled. It was hard to hear with the loud music and the bodies all moving in an almost choreographed dance. "It'll keep you company when we are all gone for the summer," she added with a shrug.

I laughed out loud at her spot-on interpretation of what my future held for me—lonely days and nights with a cat to keep me company. "Is that what you think of me?" I answered in between laughs. "That I'm an old cat lady?"

She shrugged again and smiled, one of those that reached her eyes, where they crinkled at the corners.

"Did Jacin tell you what we are planning?" she asked, speaking over the loud music. She was wearing a gold sequined dress that hit the floor, but she had it tied up in a knot at about knee length. Her dress shoes were long gone, and in their place, she was wearing her trusty pink slip-ons, the ones she usually wore at her waitressing job in town.

I rolled my eyes at her in a playful way and grinned, hoping to god that their ideas wouldn't land them in jail. I was sure, though, that Jacinto could talk his way out of anything, so I had no idea why I kept worrying about him—and Martina by association.

"I'm getting a drink," I said, turning around to head to the bar. I did a quick scan of the room again and saw my grandparents sitting in one of the lounges that were set up at the edge of the tent, having a lively conversation with the couple who had stopped by to talk to me before the ceremony started.

And he was nowhere to be seen. Just a blip in my field of vision, truly brought on by the circumstances.

The door had creaked, and I had immediately smiled because it could only have been one person at that time. "Hey," I heard him whisper that night.

I turned to look at Francisco, illuminated by the light in the hallway. The noises outside had subsided, probably because the staff was out doing their laps and had left the nurses' station empty. It was only a few minutes at a time that that happened, and he had timed it perfectly. Years of practice, he had told me once.

"Hi," I replied.

"How is she?" he asked immediately upon setting foot into the room. He turned around quietly and closed the door, making sure it latched all the way so that the nurses wouldn't notice the intrusion. He was in a complicated spot. *Entre la espada y la pared,* some would say. Their—shared—father was adamant that he not see her, but according to what I'd been told, he felt partially responsible and wanted to be close to her. Even if it was for minutes at a time and at night while she was asleep.

"Bored," I said with a playful tone. His gaze was intent on her, his brown eyes always on her the minute he arrived. He did this thing with people; he had a way with his words. It was like he turned it on. One minute it was there, and the other, it was gone. He was always *on* with her. In the beginning, the first few months of whatever that was, he had done it with me. A smile that reached his eyes, crinkling at the corners, even when it had been a hard day for everyone. A myriad of questions about anything—maybe what I'd had for lunch—and the accompanying body language that showed interest. It never looked too genuine, like maybe it was practiced, learned. He was the son of a politician, after all. So I assumed he had been trained, probably from early on, to turn on his persona.

But that had been slowly fading, and more of this— maybe his real, normal self—was coming out. Like this was a safe space for him. "It was a long day today. She wasn't allowed to go do her laps around the ward."

"And her tests?" He turned to look at me with a slight furrow in his brows. Jazmín was a social butterfly, and nothing stopped her. Except chemo and having to sit still in her bed for days at a time. Some days were rougher than others, but through the years, she had learned to listen to her body and rest. "What's the update there?"

"They are not back yet," I replied cautiously. We never wanted to give a patient's loved ones any sense of false hope. She was doing great, her spirits were up, she had no pain, but we could never be too optimistic. Just in case. "Should have them back tomorrow."

He smiled. *On.* Then he turned his whole body towards me. He took a few steps, then held out his hand and squeezed my bicep. A small greeting. "And how are you?" *On.*

This was our dance, our little routine of sorts. He would walk in, ask about his sister immediately, then turn it over to me. Ask about my plants and my family or the newest nurse drama. And there was a lot of drama to keep us entertained for hours.

"Good. I'm actually off for the next few days," I said absentmindedly. He had walked all the way to the chair in the corner of the room and angled his body in a way he could keep both me and Jazmín in focus. I was leaning by the window, flipping my view from the door to Jazmín and to him. We were careful because if the head of the service found out he was here, he would tell, and we wanted to avoid that. "Might go visit my family." I shrugged.

"Nice," he whispered, his gaze still on me. *Off.* He turned to look at his sister, who was still sleeping soundly. "How long has she been out?" *On.*

"Maybe a few hours?" I looked at my watch, then looked up at him. "She might be out for the night at this point."

"Okay," he said. "I'll stay for a little, and then I'll head out. Give me maybe thirty minutes, and then I'll be gone."

"Alright," I drawled, heading to the door. I turned to look at him and smiled. "See you in a few days."

"I'm serious about the cat," Martina said, and I blinked out of my trance. She placed her elbows on the top of the bar and rested her head on her arms. "I'm actually thinking of maybe opening a little cat café at the edge of town. You would be my first success story if you end up keeping one of the kittens."

Jacinto picked that exact moment to slide on my other side, looking down at me with those brown eyes of his. He had his puppy face on, head cocked to the side in a confused-slash-pleading look.

"Is this his idea?" I turned my body to face Martina and threw my thumb back, pointing at Jacinto behind me. He chuckled in response and moved a little closer, taking a big breath to answer, but I cut him off. "No, I want to hear what she has to say," I said, not even bothering to look at him.

Martina smiled, then looked between us, finally settling her gaze on me. "No, actually." She turned and thanked the bartender, who had set a few glasses of water on the bar. "I've been involved with a pet rescue org for a while, but there's usually much more demand for puppies and dogs. It's very hard to place cats, so I thought maybe we could promote it another way."

"And," Jacinto said, moving from behind me to just next to Martina, "I happen to have a litter of kittens that are looking for homes. What a coincidence."

What a coincidence indeed. "Why does trouble always find you?"

"Trouble?" he gasped. "Whatever do you mean?"

He let out a loud laugh, patting me on the back a few times. Martina was looking at him, giggling silently at his reaction.

"He's going to help me," she said. "And with the adjournment coming up, he'll have plenty of time to put his body to work for me." She looked him up and down with delight, but as soon as she saw I was looking, she pursed her lips. A flush formed on her cheeks, and I bit my tongue at her reaction.

"It's my pet project," he said and winked at me. "Get it? Pet project," he added, then chuckled at himself in amusement, like what he said was the funniest thing he'd ever heard.

"So are you?" Martina asked.

I frowned and turned to grab one of the water glasses. "Am I what?"

"Adopting a cat, Luli."

"I don't need a cat. I already have him," I said, looking straight at Jacinto, who was oblivious now. "He keeps me busy enough."

Martina laughed and took a large gulp from her glass. As soon as she set it on the bar, Jacinto took her by the hand and dragged her back to the dance floor, straight back to where some of their friends were hanging out.

"What's up?" Valentina asked. The question startled me

because I was focusing so much on trying to find him, I didn't see it coming. But that was Valentina in a nutshell. I never saw her coming, and she could read me from a mile away. "Who are you looking for?"

"*A nadie*," I said a little too fast, which earned me a look. She lifted her eyebrows and shook her head.

"*Aha*," she drawled, the expression coming out of her mouth quickly, following my eyesight right to the crowd surrounding Santiago. He was being thrown in the air by his friends. Some of them I recognized, and others I assumed were either colleagues or newer acquaintances. Victoria was looking up at the action from the floor, Catalina hanging off of one shoulder, laughing wildly at the scene. "Who is he?"

"Valen."

She gave me the side eye. "I also have my secrets," she said, turning her body towards me. "So I'm going to let you have yours." She lifted her hair and fanned the back of her neck with her free hand. She wasn't looking at me, and I appreciated the space, but I knew that I couldn't get away with much more of this. This thing I was doing, hiding my grief, trying to get over it but not working to get rid of it.

"Let's go dance," I said loudly, grabbing her by the hand and dragging her back to where we'd come from minutes before. And she let it go like she always did and didn't ask me about it again.

The night ended up going by in a flash. It wasn't my wedding, but brides always talked about how fast it went by, how it was all a blur of emotions and people and happiness. That was how it felt for me too. And suddenly, the sun was rising behind the tree tops, the crowds had thinned, and waiters were walking around the tent carrying trays of food.

Jacinto was standing on top of the bar, laughing loudly and throwing candy onto a small crowd that was hyping him up from below. Martina was slumped on a chair with her lids closed and a huge smile on her face.

Santiago and Victoria were still around, saying their last goodbyes to friends and family by the entrance to the tent, each of them with a bottle of water in one hand and sleepy grins on their faces.

Everyone looked happy.

"Hi," someone said to my right, draping a large arm around my shoulders. "Did you have fun?" My brother Charlie was standing next to me, the weight of his body hanging on my back. His hair was tousled, and he felt damp.

"*Qué asco*," I said, scrunching up my nose and looking towards him with more attention. His shirt was stuck to his body with sweat after what I hoped was a night of a lot of dancing. "You're all sweaty."

He laughed. Laughed. Then, with a big grin on his face, said, "I had a good time."

I beamed up at him. "It was a good party, I agree."

We both stood there, looking out at our siblings and our family. And a sense of relief ran through me because the day was over, and it was time to start the countdown again.

9

FRANCISCO

The wedding was a hit. Objectively. Everyone was having fun, drinks were going around, and the food was good.

But subjectively, it was boring. I didn't know a soul save for Victoria and Santiago, who were preoccupied with their things. So throughout the evening, I spoke to a few people I recognized from the previous days around town, stopped by to make small talk with Santiago's parents, and then found a spot in a back corner where I doom scrolled my phone for hours until it finally felt like I could leave without being noticed. By then I had enough insights on how the party went so that I would be able to participate in conversations in the next few days before everyone left town for their respective trips.

I could have turned it on and done everything my father always taught me, but it was exhausting, and it wasn't the day to do so. To do anything that remotely reminded me of him on such an important date to *me*. Having to be *on* all the time, having to be perfect and exactly what everyone always needed of me. The small talk, the million and one questions about people's lives, the smiles. God, I hated all the stiff smiling.

Because that was how I grew up. I grew up being "the child of" and never a person for myself. And for the past few years, I'd been trying to distance myself from that and be my own normal self.

Hence the extended vacation in this small town where no one knew me. A moment to step away from that chaotic life and pause. To gain back my bearings and see where I would go next. It seemed to have worked for Santiago years ago, when he took a break from work and decided that he wanted to stay in this town.

The day after the wedding, I had roamed around town at dawn, the silence following me while I explored the little corners of this place, looking to see if the answers I needed were hiding somewhere. It was a sleepy town, set awake once the sun was shining way up in the sky. But today was a completely different thing.

The town was buzzing with energy, probably because it was only a handful of hours until the end of the year, and everyone had something to talk about. Both the wedding and the new year that was approaching. Like it would magically turn a new leaf over, and anything that had happened this year would stay here.

The silence of the early morning had woken me up, the colors of the sky already changing from the cool purples and blues of dawn to bright oranges and reds. I put on my running clothes and headed out of the house, heading in the opposite direction to the town square, where Santiago had mentioned there were a few hiking and running trails. It was breathtaking, nothing like I had seen before, running under thick, lush trees. The heat wasn't bad, despite the intense drought brought on by the season. The shade under the trees even had a refreshing feel to it.

That was exactly what it was—refreshing. Like a welcome breath of fresh air. I rolled my eyes at my thoughts and decided to head back to the house, knowing that Santiago and Victoria would be back from their few nights staying at the hotel and would be packing and getting ready to go on their honeymoon.

I took a quick shower and headed to the back patio, then took a seat on the small couch facing the yard. Victoria was already sitting there, a mug in her hand and a tablet placed precariously on her leg. From what I could see, she was going over a case file, but I couldn't make out any of the finer print on the document.

"You're working?" I asked, laughing a little at the scene. Her new husband was probably inside, running around packing and getting ready to leave, and she was sitting here, working. She lifted her head and curled one side of her mouth as she took a sip of her coffee.

"I'm just reviewing something to send to Charlie, and then I'm done."

I nodded. Victoria had left her big corporate attorney job in the city once she moved to Tres Fuegos and had fit perfectly into her in-laws' firm. She looked happy.

The sliding glass door opened at the exact moment I looked up. Santiago walked through, and a blonde woman followed closely behind. Victoria was saying something right next me, but I wasn't listening, instead enthralled by the scene in front of me.

"I think I'm getting a cat." The woman sighed, almost like that was her only choice. Santiago chuckled in response, and she smiled at him brightly. She was wearing light blue scrubs with a pen tucked diagonally in her breast pocket. Her hair was up in a tight ponytail, but there were a few flyaways at the nape of her neck, where the humidity was making them stick to her skin.

All the air I didn't know I was holding left my lungs. And it felt like I was standing on a ledge, even though I was sitting down and my feet were firmly planted on the ground. My mind was reeling with the vision in front of me. That doctor from years ago. The one that was so kind to us. *Ella. Her.*

She blinked, then turned to Victoria. Her eyes did something weird, reactionary. But within a second, it was gone. Then she quirked her lips and turned to look at her brother, expectant.

"Lu, this is *Mago*, the friend I told you about," he said, looking between us. I stood up, moving in slow motion, my hands shaking with—who even knew. "Mago, Lucía, my sister."

Sister.

Sister? How was this possible? Could I have been so checked out that I didn't even notice her at the wedding?

My heart kicked into overdrive.

I could sense Victoria standing next to me, the warmth of her body close to my arm, but time stopped, and it was like Lucía and I were both inside a cone of nothingness. The universe playing a cruel joke on us both. Maybe.

My steps faltered, but I corrected myself. They were still standing right next to the sliding glass door, a few meters from where we were. I set my phone down on the coffee table, barely missing the edge of the top by a few centimeters. My movements were clumsy and erratic. Like everything I did around her.

"Hi," she said, lifting her hand and waving weakly. Did she not recognize me? "Nice to meet you." She smiled, and it was blinding.

Just like that first time I'd seen her in Jazmín's hospital room when her cancer came back. She was wearing pink scrubs then, her hair up in a messy bun, sitting askew on her head. It was past midnight then, the only moment I could sneak into the hospital to see my sister, who was getting treatment for the leukemia that wouldn't leave her system.

Since she had been born, I had been kept very separate from her life. My parents did everything in their power to keep her a secret from everyone, especially the press, but the fighting between them had escalated to violence, and they couldn't keep it from me.

She was the product of an affair—an abuse of power on my father's part—but I couldn't care less. She was my blood. And so to avoid hearing my parents fight about her, I would sneak into her hospital room in the middle of the night, on nights when her mother wasn't able to stay with her.

The hospital was aware of the challenging family dynamics, and most of the staff looked the other way, especially the night nurses.

"Hey," I had whispered to the head nurse that night. She was hunched over her phone, scrolling through her text messages. She looked up with a bright expression on her face, tucking her phone into the pocket of her scrubs and standing to give me a hug.

"What are you doing here?" she asked, a surprised look on her face. She looked around, trying to see if any of the heads of service were in the vicinity of her desk. "We just rounded, and she's passed out."

"It's okay," I replied. "I can stay until she's up if no one's going to rat me out."

She pressed her lips together, biting her smile. "We have a new doctor," she added. "She's a sweetheart. She won't rat you out, but you need to keep your distance. I'll brief her."

"Thank you." I bent over to kiss her cheek, then turned towards Jazmín's room. Once I was at the door, I winked at her, getting a big, toothy grin in response, and then walked into the room.

The doctor was leaning against the window, her gaze focused on a small notepad in her hand. She was chewing the end of her pen, lost in concentration over whatever was scrawled on the lined paper.

I closed the door quietly behind me, and at the small sound of the latch, she looked up, her nose scrunching in response. She relaxed her features and smiled, the corners of her lips ticking up just a little bit. She was stunning. Even with the wild golden hair on top of her head and those loose pink scrubs draping on her body. Her big, blue eyes shone in the dark of the room.

And now I was seeing her again after so many years of so many missed moments and things that were never said amongst us. Movement to my right snapped me out of my memories. Santiago moved to be closer to his wife, backing her body up against his front and draping his arm around her shoulders. He whispered something in her ear that made her light up and look up at him.

"She's going to be around this summer," Victoria said. I turned to look at my friend's wife, ping-ponging my attention between her and Lucía. I could see her mouth moving, her eyes fixed on me, but I couldn't make out a single word. "Whatever you need," she concluded.

"Francisco," I said, moving a step or two closer to Lucía

and kissing her cheek as a way of introduction. She hummed, and her hand hovered over my arm. She smiled in response and turned back to look at Victoria, who started asking her questions that, again, I couldn't make out between the rush of what was happening in front of me.

Shit.

10

No.

No. No, no, no, no.

"Mago, Lucía, my sister," Santiago said, waving a hand between us both. Victoria was standing right next to him, adding on to the comment and moving her mouth, possibly saying words out loud. Maybe something about watering the plants while they were gone because according to them —*allegedly*—I had a green thumb. I didn't, but I wasn't going to blurt that out now.

"Hi," I said weakly, my words (what even were those?) barely a whisper. I thought I gave him a weak wave, but my brain was reeling. "Nice to meet you."

What? No. No, this couldn't be happening. How? What? When? I—

Santiago moved towards his wife, standing behind her

and putting his arm around her shoulders, tugging her close to him.

"She's going to be around this summer," Victoria said. "She lives at the big house and will probably stop by to take a look at things, water the plants, whatever you need."

I nodded and kept that smile on my face. Did he not recognize me? He was doing the same thing, looking between Victoria, Santiago, and me, following the conversation. He looked good. *So good.* Better than what I remembered. His hair was longer, and his brown eyes were softer, somehow. Maybe he was tired, but it worked for him. The lines around them were much more pronounced. Like he'd spent the past few years just laughing wildly at life. He had a smile on his face too. It didn't make sense compared to my grief. Why would he look better? The time after Jazmín's death was rough for everyone, and I would imagine it was especially hard for him too.

"Lu, this is my friend from the firm I told you about that's going to be staying through the end of January and house-sitting for us."

More nodding.

"Francisco," he said. And he took a few steps and leaned forward to kiss my cheek. I blinked again, incredulous at what was happening, hoping to god everyone here was none the wiser. And his smell. *Jesus*, I had forgotten exactly what he smelled like. My nose tickled, and my eyes watered a little at the memories of the past. The last time I saw him. The last time I saw her, his sister.

"Anyway, what were you just saying about a cat?" Victoria asked, taking a step away from my brother and sitting back down where she was when I first came in. "Is this one of Jacinto's antics?" Her lips kicked up, and I responded with a similar expression, one I reserved for my patients' parents. Tight and fake. I huffed a laugh. Also fake. There was no joy in that moment, and I needed to get out of there, fast.

"Yeah, they guilt-tripped me into it." I shook my head and smiled again. "I actually have to get going because I have to check in on her." I looked up at them, moving my eyes back and forth between the three of them. "I'll see you later, Vee?"

Santiago and Victoria nodded in response, and I turned on my heel, not daring to linger or look back at him.

I walked through their house, straight for the front door, and closed it behind me with a little more force than I wanted. I beelined it for my parents' house, straight into the large entryway, up the stairs, and into my room.

Because I wasn't *seeing* ghosts. I was actually living among them.

———

I paced my room for what felt like hours. It was probably hours because by the time I looked up and was out of my daze, it was dusk, the sky a bright purple and a few stars blinking back at me, not a single worry on their metaphorical shoulders. The cat sat perched on the bed, a glare on her face as she tracked every single one of my movements inside my room.

Back and forth, back and forth. Like I'd seen him do so many times during those long hours we had been confined in the same space years ago. Sometimes he did it out of boredom, I'd learned after a few of his visits. Others, it was stress-induced. But every single time he did it, the pacing stopped as soon as his sister woke up. *On.*

Once she was awake, his eyes were on her. That was why when she died, his light probably died with her.

That one particular night, the night I figured out his pattern, was a happy one. He had been sneaking into her room to see her for a while. She was in with a nasty infection, and she knew it.

Nurses would move in and out of rooms, checking patient vitals. I would do a few rounds, but in the early morning hours, my body would complain and take me to the on-call room for a much-needed nap. The nights he was there, my body gravitated towards him, feeding off his light.

Mago. I'd never heard my brother talk about this friend. In fact, when we discussed the possibility of them having someone over to house-sit, Santiago had mentioned *Fran,* his best friend from work. I always thought he meant Franco, *not* Francisco.

Mago. That was what she called him too. She said his friends started calling him that when she was in the hospital the first time because he was always doing disappearing acts on them to sneak into the hospital to see her. She laughed and thought it was so amusing. So she kept it up, and he loved it. On some of her rougher days, he would show up in all-black clothing, doing stealthy moves like a ninja just to get a chuckle out of her. Too bad he only showed up at night, in the dark, because the other patients in the ward would have probably gotten a kick out of it. Of trying to make light of a situation that was as dark as could be.

The first time I'd ever seen him was on one of those nights. He was wearing all-black clothing and trying to sneak into the room. I had heard mumbling coming from the hallway, followed by a light click of the door. He stood there, taking in the room and his sister asleep in the middle of the bed, the IV drip hanging from a pole right behind the headboard. He stood there for a moment, looking at me with curious eyes, his gaze burning a hole in the side of my face. And then I looked up from my notes and beamed at him.

"*Mago,*" he said as he approached. His mouth opened and closed a few times, like he wanted to ask a question but couldn't quite verbalize it.

I lifted my hand. "Lucía," I said. "Nice to meet you."

We stood in silence in her room, the beeping of the machines taking over any conversation we could potentially have. He looked like he wanted to ask me questions about her but was still feeling me out. I was only a resident, and we'd never met before, so he had no reason to trust me beyond the care I was administering to his relative.

He turned, his body slumping on the companion's chair right next to the bed, his backpack discarded by the door.

"Are you staying over tonight?" I asked, his gaze bouncing from me to his sister. He grinned, focusing on me. She almost never had people stay over with her, so we took turns with the nurses to wait until she fell asleep and hung out with her in between rounds. His reaction surprised me, a big smile pointed my way.

"I'm…" he said, his words cautious out of his mouth. "I'm not really allowed to be here," he whispered, looking over at his sister to make sure she was still asleep. "But I'll stay for a bit."

I nodded, tucking my notebook inside my scrubs pocket and shoving the pen into my messy bun. The nurses had mentioned this particular case. A high-profile family that was messy. Messy with their secrets and their stories. But it was none of my business because I was there to take care of a patient, so he stayed and came back consistently to see her. His light in the dark of the hospital.

The cat jumped off the bed abruptly and sauntered over to me. She rubbed her lithe body between my legs. The movement relaxed me, bringing me back to the present, shaking off those memories.

"You need a name, sweet girl," I said as I crouched down to grab her soft body. Her purring was still low and cautious, developing together with her confidence and slowly getting her out of her shell. "You and me both, bud."

The lights flickered once, twice, before they were

completely off, and the cat scurried from my arms and slid right under the bed at the unexpected darkness. I sighed and face-planted on my bed, waiting to see if this one was going to be a classic summer blackout or if it was going to be one of the milder ones, just the warning before the big ones started.

A few moments later, the lights were back on, and the cat immediately jumped on the bed and curled against my side.

How could he not remember me?

11

FRANCISCO

DEEP BREATH.

New year, new me, right?

Except that, no, wrong.

Victoria and Santiago were walking ahead of me, hand in hand, in the direction of the big house, where the wedding had taken place only a few nights earlier. Turns out, the place was Santiago's family home, and apparently his sister lived there with their parents.

And she didn't remember me. "Nice to meet you," she had whispered, then kept going on about a cat and yet another person I didn't know in their town. It had been well over twenty-four hours, and I couldn't figure it out for the life of me.

It had to be her. It clicked now, the last name and when she talked about visiting her family in her hometown. I always thought she was talking about spending time with her parents, like she lived in the city and they were farther out in the suburbs. I never knew they were so far away in this mountain town.

She talked about her plants, about her job. She told me a little about what made her become a doctor, about Jazmín. But we never spoke about much else. Or at least, nothing too deep or intimate. Because I was just her patient's brother, and she was that, my sister's doctor.

We walked through the driveway towards the front door. It was left ajar, and we could hear the conversation from the sidewalk. Daylight was still clinging, holding on tight and never wanting to leave. It was technically night-time on New Year's Eve, but it still felt like a long, endless afternoon. I was carrying an impossibly large salad in my hands. Santiago was clutching a bag with a few bottles of wine he had brought in from his hotel that same day.

Apparently, the new year was a big deal in Tres Fuegos. Maybe everyone lived up to the motto of *new year, new me*.

The house was loud with laughter coming from all directions. As soon as we walked in, a toddler came running our way and jumped into Victoria's arms, her mother following behind with a stern look on her face.

"Oh, it's you." She sighed, but then she grunted, and her mouth curved up as she walked in our direction. Victoria switched the small girl to her hip and then hugged her sister-in-law with one arm, hooking it around her neck. "Finally."

Santiago kissed her on the cheek and kept walking

towards the back of the house, turning his head and nodding in the direction for me to follow him. The entry hallway dead-ended onto a large doorway, and I could see all the lights on from the front door.

"How many people are here?" I asked Santiago. Between the door being left ajar and the loud noises coming from the back, it had to be a few dozen at least. It was a stark contrast to how I'd spent the past twenty holidays of my life, at least. Either surrounded by people I'd never met before or alone in a dark house because my parents couldn't bother with me. Since college, I had started spending New Year's Eve with friends, but other holidays were a little lonely still.

"It's only our siblings and some close friends." He smirked and scrunched his nose. "We are a loud bunch."

We walked into the kitchen and dropped the food and drinks on the island, where someone had laid out a massive spread of food for the guests in the house that evening. I said hello to the few people around the kitchen table who were too engrossed in a conversation about who the best Power Ranger was to be interrupted.

And then we walked out into the backyard. The large tent was gone, and in its place, there were three different seating areas, a larger one closer to the back of the lot around a firepit that was all embers and ashes. Right next to the entrance to the house, they had set up a long table with drinks, so I headed that way while Santiago made his rounds. I could hear squeals coming from inside the house, followed by some laughter and then more high-pitched screaming.

This family was a loud bunch indeed.

I walked towards one of the seating areas farther out into the lot, next to the neighboring house. A few trays with appetizers lined the table, and there was a full bottle of wine in the middle, glasses stacked right next to it. There were a few board games piled on the tabletop, a game of Monopoly mixed in between. I circled the table, drifting my fingers along the edge of the box, completely immersed in my thoughts, then sat down and stared at the bright colors on the board game taking me back to a different moment in time.

It was a quiet night, that one. The nurses' station was only inhabited by Sonia, the charge nurse, who had learned to ignore me. Although occasionally, I would catch her small smile as I walked by her desk. Lucía wasn't standing with them that night, but instead I could hear her whispering from down the hall, discussing something with another one of the staff. I looked her way, and almost like she felt my eyes on her, she lifted her head and brightened in return. I winked at her, then turned to head towards my sister's room. I had texted her in advance to let her know I was coming and to wait for me. Usually, when she was in for her multi-day chemos, she was tired and was not able to stay awake for long periods, but this time, it was different.

"*Ey*," I whispered as I walked in, looking into the room to make sure the coast was clear. I was technically allowed in to visit her since I was family and our last names matched. It was a common last name, probably so common that my parents had hyphenated mine, combining both of theirs, to make us a little bit more distinguished amongst *others*. And I was cautious because I never wanted to bring any extra attention to myself. Somehow everything I did always got back to my father. "*¿Cómo te sentís?*"

She was smiling with her lids closed, but I could nonetheless picture her eyes rolling at me. Her brown hair was short, finally growing in after the last round of chemo. She reminded me so much of a younger version of myself, except for the eyes. Where mine were brown, like my father's, she had bright green ones after her mother, Florencia. Someone had to be blind to not realize we were siblings. And for half-siblings, we were too much alike. Because we both took after our father.

"Fine," she answered, sitting up and leaning against the pillows behind her body. "Did you bring it?"

I snickered as I closed the door quietly behind me, then took off my large backpack and unzipped it at the foot of her bed. I wiggled my eyebrows at her and snatched the box from my bag, doing spirit fingers with the other one. Jazmín clapped her hands and hooted, her loud laugh echoing in the bare room.

"Shhh," I said in between chuckles. "They're gonna find us out."

She smiled one of her giant smiles and then whispered, "They already know what we are up to, *bobo*." Dumb-dumb.

I laughed at her, then moved over to the other side of the bed to set up the game. She looked healthy that night, like the medication was finally working and she was able to fight the infection. She had been through so much, and she was missing out on the last few weeks of her last year in school because of her constant infections.

"Alright, you get the car," I said, and she rolled her eyes at me, almost like she was saying, *like, duh,* to me. As if I had forgotten. "I get the dog."

"Oh, save the top hat for Lucía. She's always the top hat when she plays with her family," she said casually. I turned to look at her, a question on my face. "I told her we were playing tonight, and she said she would stop by if she could for a few rounds."

"Alright." I looked at her and handed her the dice, her small hand reaching out towards me. I looked at the door, then back to the board game, a small flutter in my belly at the possibility of seeing that kind doctor.

"Ohmigod," she gasped. "You like her!" She was squealing in her bed, moving her legs up and down and clapping her hands like an excited toddler.

I smiled and shook my head, reaching for the dice that were still cupped in her hands. "*Estás delirando,*" I said, a grin on my face. It was the happiest I'd seen her in a long time. The disease was definitely taking a toll on her. She was diagnosed in her early teens, but it had come back in the last year, and it was doing so with a vengeance. Everything and anything would give her an infection, and she would be in the hospital for weeks at a time. It was so hard to watch her bored to death in that little room. The only thing keeping her sane was that doctor, probably, and her books. "We're just friends."

"Just friends, *las bolas,* Fran," she said. "Even the nurses say so."

I snapped my head towards her, my eyes widening. She cackled like a mad woman, screaming with such delight that I couldn't help but laugh too.

"You're a lost cause," I added, setting up the game in between us and sitting at the foot of the bed. She tucked her small legs under her, dragging the table towards her with a big smile on her face.

"Whatever." She rolled her eyes, but her smile lingered, even as we got into the game. She started telling me about her day, catching me up on some nurse gossip, then talking about how the pretty doctor—wink—was not taking good care of herself and would normally not have lunch during her shifts.

"What happened here?" I asked, looking at the back of one of her hands. The bruises extended all the way up her forearm and towards her elbow. "What the fuck?" I stood abruptly and walked to the door to look for the doctor.

"Fran," she said from her bed, sitting up straighter and rolling her shoulders back. "It's nothing!" she uttered quickly. "They drew blood the other day, and it just bruised. Calm down."

"Does it happen often?"

"*Duh.*" She rolled her eyes again. "I have leukemia, dumb-dumb."

"So what?"

"Oh my god." She sighed. "Let's just play, okay?"

"I'm going to ask the doc—"

"Double sixes!" she interrupted. "Yesssssss."

I made a mental note to talk to the doctor about her bruises. Jazmín moved her car all the way to the electric company and purchased the property, taunting me a little because she already had a leg up from her double roll. We played like that for a while, going back and forth between purchasing properties and paying rent to the other one. A few rounds in, Lucía peeked her head into the room, a playful smirk on her face.

"Hey, you," she said to Jazmín, walking directly to the foot of the bed. She had a notepad out and was looking at the monitor right behind her, taking quick notes of my sister's vital signs. "How are you doing?"

Jazmín's face lit up at the sight of the pretty doctor. We had lucked out with her because in the last few months and since my sister had been in and out of the pediatric unit, she had become close to Lucía. She had kept her company when Jazmín's mother wasn't able to be there and I was either running late or wouldn't be there either.

"Ugh, you guys are exhausting," she said with a big smile on her face. "Sit. You get the top hat."

Jazmín handed her the Monopoly piece, then the dice, and then we played until my sister fell asleep with the dice in her hand. It felt so normal, even with our surroundings and the constant beeping of the machines around us. Like what *normal* families would do on free nights to spend time together.

"Do you mind if I join you?" a soft voice said from behind me. I turned my head at the same time as Lucía moved in my direction. I had been absentmindedly stroking the Monopoly box while lost in my thoughts. She took a few steps towards me, standing right in front of me on the other side of the table.

"Ohhhh, Monopoly," one of the brothers said from the other side of the pool while rubbing his palms together. "Dibs on the thimble," he yelled, jogging towards us and taking a seat beside me on the long bench.

"Jacinto," someone groaned from the back porch. "Calm down."

He was bouncing on the seat next to me, eagerly opening the box and setting the board down. "Luli is always the car," he said and grabbed the small piece to hand it to her. I snapped my head in her direction, trying to find answers on her face. She was sitting across from me, her hair cascading down her back and a colorful headband decorating the crown of her head. She was wearing a white dress, much like the majority of the women there. But hers made her eyes stand out. Even in the dim light of the dark night, she was shining. "Sucks to be you if you were going to pick that piece."

"I'm good with the dog," I added and shrugged in

response. Lucía smiled at me, and if I weren't looking so intently at her, I would have missed the tiny squint that came my way. A second there and then gone.

"Jacinto," someone else warned as they walked in our direction. "Please don't scare the innocent." There was laughter around the table, and Lucía laughed in her brother's direction, rolling her eyes discreetly and then looking back at me with a watchful expression.

A few others joined us, and we played for a few rounds until people started getting up, walking around the yard, and chatting with the small groups that were huddled around the different seating areas. Santiago was now sitting at the table with me after dragging me inside to grab some food, then bringing it out to the table to eat. Victoria sat on his lap, but her body was turned towards Lucía, who had moved to the other side of the bench at some point during our Monopoly game. They were talking about Victoria and Santiago's trip to the South of France, how one of the planned excursions fell through, but they were happy about it because they realized they had been overzealous and packed too much into it. Apparently, Santiago hadn't taken any time off since he moved back to Tres Fuegos for good, so this was a very welcome time off for both of them.

"Maybe you should move the plants here," Victoria said casually. Lucía eyed me quickly, then went back to her sister-in-law. "It might be easier to have them all in one place instead of going back and forth."

"Yeah, no," Lucía said with a smile on her lips. "There's

no way I'm going back and forth tomorrow to grab them all." She shook her head and took a sip of her wine.

"Just trying to make it easier for you, you know. In case there's a blackout or if there is a storm, you won't have to run to the house."

"Pft," Lucía replied. "It's much easier this way. Besides, I have literally nothing to do. I can go at any time."

"Do you have a green thumb?" I asked, cutting in on their conversation.

Victoria turned to look at me and smiled. "The green-est," she said, laughing.

"Allegedly," Lucía added with a wink towards her sister-in-law. "I haven't taken care of plants since I moved back into town."

"It's like riding a bike," Santiago said in between bites of food, but then laughed and shrugged. "I wouldn't know because I kill them all. She's the one that keeps ours alive." He kissed his wife's shoulder and draped a hand around her waist, bringing her closer to his body.

"Well," I drawled, "maybe you can teach me a thing or two?" I smiled at Lucía, hoping... for what? Would she remember me if I brought up things from our shared past?

"Sure." She shrugged. "I'll walk you through it."

12
LUCÍA

Qué te pasa. Valentina was right. There had to be something wrong with me.

I'll walk you through it? Who the fuck said something like that to a man who belonged very far in their past?

"It's too hot for a fire right now," Charlie harrumphed from the other side of the yard, where Jacinto was laying down a few logs in the firepit. "I just can't with you," he said, shaking his head back and forth in disagreement.

"Charlie, you are such a party pooper, man," Jacinto argued back, making a large pile of logs inside the brick circle that would contain the fire. "If it's too hot, then you don't have to stand here."

"Jacinto." Charlie was standing by the unlit fire, inching towards the pile of logs to start removing them, his face stoic and his fingers on his other hand tapping lightly on his leg. He sighed, then turned to look at me, his eyes pleading for something. Intervention, probably.

I shrugged and smiled at him, chuckling a little under my breath. He glared at me, then turned back to Jacinto, mumbling something to him and squatting down to the grass to remove a log.

"*Dale*, man," Jacinto said, his features tightening at what Charlie was doing. "Just leave it."

"Shit," I said and stood from the table quickly. "Be right back."

I speed-walked towards the firepit, knowing well that this was the beginning of a long-standing fight between them. Charlie was too serious for any of Jacinto's shenanigans, and Jacinto was usually extremely rowdy at the end of the year, when the nice weather and the long days gave him too much free time with his thoughts.

"Uh-uh, nope." I looked at both of them and crossed my arms across my chest. "Immediately no."

"But he—" they both said at the same time, pointing fingers at the other one.

"No," I said, cutthroat. I looked at Charlie. "You are a grown man, and you don't live here, and if you think it's too hot for a fire, then you don't participate. Period. Go inside with Granny and Grandpa and keep them company. And you." I pointed at Jacinto. "*Dale*, you know better."

"It's too funny," he said, chuckling while he added more wood to the firepit. "He gets riled up too easily."

Charlie glowered at him, then turned around and

stomped towards the house, his arms dangling by his sides and moving intentionally with his strides. He had been extra grumpy since the wedding, hiding in the big house and avoiding town at all costs. He had even slept in his old room a few nights instead of walking the six blocks—literally—to his house to spend the night. He was jumpy and jittery, more than usual.

I laughed because it was true. It was easy to get him riled up. But I was the only one allowed to do it. Jacinto drove him absolutely insane, and the age gap between them didn't help. They were ten years apart and in very different moments of their lives.

"Behave, please."

"Fine, but I'm telling you, it's going to get colder later on, and this will be nice." Jacinto stood next to me, the sudden feel of the warm fire on my bare legs was comforting somehow. Then he turned towards the big house, a cheeky smile on his face.

I scanned the yard. Victoria and Santiago were sitting under the big tree where they were married, sharing a small metal bench that my mom usually had there. She had placed a rustic coffee table in front of the seats, and they both had their feet propped up on it, Santiago's crossed at the ankles. They both looked so relaxed, and Victoria was beaming, looking at my brother.

I wasn't jealous of them. I actually loved how they had grown together since they decided to give their relationship a go, but it was so different than what I was doing. For many moments in our lives, it seemed like Santiago and I had walked in tandem, approaching our adult lives in similar ways. But now it seemed like he had taken a side road, and I was stuck in this small town, in my parents' house, being treated like a teenager all over again.

I'd moved to Buenos Aires for med school and had all the intentions of becoming a pediatrician and then following that up with a fellowship and specialization in pediatric oncology. It was a coveted program, a single spot at that hospital. I was on my way there, and it was going well. And then the Francisco train hit me hard in the middle of the chest when I least expected it. And between Jazmín's death and what happened after, I was lost. Drowning.

Jacinto came running out of the house, holding fire-crackers and sparklers in his arms, cradling them like they were his newborn kittens. Martina followed behind, a glimmer in her eyes as she turned the corner towards the street. That had been our signal for years—someone walked out of the house with our small kit of fireworks, if they could be called that, and then we all huddled towards the back of the property so we could watch the show from behind the big structure.

It was our own way of welcoming the new year.

My parents sat with my grandparents by the pool, enjoying their drinks and a few desserts. The men were having a conversation, and my mother was looking around the lot, smiling at the scene in front of her. Charlie was scowling in a corner, sipping something from a low glass, sitting with Victoria's brother and sister-in-law, who was holding a sleeping toddler in her arms.

And Victoria and Santiago were cuddled under their tree, his arm around her shoulders, bringing her closer to him. Her head was lying on his chest, and her lids were closed while Santiago spoke into the top of her head, kissing her hair every few words.

Ugh.

Francisco was sitting on his own, still looking at the discarded Monopoly board, toying with the car piece between his thumb and index finger. His gaze was far away, probably in the same place where my thoughts were. Back to her.

It had been a few grueling days. Since the wedding, since the day of that anniversary, I hardly had time to think of her.

Five, four, three, two, one. New year. New countdown.

It was a flash. A moment of darkness around us, followed immediately by sparks lighting up the sky behind the house. Jacinto's laughter could be heard all the way from the back, giddy with excitement at the show he was putting on.

And then when I turned to go hug my parents, Francisco was standing there, frozen solid and squeezing his eyes shut. Everywhere around us, people were hugging and kissing each other, screaming with joy at the new year. The pops of fireworks were loud in the background, but instead, Francisco was standing to the side, his fists tight, his knuckles white from the intensity of his grip.

"Happy New Year," I said as I got closer to him. His breath was heavy, but he snapped his eyes open to look at me, immediately searching my face for... what? "*¿Estás bien?*" I asked with a smile, trying to diffuse the tension a bit.

"Yeah, I'm okay." He huffed and gave me a weak smile. "It's been a tough year."

I smiled and rolled my eyes. "Tell me about it. Imagine living with your parents when you are in your thirties."

I giggled, but he remained stoic, his hands still curled in fists to his side.

"You can tell me," I whispered, hoping for anything that he would remember. The lights flickered on, and his hands relaxed. His jaw was still tense, but he moved his body, a tiny sigh of relief leaving his lips. "We are a lot. I get it."

I smiled, and he turned to face me, his lips curling up in a polite smile. *On.* He tucked one of his hands in the pocket of his Bermuda shorts, then ran his fingers through his hair, tousling it a little bit. I blinked because for a split second, he looked so much like that man I'd met years before, hanging out in a hospital room, hiding from the world and laughing together.

It was a different time; moments when my life wasn't so heavy. Before her.

"Lu," my mom said from the door to the house, interrupting my thoughts and bringing me back to now. "Do you want some champagne? Francisco?"

We both turned to face her, a big smile on my face. "*No, gracias, Ma.*"

"How's your cat?" he asked, his eyebrows rising in question. "I heard you were getting one?"

"Oh." I snort-laughed. "Jacinto practically bullied me into adopting one of the cats he found last week."

He scrunched his nose. "Not a cat person."

"Everyone is a cat person," I said with a scowl. "You just don't know that yet."

He laughed, and I couldn't help but follow him because that was who he was. A lighthearted man who enjoyed my company, and we laughed at the silliest of things.

"Does it have a name?"

"Not yet. I'm still trying to figure it out."

"Hmm," he added, running his fingers through his hair again absentmindedly. He wasn't smiling, but he wasn't frowning anymore. So I would consider that a win. He turned again, walking towards the table where we had sat all night and tucking his long legs under it. He scanned the top, then started collecting all the discarded pieces of the board game, meticulously piling the cards and grouping everything together. It was almost like they were practiced movements—muscle memory from the many nights he'd done it with his sister in the hospital.

"So." He looked up and turned to me, a small smile on his face and all traces of his meltdown erased from his expression. "This thing with the plants." He cocked his head to the side, expectant.

I snorted in response because it wasn't a thing. Maybe it had been one back then, when I lived with my siblings during med school and residency, and it was something we'd talked about a little. If he remembered me, would he be asking about it? "Oh, nothing. I volunteered to water their plants when they were gone, but I didn't know anyone was staying at their house," I said dismissively.

"It wasn't the original plan, you know?" He was looking down to the Monopoly board, moving the cards just so. Like he didn't care that they would move the moment that box was lifted from the table. "Not sure what changed."

"Guilty," I said, lifting my right hand in the air. "I was going to stay there for the summer, but my parents needed me here."

He nodded, closing the lid to the board game and looking at me, his eyes intent on mine. And then something cracked, and Jacinto laughed, and the moment was gone.

13

FRANCISCO

"THIS PLACE IS CALLED LIGHTHOUSE POINT," she said, looking around us.

We were high up in the mountain, a valley visible from our position at the peak. A slow smile started forming on my lips at the irony of a land-locked point in the middle of the country being referred to as a lighthouse, a beacon for ships in the night.

"I can feel you laughing behind me," she said, her smile evident in the tone she was using. That morning I had woken up earlier than usual, the quiet moments of the small town still taking me by surprise, even after consecutive nights of being alone in that house and moving to a new rhythm. I sat on the living room couch, a favorite spot where I could look outside both the front and back windows and see the movements of the trees beyond the clear glass.

A tall, leggy figure ran past the window, her golden hair

catching up to her as her body moved. I stood abruptly and followed her with my eyes to see her stop at the corner of the street and immediately turn back. For a second, she hesitated, turning her body in opposite directions, her nose scrunched up as her thoughts probably moved inside her brain.

Her hair was longer than the night before and blonder somehow. Wilder. I had only seen her with her hair up at the hospital. A few times it had been tousled, like she had gotten out of bed in a hurry and hadn't had a chance to fix her ponytail before having to do her middle-of-the-night rounds with the nurses.

I walked to the front door and jerked it open, startling her in the process. She had jogged back the way she had come from, slowing down noticeably once she had reached Santiago's front door.

"*Buen día,*" I drawled, my voice still raspy with sleep. Her hand went to her chest, right above her heart. Definitely startled. "What are you doing up so early?"

It was a ballsy move, to be so direct. I left abruptly from her house the night before, uncomfortable with the intimacy of the situation. Of her witnessing my panic during the few seconds of total darkness before the light was back on.

"Ah, good morning." She smiled, her eyes squinting in an unnatural way, like she was faking it or slapping it on for my benefit. Her hands moved down to the sides of her body, and she clenched her fists. Open, close. Open, close. "Uh, I was going for a run," she added, her head turning towards her house. She bent her knee, moving her right ankle in circles at the same time. The movement was so natural, like this was muscle memory for her. Back then we never got into such details, choosing instead to talk about minute things and focus on my sister's well-being instead. Maybe she had been a runner all this time?

"Cool." *Idiot.* I cleared my throat and leaned against the door frame. "This early?"

She messed with the hem on her T-shirt with one hand and twirled a lock of her hair in another. "Ah." She shrugged. "A blessing and a curse, this whole doctor thing. I can fall asleep almost anywhere, but my body is also ready to go the moment it wakes up."

That explained the messy ponytails on those nights I remembered so vividly.

"Cool." *Ugh.* I opened my mouth to say something, both to apologize for the night before and thank her for being so kind to me, but nothing came out.

"Anyway." She pointed her thumb towards the house behind me. "I was wondering if I could water the plants real quick?" She blinked once, almost in slow motion, long lashes reaching to touch the tops of her cheeks.

"Oh," I replied like an absolute fool. "Um, sure, yes, yes, of course." *Shut up.*

I moved to the side, and she took a few tentative steps into the house. It was completely dark except for a handful of candles on the hearth, remnants from the night before.

She eyed them cautiously, walking in a straight line to the back and through the sliding door to the patio. She mumbled something unintelligible and tugged at something under the grill, then stood up abruptly and smiled at the scene. Within a few seconds, her expression was back to neutral, a watering can in one hand, the other one draped over the faucet while she waited for the water to fill up.

She moved quickly, her movements almost featherlight around the house. And I stood like a fool in the middle of the living room, just looking at her. I could have said something, but instead I was dazzled. Stunned into silence by the familiarity of having her around me.

Lucía dropped what she was using back where it belonged, then locked the door to the backyard and turned to me. She opened her mouth to talk, but no words came. So we stood there for a few seconds, looking at each other. I cocked my head, and she shook her head in response, like she was clearing her thoughts.

"Alright," she drawled. "I'm going to head out." Her eyes were shining in the faint light of the morning.

"Okay," I said with a smile on my face like an idiot. "Enjoy your run."

She smiled in return, a genuine one, I thought, and turned on her heels, taking a few steps before turning back to face me again. "Would you like to join me?" she asked, a frown immediately forming on her expressive face.

And that was how we ended up on the top of this peak,

looking out onto the valley with houses scattered all around, at sunrise.

"I'm not laughing," I said, eyeing her cautiously. She was wearing long, black leggings, and a pair of very colorful shoes. Her top was tight against her slender body, a totally different sight than the many times I'd seen her in those loose pink hospital scrubs. "I just find it od—"

"It's a small town, Francisco." She sighed and turned to face me. But she was smiling, her expression shiny with something I couldn't quite place. Hopefully levity.

"I didn't say anything," I said, a loud laugh leaving my mouth, echoing slightly in the valley below us. "I just find it amusing that, quite literally, in the middle of—"

"I know," she blurted. "I guess they didn't have much to do when they named these peaks, right?" She turned to her right, focusing on a small clearing close by on the side of the mountain. "See right there?" She lifted her hand and pointed her finger towards that location. "It's called Eagle's Nest." She smiled. "Ask me how many eagles I've seen in my lifetime."

She laughed. This time, her smile finally reached her eyes.

"*¿Ves?*" I said. See? "*Tengo razón.*"

"There're people in this town who have never, ever left. Not even to go to the small city that is less than an hour down the mountain. I'm not talking about Buenos Aires, you know?" She sighed.

From what I could tell from my conversations with her

brother when we worked together in Buenos Aires, all of their siblings had moved to the city for their education. Her brothers had chosen to go straight to law school, following in their father's and grandfather's paths. But she went to med school, obviously. It wasn't clear to me why she had chosen a different career, especially if her family had a long and successful legacy in what they all did. Her father and grandfather were really respected family attorneys in the area, and her sister-in-law had joined them too. She didn't owe me any type of explanation, of course, but that didn't mean I wasn't curious.

"Why—"

"I don't get it," she interrupted my question. I wanted to know more. She raised her eyebrows at me in response, urging me on with my question. But at my silence, she kept going. "Why would you not at least go and *see* what is out there?"

"Well." I turned to face her. The sun was slowly inching up beyond the mountain peaks, coloring the tops of the trees in a bright orange that I hadn't seen in years. "I guess it could be said the same of people who never leave the city." She looked at me, her eyes studious over my face. "I'm partially guilty of that myself."

I smiled, even though the reasons for that statement were not worthy of happy memories. Jazmín was born when I was in my early teens, and everything after that was chaotic for me. For my family.

My upbringing was already nontraditional, the son of a

very prominent political figure. I never had structure, being carted around from event to event. Missing out on school because of my family's obligations. And then when my sister was born, everything for me just... stopped. I stopped going out in public except to go to school and back. My parents fought a lot. Things in the house were tense.

"It's the first time I've been to this province." I shrugged. "To any of the provinces, really."

"You're lucky, then," she drawled, cocking her head to the side. Her eyes roamed my body for a fraction of a second, and then she turned her body to look out onto the large valley behind her, bright blue sky engulfing her frame. "It's the best province."

"Yeah," I agreed.

"And the best time of the year too." I took two steps and stood next to her at the edge of the trail. Voices got louder and louder behind us, and the sound of gravel under shoes lingered in the air. "Ready to head back?"

"Yeah."

Her so-called run ended up being a leisurely and quiet stroll through the trails that wrapped around her small town. By the time we made it back to the town square, the sun was burning hot high in the sky, and the townspeople and tourists were out and about, moving in practiced motions through the streets. Lucía took a deep breath once we reached her brother's hotel, her eyes looking straight ahead in the direction of her parents' house. It was the first day of the year, and it felt exactly like it. People were moving about in fast, hurried movements with a sense of urgency, like their resolutions started right then and there, and if they didn't hustle, they would catch up to them.

The polar opposite of what our morning had been. There was a sense of intimacy to what had just happened, like we knew each other.

Because we did. But so many years had passed that maybe, definitely, we didn't know the next thing about each other.

"I love the smell of this town in the summer."

I laughed in response because of all the things she could have said after those moments of silence, this was what she came up with. "What do you mean?" I chuckled, waiting for her response.

She smiled, the movement making her features light up with eagerness. She took a deep breath, then exhaled dramatically, smiling and rolling her eyes at me. "The smell of the flowers is addicting."

Huh. "I don't think I've ever paid any attention to the smell."

She shrugged. "It's my favorite thing ever."

She kept walking, and I trailed behind, following every single one of her movements. Paying closer attention to the things she had mentioned during our walk. The smells, the sounds, the colors. Anchoring me to the town.

"Hey," I whispered, reaching out to grab her elbow. She looked over her shoulder at me, her arms relaxed at her sides. Her skin was flushed from the heat and the long walk, and a few tendrils of her hair were sticking to the side of her face, damp with sweat.

"Mm-hmm," she answered.

I stopped. "I..." I ran my fingers through my hair. "I wanted to say thank you for last night." Her eyes widened in response, a kind smile on her lips.

"No problem," she said, lifting one shoulder almost dismissively. I hoped she was doing it for my own good, to spare me the embarrassment of the whole thing. Of a grown man being afraid of the dark.

"Thank you."

"Okay, well," she replied and lifted her hand in a small, awkward wave, "I'm heading that way." She gestured with her head behind her in the direction of the house.

I took a step forward as she turned, lifting my arm to squeeze her bicep. It was a move I'd done a million times in the intimacy of that hospital room, the darkness of those days enveloping us and keeping us separate from the world in our own bubble. But today, in the stark daylight, she froze. And I froze in response.

Her gaze snapped to mine, her posture stiff in front of me.

I dropped my hand and said, "See you later." Then I turned on my heel in the opposite direction of where I should be heading because... fuck.

14

FRANCISCO

THE THIRD TIME IT HAPPENED, the storm was loud. Compared to those first times, where lights flickered in warning and they were back on within a few minutes, this was much more momentous. One second, the lights were on. The next, it was pure darkness.

Darker than those times.

But thunder rumbled and lightning promptly lit the sky like in an end-of-the-world movie. And everything shook in this small town.

That night, on New Year's Eve, Lucía had immediately noticed something was wrong. She walked towards me, bypassing her family and her friends to talk me out of it. My thoughts immediately took me to that time many years ago when everything was dark and scary.

I had worked for years to get over my fear. And all my effort was paying off. I was slowly inching towards managing my triggers like an adult. But then my sister died, and everything went to shit. Because not only had she died, but then many things happened in succession, and a lot of family things were unearthed after she passed.

I found myself sitting alone in the middle of the empty house, paralyzed by the darkness, unable to move even to grab the matches to light some candles. I was getting ready to go for a run, something I had been doing frequently to both get out of my thoughts and to get to know the town better. There were a few trails along the hillside that I saw when I went for that walk with Lucía. But the storm and the blackout that followed took me by surprise, and I didn't know how to react or what to do.

I turned on my heel, keeping my breaths even and focused on the things I could see—Victoria's plants in the corner of the living room, the small entry table with the bowl on top for keys, and the wind blowing outside, making the leaves move in synchronization to the noise it was making.

I knew that if I walked out that door and headed left, I would eventually make it to the big house, and the chance that she was there was pretty high, considering she had mentioned multiple times that she had not a single plan during her time off this month.

So I took a shot in the dark—literally—and walked in the direction of her house, uttering a silent prayer that she would open the door. It was raining hard. My whole body was soaked the second I stepped outside Santiago and

Victoria's house. My running shoes squelched on the pavement, and I could feel the slosh under the bottoms of my feet. It was, luckily, calming to focus on something else and not the darkness around me.

The house was completely black except for a dim white light coming from a window in the upstairs of the house, right above the front door and visible from the driveway. It was slightly open, and the curtain inside was moving with the wind blowing inside.

I walked fast up the driveway and right to the covered porch, knocking loudly once, twice. A clap of thunder followed the knock, but I waited for a minute. Water was coming down hard, my calves getting splashed despite being under a roof. The entry porch was small, just enough for a few people to stand at the same time and as wide as the double front door. There were bushes on either side of the house under the large windows.

I knocked again, this time harder than I intended. Goosebumps erupted across my spine because this was taking much longer than I was comfortable with. If she didn't open the door within the next few seconds, I would have to run back to Santiago's house alone and stay there until the lights came back on.

"*¿Quién es?*" I heard from inside the house, the voice a little weak and weary.

"Lucía?" I croaked, my body deflating with relief. I rested my forehead on the door, taking a deep breath.

"Jesus," she said, her eyes widening as she took me in. I

was smiling uncomfortably and dripping water from every-where on my body. The force with which she opened the door made her hair move, a tendril landing in front of one of her blue eyes. "What are you doing here?"

I startled her; it was clear by how she was blinking. She moved a hand to her chest, touching above her heart. It was the second time I'd seen her do that same thing. Like every move I made took her by surprise. Her other hand went to her hair, tucking that lock that had moved and was blocking her vision behind her ear.

"I went for a run and got caught in the rain," I said, lifting my shoulders nonchalantly. "I couldn't find my way back to Santiago's house in the dark," I blurted without taking a breath. Then I smiled again, hoping to get a reac-tion, any reaction, from her. I'd never been happier to see someone in my life.

"Francisco." She *grinned*, doing a once-over and looking at the whole scene in front of her, my hair soaking wet and dripping all over my face. "His house is literally two doors down! On this side of the block! It's not that hard."

I shrugged again. "Are you going to let me in or what?"

"Fine," she said with a big smile on her face. "Did you have dinner yet?" She turned towards the house and moved to the side to let me in. Her hands were on the door, and she was standing partially behind it, getting ready to close it once I was inside. Even in the darkness of the house, she was shining. It was such a different scene to see here in her hometown. Her hair was almost always down, compared to the many times I'd seen her at the hospital with her hair up, away from her face.

"No," I replied, taking a few steps into the foyer. My clothes were dripping on the floor, and my sneakers squeaked as I moved. "I was planning to go to the hotel restaurant, but now that the power is out, who knows when it'll be back."

"There's food here if you'd like," she said, walking towards the back of the house. I followed. "I'm going to get you a towel."

She turned her body once more and ran straight into my chest. I grabbed her shoulders to stabilize her, catching her gaze and her small gasp of surprise.

"*Que susto*," she whispered, then straightened herself and cleared her throat. I squeezed one of her biceps like I'd done many times before, and her eyes snapped to my hand. We both swallowed audibly. "Take your shoes off," she said finally after a few moments of silence. "I'll be right back."

She hurried up the stairs, and I took the time to listen in on her movements upstairs. Her even steps, a door opening, some rummaging inside what sounded like a closet. I took my shoes and socks off and left them to the side, making sure to stick to the tile of the entryway and not the hardwood floor of the family room right on the other side of the doorway. I took my soaking wet shirt off and held it in my hand, making sure the sleeves were tucked in a tight ball to avoid any more dripping. "Which way to the laundry room?" I yelled over the sound of the storm and the movement upstairs.

She didn't reply back, but at least I heard a door closing and her steps coming back down the stairs, a soft mumbling coming from her lips. Then she stopped dead.

Midway down the stairs, she stood frozen, looking at me waiting for her in the entry to her parents' home. And she was striking. She looked so much like those many moons ago. Just standing there, with a soft smile on her face and eyes taking me in.

She shook her head, then moved quickly, shoving the towel at me and turning in the direction of the kitchen. The power was still out, but Lucía had candles all over the coffee table in the family room and a few on the kitchen island.

"Shit," I mumbled, the pain from my toe radiating all the way up to my hip. I lifted my foot and held it in my hand, doubled over it, not being able to take a step further. The freaking darkness and the unfamiliar setting was making me clumsy. Or maybe it was her. So clumsy and awkward around her.

"What?" she replied, moving her eyes all around me to try to figure out what was wrong with me.

"Stubbed my toe," I answered through gritted teeth. "I don't know this house like you do."

She cackled with laughter, bending over and wheezing a little.

"It's not funny," I said, smiling back at her.

"It's a little funny," she finished, turning her back and

walking in the direction of the refrigerator. And this was the Lucía I remembered. We had never been so *domestic* when we'd known each other then. But she looked carefree, happy even. The woman I'd seen in the previous days was a different woman. It seemed like she was a problem-solver, bubbly and excessively upbeat to the benefit of no one but her family. She reminded me a little of how I'd been raised, taught to turn it on and off depending on where we were. Except it looked like she was doing it out of habit, like she was expected to be that way.

We ate leftovers at the kitchen table, talking about the Monopoly game we'd played on New Year's Eve in that same house, the weather, and some of her brother Jacinto's pranks throughout the years. Like the time he booby-trapped the whole upstairs of their house when he was a tween and Charlie rolled down the stairs. Apparently, that earned her youngest brother a whole year of silent treatment from the oldest Williams sibling.

She told me she had returned to Tres Fuegos after her residency, settling down in the town practice and finally taking over for the town doctor that had been overdue for retirement.

"We are still going through all of the patient files to put them into the system," she said with a roll of her eyes. "I've found folders with the medical history of people I went to elementary school with." She laughed at that comment, maybe thinking something she wasn't saying out loud, maybe too early to share with me.

She told me how she and Valentina had painted medi-ocre animals on the walls at her clinic, and although they were a little cringey, her little patients seemed to love it.

And then, like nothing had happened, the lights came back on. Marking our return back to normalcy. To a moment in time when we coexisted in the same space for a limited period, just because.

15
LUCÍA

Despite the massive storm of the previous night and the long, lingering blackout, the next morning, the sun was shining, and it was promising to be a hot day. Valentina had left after the wedding to visit her sister in the city, and I was going to use a few of my days the first two weeks to clean up our files.

Dr. Martín, *bless his heart*, had kept meticulous records of all his patients, including copious notes in his terrible handwriting. It was my job to try to decipher what they said and then figure out whether to hold on to them or get rid of them. Some of those records went back decades to patients that were now bringing their own children to our practice. It was antiquated, for sure, and nothing like we'd done during my training, but it was still entertaining to try to figure it out. Peek at what the past had been like.

The sidewalks were still wet from the rain, a few puddles gathered where the pavers met each other. I passed my brother's house, taking a quick peek inside through the living room window to see if I could covertly watch Francisco moving around, but it all seemed quiet inside.

I was due for a visit anyway, so I could maybe ring the doorbell later and *pretend* that I needed to water the plants. It was not at all to find an excuse to maybe talk to him.

The moment I crossed the street to get away from the image of him standing practically naked in my foyer, a woman stopped me.

"Oh, hey," she said, a big smile on her face. "How are you doing? I haven't seen you in *ages*. How's your family?" she continued, smiling at me with a smile that didn't reach her eyes. Maybe she was just being polite. "I heard Santiago got married. *Finally*, you know? How are your parents? Your brothers? How was the wedding? What are you up to this summer?"

She spoke slowly, like she was trying to get something through me. Like maybe I was too dumb to understand what she was saying. I blinked a few times, trying to place her. She clearly knew my family and our comings and goings in this town. Everyone knew my family, but I could quickly place the majority of those who interacted with us beyond just *knowing of us*. Maybe she had gone to school with one of my siblings?

She pulled out her phone. "I'm *so* glad I ran into you."

She chuckled, like it was the funniest thought. "What a coincidence. Anyway, can you look at this rash? I think it might be viral but just wanted to check, you know, in case I have to drive all the way to the hospital. You can never be too safe when it comes to little ones, right?"

She flashed her phone screen to me. There was a photo of a young toddler covered in red hives, her cheeks red like someone had slapped her, and her arms displaying the same rash but more spread out on the surface. "Is there a fever?" I asked, and she shook her head in response.

"Any allergies that you know of?"

"No, none of that."

"I would like to see her," I said, reaching into my tote bag and rummaging for one of my business cards. She wasn't a patient, that was clear, because I would have recognized her. Maybe she took her child to the nearest hospital, where they had a few pediatricians on staff that would see children for their well visits. "The office is closed, but I'll be there all day, so if you want to come over at around three, I can do that."

I extended my hand and offered her the card, but she dismissed me with a wave.

"I was hoping we could avoid that," she said, a polite smile on her face. "I mean..." She laughed. "I don't want to impose."

Impose? *Imposing is exactly what you are doing! Stopping me in the middle of the street in the dead of summer to ask me to diagnose a child by just looking at a photo taken with a camera phone.*

"Oh." I waved my hand. "None of that. I'm happy to see the kiddo."

She glared, and my first reaction was to yell. But I was too polite for this town and its intrusions, so instead I took a deep breath and smiled, that one single smile I reserved for my patients. "Well, at first glance it looks like it might be Fifth disease, which is totally viral and should clear up on its own. Just make sure you manage symptoms. But again, I'm going into the office now if you want to bring her over, and we can check her out later today." I smiled.

"Oh, no need, right?" she chirped, tucking her phone back into her large purse. "Thanks *so* much. You saved me a trip to the doctor."

And as quickly as she showed up, she was gone with a small chuckle on her lips, and I was left standing in the middle of the street, the birds chirping around me and the summer sun burning my back.

"Damn it," I mumbled. People were so weird sometimes. Everyone knew I was a doctor, and I had many of these interactions on the daily. Some people even went as far as asking me point blank about their ailments. At least this woman pretended to be interested in me and my family. I didn't have a single second to respond. Could have been worse.

When I finally made it into the office, Francisco was standing outside, one hand inside his jeans pocket and the other holding a to-go cup from the hotel's restaurant. He smiled when he saw me approach, then immediately followed it with a frown. I looked behind me to try and figure out what he was looking at but didn't find anything that could have warranted the displeasure on his face.

"Hey," I said with a big smile on my face, my heart hammering inside my chest. "What are you doing here?"

"Oh, um…" He shifted on his feet, weight going from one leg to the other. "I took this by accident," he said, taking a tongue depressor from his pocket and shoving it towards me.

I stood there for a second while my brain computed what was happening. And then I barked out a giant laugh, something I hadn't done in a long time, not even when teasing my oldest brother for being a weirdo. "What?" I squeaked.

He smiled, then shrugged his shoulders. "What?" he asked with a glint in his gaze.

"Where did you get this from?" His eyes were shining with levity, and those damn corners crinkled with his smile. "These are disposable," I said. "I have no use for them." I giggled a little more at the ridiculousness of the situation.

"I think I took it by accident the other night when I got rained out." One of the sides of his mouth lifted, giving me the most adorable, crooked grin ever. "Oh, and here," he said, handing me the to-go cup. "Someone at the little café by the square told me how you take your coffee. So I brought some."

My eyes narrowed, and the corners of his crinkled in response. "What for?" Now I was curious. Because just minutes ago, I was standing outside my brother's house, hoping to sneak a peek at him. And now, he was standing in front of me with a lame excuse and coffee.

"For dinner last night," he mumbled, tucking both of his hands in his pockets once I took the cup. He was wearing a loose button-down shirt and jeans despite the heat. His feet were covered in *alpargatas*, and his hair was wild on the top of his head, like he'd slept with it wet and tossed and turned all night. "And for taking me in like a stray puppy."

"You're more like a cat." I shrugged but then scrunched my nose at my awkwardness.

"I already told you, I'm not a cat person," he said, his smile growing bigger the more he looked at me.

I laughed again and turned to unlock the gate outside of the small house that was home to the clinic. It still belonged to Dr. Martín, but he and I had worked out an agreement for me to slowly pay for it so that I could own it eventually. Francisco stood behind me, waiting for me to unlock the door, then pushed it and held it for me. He walked in and closed it behind him.

"Wow," he said, then chuckled lightly.

"Hey," I scolded, turning around and swatting at his arm. He deepened his laugh, then squeezed one of my biceps. I froze but quickly recovered. Because he didn't remember me, but he did it nonetheless. It was the third time. Our *thing*. The squeeze. Like a signal but in not as many words. In no words, as a matter of fact. "No laughing."

He lifted his hands up, palms facing out. "You said it last night," he said with a smile and stared at the mural. "It's something, alright."

I grinned, then moved towards the reception desk to drop my things. Valentina had left it pristine, all her paperwork put away for the year. She would be back at the end of February after an extended summer break visiting her family. I would make do without her for a few months, and Martina promised to help around a little, so I was confident I could manage.

"Does that happen often?" he asked. My brows furrowed, and I angled my head in question. "People stopping you on the street and harassing you for a diagnosis for their kid?"

"Oh." I pursed my lips.

"Yeah, oh," he said, walking towards me and taking a seat at the chair by Valentina's desk. He crossed his leg, setting his ankle over the opposite knee, then relaxed his forearms on the arms of the chair. He cracked his neck, then looked at me again, waiting for a response.

"Sometimes." I shrugged. "It's no big deal."

"Luli," he deadpanned. "She *literally* said that you were saving her a trip. Just a little too convenient, don't you think?"

I sighed.

"Not you too," I mumbled, then turned to grab my

laptop from my bag. I didn't use it much at the practice, but I was hoping to catch up on some of my reading of recent research papers. "It could have been worse." I tried to lighten the situation, although why would he even care? "It's fine."

"How is it fine?" he countered. From the corner of my eye, I could see his spine straighten. We didn't know each other, not in this life, so he wasn't anyone to question me and my processes. What I liked to do for the people in this town. Even if this woman never brought in her child, I liked it. Because sometimes I preferred to go the extra mile to avoid something else, something worse, happening to my patients.

Logically and in my brain, I knew I couldn't save them all. But I could try. And damn it, I was going to try, every single day.

"Why do they call you Mago?" I asked, finally taking my computer out and setting it on the desk. I walked to the other side and sat on the chair across from Francisco, opening the screen while waiting for his response. He was silent for a minute, searching for answers on my face. I smiled a cocky one, trying to convey that I wasn't going back to the previous topic of conversation. "That's a unique nickname."

He chuckled, all the tension gone from his shoulders and neck.

"It's a silly thing," he replied. Francisco shifted in his seat, crossing and uncrossing his leg, then finally setting both feet on the floor and leaning his upper body towards me. He rested his arms on the table, then took a deep breath. "My friends started calling me that because I would always sneak out without telling them."

"Like Houdini," I said. The words flew out of my mouth before I could give them a second thought. And that had been the same exact explanation his sister had given me once, when I walked into her room and they were both there playing a card game that looked to be one hundred percent invented by them, no rules or regulations or even logic to us outsiders.

I smiled awkwardly, the panic creeping up on me at just any mention, whether implied or not, of Jazmín, her memory everywhere now. Whereas before, I could shake it away, now having him here was a constant reminder of her.

A blip.

My field of vision went black, and the room started spinning on me, a tight grip on my chest. My breathing was labored, or so I thought because I couldn't feel anything, just darkness.

It came like lightning. And like lightning, it was gone.

"Sorry." I cleared my throat. "Did you say something? I spaced out."

He nodded, following along with what I was saying. I smiled, knowing very well it was fake and stiff.

"Anyway, glad we cleared the whole tongue depressor fiasco," he said with a shy smile on his face. "I'll get out of your hair."

"Okay," I said in response and stood to walk him to the door and lock it behind him. "Thanks for the coffee."

"No problem." He saluted, then walked out the door, down the few steps to the sidewalk, and back in the direction of the town square.

16

FRANCISCO

"*¿Dónde estás?*" he asked, his voice deep and raspy from his many years as a smoker. "I've been calling you."

A statement. An expectation.

"Hello," I drawled. "Happy New Year." My phone started buzzing incessantly while I was sitting in Lucía's office, and without even looking, I could tell who it was. The street outside the small house was quiet, the mid-morning sun shining in between the tall trees, creating random shadows on the sidewalks.

"Are you done with your stupid games, Francisco?" he sneered, his steps moving quickly in the background. He was probably walking in the house, an annoying habit he had when he needed to think. He would pace the hallways, back and forth, back and forth. "When are you coming back?"

"Father." I took a deep breath, my jaw already clenching in response to his small inquisition. "I am on vacation."

"We don't take vacations, boy."

He was right; we didn't. Because politics never slept, according to him. I sighed, trying to control my temper. Another one of those things that I had been working on, along with that stupid, childish fear. It was easy for me to just revert to the old ways—the screaming and the arguing and the constant gaslighting. It was how I was raised, and logically, I knew better, but it got out of control.

As I grew up, I started realizing some things about my family. Mainly that it wasn't normal to be treated like a publicity prop, paraded around from the moment I could form sentences. I clearly remember going to late-night talk shows with my father, a toy in hand to keep me quiet and proper next to him. Why would someone do that to a child? My parents worried more about keeping my clothes free of dirt stains than putting me to bed at a decent hour. It was all for show.

And it still was, even in my early thirties as I tried to separate from that by choosing a different path.

"Okay," I said, my jaw clenched. "How's Mom?"

"You need to come back," he said, the sound of his footsteps lighter in the background. "I'm starting the campaign soon, and I need you here with us."

Deep breaths. "I'm on vacation until we are back up and running. So, February."

"What do you mean?" I could picture him furrowing his

eyebrows in confusion. "That's six weeks of vacation, Francisco."

"Yes, I'm aware." *I know how to count, old man.* I wanted to hang up on him and run back and hide. Maybe tuck myself inside that bed in Santiago's guest room and sleep for twelve hours straight.

"Where are you?"

"Córdoba."

"What are you doing in that god-forsaken province?" he sneered. He'd historically clashed with the representatives from this province, my father's ideas too conservative for some of the elected members of this area. He scoffed and then took a long drag of his cigarette, the burning sound of the thin paper crisp and clear on my end of the phone.

"Okay, good talk." He was playing his silence game. Something he did a lot to my mother on purpose. To get her to crack, to make her look weak. "Say hi to Mom for me."

"*Chiquito,*" he said with a *tone* I hated. Not only was it derogatory, but also calling me little boy? That hurt. "Have you spoken to her?" he asked, his tone back to casual and conversational. I knew he was referring to Jazmín's mom because he never called her by her name and tried to be casual about it.

"Mom?" I played coy, acting casual but knowing exactly what he wanted. "No, I'm going to call her a little bit later. I thought you had that luncheon with the Díaz people."

The Díaz people were actually his biggest supporters. They were a well-to-do family in the country with a lot of money to burn who used it to advance political campaigns that could—allegedly—tip the scales to their favor. Nothing was done for free in politics, that was for sure, and my father bent over backwards for them so that he could get a couple million *pesos* in return to fund his campaign.

"Yes," he said. Another drag of his cigarette. "That is why I'm calling you. There's an... issue."

Interesting.

He never involved me too much in the logistics of his campaign. He wanted to show a united front in front of the press and the opposition, showing how his family was a strong unit with traditional values so that his constituents could see themselves reflected in us. But ever since Jazmín's death, he'd become a little bit more paranoid of being caught.

His biggest dirty little secret yet. The one kept tightly tucked in the past.

That day, I had been hiding in the hallway, stuck in between the stairwell and the door to the pediatrics rooms. A few meters past the door, the nurses' station sat, almost forgotten amongst the chaos of the night. I had snuck in earlier than I usually did, and the staff was busy doing their shift change, lots of people roaming the hallways.

I was scrolling my phone, waiting for movement to die down, when it started buzzing, my father's name blinking at me from the screen. I hadn't spoken to him in a few weeks, our last interaction having ended in a bout of screaming that even my mother couldn't shut down.

"*¿Dónde estás?*" Fuck. He already knew the answer, I could bet my life on that. "*Cuántas veces te lo tengo que decir,*" he said tersely. How many times do I have to tell you? He spoke to me as if I were a child still cowering behind the furniture in the exact same way I did when I was young.

"Eugenio," I said, using his first name instead of calling him Dad. He didn't deserve it, especially not in the last few months or so. His daughter—my sister—was in the hospital, and he moved heaven and earth to make sure no one knew who she was. And that meant that I needed to stay away because some people recognized me even if I had separated myself from his image. That was why he was probably calling me now. One of his spies had called him to tattle on me.

"Francisco, *basta.*"

"No. You stop. I'm not having this conversation again—"

"If the press finds out..." he said. He was seething, I could tell. I'd had years of practice.

"Not my problem, Eugenio," I added, shrugging my shoulders despite not having him in front of me. A door sounded above me, a few steps coming down the stairs and the sound getting louder and louder with each step. "You should have thought about this seventeen years ago, *Father.*"

"*¿Qué dijiste?*"

"You heard me," I replied nonchalantly.

"*Mirá, mocoso. No te me llegues a cruzar porque te reviento,*" he threatened. Five years ago, this would have scared me, the threat of physical violence. Today, it did nothing to me because my priorities lay elsewhere. I was done trying to bend over backwards for him, and I was damn proud of it. The steps were getting closer to me.

"*Chau, Papá.*" I hung up the phone and tucked it clumsily into my slacks pocket, my hands shaking from the harshness of the conversation. Harsher words had been said in the past five years, for sure, but that didn't make this less intense.

I rested my head on the cold concrete of the wall. I was stuck in that small landing, the lights dim and dull, until the shift change was over and I could slide into my sister's room unnoticed. I took a deep breath, trying to calm down before going in to see her. I hated that she was in the middle of all this. Not her fault for being born into this fucked-up family.

I felt a tap on my shoulder, then a gentle squeeze.

Our signal.

I turned, and there she was, standing in front of me, her mouth pulled into a blinding smile and her hair away from her face like she preferred. She wasn't wearing pink scrubs today but instead dark jeans and a colorful shirt under her white coat.

"Hi," she said, her smile turning brighter at the edges and her eyes soft on me. She squeezed my bicep again, then released it. That hand joined the other one holding a laptop tightly against her chest. "What's going on?"

She had concern in her gaze. I'd seen it a few times in

passing while with my sister but never directed at me. I liked it. A lot.

"Long day," I said, trying to dismiss her concern and adding some lighter tones to the whole thing. "And it's chaos out there, so I'm hiding until I can sneak in."

She chuckled, but there was still a small frown on her face. "Is Sonia not here?"

I sighed. "The nurses' station was deserted the last time I peeked."

She reached into her coat pocket and grabbed her phone, typing furiously on the screen. Her forearms were still holding on tightly to her device. Her phone buzzed in her hand, and then she looked at me with a big smile on her face.

"She said we can go in in three minutes and straight to her room. They are finishing rounds now."

"Thank you, lifesaver."

She blushed but smiled at my compliment. "So what's going on, really?"

"It's a thing with my dad. It's a long story."

"I have… mmm…" She looked at the screen on her phone and then smiled at me. "Two minutes."

I barked out a laugh, the last of the tension leaving my shoulders. "He somehow found out I'm here, so he called me to yell at me. It's complicated."

"Hmm," she hummed, her attention fixed on me. Her long hair swayed behind her head with her delicate movements. Her weight shifted slightly from foot to foot. She was breathtaking. Even there in that dim, cold hallway. "Time's up, *Mago.* Go do your magic."

She spun on her heel and opened the heavy door, turning her head to look at me with a big smile.

"Francisco, did you hear me?" His raspy voice interrupted my thoughts, bringing me back to the present.

"No." And if I had been standing in front of him, he would have tried to punch me for my attitude. "*Chau, Papá.*"

17

LUCÍA

WHAT I HAD INITIALLY PLANNED to be a relaxing time off ended up being a string of endless days with nothing to do. Summer in our town was a sleepy affair, but it was also full of tourists that were here for the many things to do. Hikes, lazy floating in the river, tanning by the creek beds. There were a large number of paragliders, too, but the starting point for that was the other side of the mountain, so they mostly just came through on their way to the top.

So my days were long. The blackouts had been relentless, coming at all times of the day, not only at night like other years. The ceiling of the family room looked particularly gloomy from my spot on the couch. It was so hot, all the windows were open, and there was a light breeze coming into the house, but nothing was helping.

And not to sound dramatic or anything, but they really did reflect my mood so accurately. It was the worst because the only things I could do during those times were either scroll my phone mindlessly or get in my thoughts about Jazmín, her death, the things I could have done differently.

Francisco. And the night that I felt like things had changed between us.

Sonia had been standing by her desk that night, the phone trapped between her shoulder and ear. She was nodding, snacking on crackers that she had tucked inside her scrub pockets. In her other hand, she had a pen and was taking occasional notes of the conversation, mostly numbers, so my guess was that it was the lab, delivering a batch of results for our patients.

It was late, probably close to midnight, and it was *quiet*. Which was always a bad sign in a hospital. Because it was literally when everything hit the fan and chaos quickly ensued. From the corner of my eye, I could see a shadow lingering in the hallway, their chest moving quickly like they'd run up the stairs at superhuman speed and were not catching their breath. It stayed there for a minute, then turned its body, and I could see him.

I smiled coyly, looking back to Sonia to see what she was doing. She didn't give a shit, quite frankly, because our pediatrics patients were always supposed to be accompanied by an adult, but Jazmín was a special case. And for some reason that was *way* above my pay grade, she was granted an exception. She spent a lot of nights on her own, her mother coming in daily but not being able to spend the night during weekdays.

I went back to Sonia's side, looking over her shoulder as she took her notes and smiled. Jazmín's labs were looking good, and she could go home soon. That was the goal for all our patients.

Francisco scurried past us, walking in the shadows of the hospital hallways, pretending we couldn't see him. He hurried past the first few sets of doors and walked into Jazmín's room, closing the door quietly behind him. Jazmín had been asleep for a while, and she'd had a rough day, so he might have missed his opportunity to talk to her.

Sonia finished her conversation with the lab tech, then turned to me and started spewing numbers, asking a few questions and corroboration for courses of action with our patients. The attending was in the on-call room napping, so I made sure to take notes to ask questions later. I was almost at the end of my residency and comfortable with what I was doing, but some patients gave me more anxiety than others, and it never hurt to double check with those with more experience.

She looked up to me with her big, brown eyes. "*Andá,*" she said and bit her lower lip to hide her smile.

"*¿Qué decís?*" I tried to evade her comment, but I couldn't help the blush that was creeping up my neck towards my cheeks. I was in my late twenties, but I still blushed like a schoolgirl with a crush when I even thought of Francisco. Who was no one, just a patient's brother. That was it.

"Go say hi," she added, turning back to face her computer screen, then looking up at the monitors against the wall. "If I need you, I'll come find you." She winked, then turned and chuckled to herself, grabbing one of the crackers from her pocket.

I walked the few steps to Jazmín, peering into the darkened patient rooms as I went. All of the littles were asleep by then, their adults also sleeping soundly despite the constant beeping of the machines and the noises in the hallways.

The door opened with a creak, and Francisco's face lit up, immediately boring into me. He swallowed, then stood from his spot in the corner chair, where he had been sitting and watching his sleeping sister. I smiled, then took two steps and closed the door behind me.

"I thought that was you," I said, smiling wider at his grin. "You are not as inconspicuous as you think you are."

He laughed and immediately covered his mouth with one palm to stifle it. It was in those moments that he looked like a boy: no worries, no sick sister, no messed-up parents. Just there, passing the time and enjoying my company.

"How is she?" He walked to me and squeezed my bicep before immediately turning towards his sleeping sister on the bed. "Are the labs back?"

"Sonia was just on the phone with the lab as you were sneaking in."

"What did they say?" He was impatient, always checking in on her first. "How is she looking?"

I turned to look at him, my whole body facing his. We were so close, I could see the flecks of green in his eyes, even in the darkened room. It took me a moment to collect myself because we did, indeed, have good news. She would most likely leave the hospital within the next few days—I just needed to confirm that with my attending.

"Looks good," I said and grabbed my notepad from my coat pocket and looked up. But I wasn't ready for that smile, a blindingly spectacular display of joy. "Oomph."

The next thing I knew, he was hugging me, pressing his body against mine, *hard,* in the most unexpected way. And his happiness was contagious, so I hugged him back, my arms hooking under his and wrapping around his shoulder blades. His whole body shook with laughter, and the only reason there wasn't a sound coming from him was because he was using my shoulder to hold it back.

I was frozen but burning at the unexpected contact. I was scared to move because I didn't want to. I wanted to stay in that spot *forever.* But I *had* to. *This is a patient's brother!* my brain screamed. My body wasn't responding to my commands, and my heart was yelling at me, asking for more. I licked my lips once, then took a big breath, not ready to take a step back.

And then, a soft knock at the door startled us, and he jumped back three meters and straight to the chair in the corner, his hands running nervously through his hair. He peeked one last time through his lashes, then turned back to face his sister. Sonia was at the door, holding a phone to her ear, apprehension on her face as she listened to whatever was being said on the other end of the line.

"Dr. Williams?" she whispered, popping her head into

the room. "We need you in room 203, please." She spun her body around and started walking fast to the opposite side.

I blinked, and just like that, the moment was over.

The lights flickering at my parents' house brought me back from my thoughts. The cat was cuddled against my hip, her furry body tickling the bare skin where my jean shorts had ridden up. We were on day six or seven—or who even knew at this point—of consistent power interruptions, no rhyme or reason. Because it happened on even the mildest day of summer, when not everyone was inside sheltering in front of their air conditioning units or maybe running their fans at full blast.

"Lucía," my brother Charlie said. He was standing in the doorway to the kitchen, just watching me. He looked at the cat, then looked back at me. He was sweating, drops running down his face and dropping on the tile floor beneath him. "What are you doing?"

I blinked, still fuzzy and in my thoughts. "What are you doing here?"

"Do you want to go have lunch?"

I cocked my head, not following the conversation. This was common with this brother, taking a lead and never bending from his objective. He wanted to go to lunch and wouldn't answer my questions until we were actually sitting, facing each other.

"Sure." I stood from my perch on the sofa in the family room and put my shoes on. The cat lifted one eyebrow and watched me for a second with an uninterested look, then tucked her head between her legs and started purring. "Your house?"

He scoffed. "No, the mountain."

I rolled my eyes. "No, Charlie, it's going to be packed with people." And I didn't want to run into any of the locals, who would find me immediately among the crowd and expect free medical advice.

"You love people."

"Not when I'm on vacation," I admitted. "And it's getting a little out of hand with the amount of people stopping me and flashing me their phones or sending me pictures of their rashes." I chuckled at his grunt, his face annoyed at me.

"I told you, boundaries."

"Shut up."

We ended up settling for the restaurant hotel because it was a more popular spot for dinner and not as crowded for lunch.

"I thought you were going to Mendoza with Mom and Dad," I said as we walked towards the town square, where Santiago's hotel was. He had purchased the property from our aunt and uncle, who were ready to retire, as he needed a break from his law practice. It had worked out perfectly because the job he decided not to take at our family's firm went to Victoria, who moved to our town after things with her family imploded.

Another grunt. "I'm a grown man. I don't go on vacation with my parents."

"Okay, grumpy." I smiled at him, this one reaching my eyes because this teasing had quickly become one of my favorite things. "What's eating you up?"

He stared at me for a long moment. "Are you going back to work in February or March this year?"

"February, but the more I think about it, the more I want to wait for Valen to open the practice because I'm already exhausted at the idea of running it on my own."

He tripped on an uneven tile on the sidewalk but quickly composed himself. "She's not here?" he squeaked.

"No, she went back to visit her sister for the summer."

He glared at me, standing in the middle of the sidewalk under the blistering sun. "Is that why you are so prickly? Because she's not around?"

"Is that why *you* are so testy?" I laughed.

"Shut up," he said with a small smile, his lips hardly lifting from the corner of his mouth. It was barely perceptible, like everything he did, all his gestures. He blended in but stood out at the same time. An odd combination of things, for sure, but it worked.

I smiled at him, looking up to study his face closer. He was poker-faced, not giving anything away but clearly holding on to his secrets. "I know you are hiding something, and I'll pry it from your lips eventually."

A third grunt in response, followed by a spark of something—annoyance, probably—in his glare.

The hotel restaurant was practically empty. Only a few

tables by the entrance were occupied. Charlie and I sat towards the end, by the entrance to the kitchen.

"Are you bored yet?" I asked him, knowing damn well that he had been bored since the moment they locked the door to the firm for the summer. He wasn't a workaholic, per se, but he didn't do much outside of work and his reading.

"Not yet," he said, looking around the restaurant. "I'm enjoying the quiet."

"*Aha,*" I drawled in reply, not believing a word he said. "What have you been doing?"

"Reading. I went to the city yesterday to pick up a few books." *The usual.* He didn't say it, but I was sure he was thinking it.

"What's up with Jacinto?" His gaze was fixed on the menu, even though we knew exactly what we would order. We were creatures of habit, Charlie and I. "I haven't seen him since New Year's."

"He went camping." I shrugged. It wasn't my thing, but every year since they had finished high school, my youngest brother and his group of friends would go camping to a different spot. A way to travel around the country and explore "the majesty" of it all, as he would say. "He'll be back by the twentieth."

"Hmm."

"Do you ever think Mom and Dad don't like that I'm a doctor?" The question was out there now. It was the first time I'd spoken about this out loud ever since coming back, but also since leaving for med school. They were supportive, yes, but my father especially treated me differently. Charlie frowned, his thick eyebrows scrunching together in question.

"Where is this coming from, Lu?" His head was angled as he tried to figure out what I meant.

"I just..." I shrugged. "Sometimes it feels like I'm a teenager all over again, you know?" Like when they reminded me to wash my hands after coming back from work or when my father would give me a small lecture about keeping all the windows closed if the A/C was going to be on. Like I didn't have a medical degree and hadn't lived on my own for years before moving back to live in their house with them.

"I think it comes from a place of concern," he replied. His gaze was fixed on me, but I couldn't look at him. I was embarrassed, a little, because I wasn't able to do what I intended to do, so I returned home with my tail tucked between my legs and was now doing something I didn't fully enjoy. "You basically showed up back in town and haven't discussed it with anyone." He eyed me cautiously. "Which is fine with me, you know that, but—"

"I told you," I interrupted. "I told them too." My heart was hammering in my chest, trying to take flight because I was still not ready to talk about it, despite Francisco's presence, and the date coming and going, and time passing. "It wasn't for me."

"Luli." His eyes softened. He hadn't called me that since

we were kids, going for the much more formal Lucía more than anything.

"I like it here." A lie. "I like being back here with everyone, especially now that Santiago is here." But the truth was that I'd never felt as alone as I did then. Despite being surrounded by my family and friends, despite more of the people I'd grown up with moving back to town soon. Because deep down I wasn't happy with my career—my calling—and that made the days drag on. *Interminables.*

"If anything, they are insanely proud of you being a doctor," he added. "It has absolutely nothing to do with you not being a lawyer."

Charlie's words gave me some relief. Knowing, at least, that I wasn't a huge disappointment to them. I was just a disappointment to myself.

"Let's order," he said, lightly changing the topic. "I'm starving."

"Okay."

18

FRANCISCO

SHE WAS WAITING for me outside the house, leaning slightly against the door frame. The cat sat at her feet, facing the street, its nose in the air like it was trying to smell the rain. As soon as she saw me turn into the driveway, she smiled and straightened, then grabbed it from the ground and cradled it against her chest.

"What are you doing here?" It was the same question she asked every time, and I was running out of excuses by now. The driveway was dark, but I'd done that trek so many times in the past few days that I could mostly walk it with my eyes closed. There was a dim orange light coming from the house, like she'd lit all the candles in there so I would be able to see everything.

Uh. Crap. *She's catching on.*

"You might need my help feeding the cat," I said and walked straight into the house, her steps following behind me with their regular cadence. She snorted, then laughed louder, the sound echoing in the large hallway. It was warm and pleasant. Cozy. It made me feel like I belonged there.

"You don't even know where the food is." She caught up to me, the cat jumping from her arms and running up the stairs and into one of the open doors that were visible from the ground floor. "You know that I can handle myself, right?"

"Maybe you're scared." I smiled. "And need a big, strong man to protect you." I lifted my arm and curled my bicep, squeezing it with my opposite hand.

She quickened her steps and stood in front of me, lifting her hand and pinching my skin. Her body was warm next to mine.

"What's that for?" I asked, lifting my hand to touch her bicep in that reassuring way we'd done dozens of times. She laughed, pushing my hand away from her and walking past me into the family room. The coffee table was covered in candles, almost to the point where it would be a fire hazard, and the flames flickered with our movements around them.

She sat on the couch, then lifted her legs onto the cushions, sitting sideways, facing me. She studied me while I lowered myself to mimic her position, eyeing me up and finally focusing on my eyes. I wanted to keep her gaze there, focused on me forever.

"I wish the power was back," she said, leaning her head against the back of the couch and closing her lids, a sleepy smile on her face. "This is awful."

"It's not that bad," I lied. Even though it had been brutal. The whole situation with the dark was getting out of hand, the panic setting in earlier and earlier every day as I hoped to whoever was up there that the blackout would hold off until I was asleep for the night. "I have the slider open at the house, and there's a nice breeze."

"Shit." Lucía sat up and ran her fingers through her hair, dragging the flyaways up to the knot at the crown of her head. "I need to go water the plants."

I chuckled lightly at her over-the-top reaction to having to do that small favor for her brother and sister-in-law. "What happens if they die?" I asked, genuinely wondering what the answer to that could be.

She shrugged, leaning her body back on the couch and shifting her legs so that they were angled towards the back cushions. "Nothing." She scrunched her nose, a little nervous habit I noticed she had. She did it when she was thinking or talking about her family, probably because her brain told her something, but her heart told her to do the complete opposite.

"Then why are you stressing about it?"

"I promised I would do it, so... I keep my word."

I nodded, taking stock of what she was saying. She did keep her promises, or that was how I remembered her from back then.

"I thought you were going to walk me through watering the plants." I draped my hand across the back of the large sofa, inching my fingers closer to her. I felt my skin flush with embarrassment at the ask, almost begging for excuses to see her again.

She chuckled, her eyes drifting closed in a peaceful rest. It was hot and muggy. The candles didn't help the situation at all, and she was probably exhausted from being in this big house all alone, trying to figure out what to do to cool herself down. I knew I was in the same boat, and that was why my body gravitated towards her. Both from the fear of not having her close but also from the dead silence of the dark and what her company meant.

"Yeah," she rasped. A soft smile formed on her lips, the corners barely tipping up with the movement. "Sure."

"How was your day?" I wanted to keep hearing her voice, those wonderful notes that came out of that mouth with the inexplicable power to calm me without even trying.

"Umm," she said again. "Hot."

A loud crack of thunder sounded in the distance, and the cat chose that moment to jump in between us, placing its soft body on Lucía's feet. She curled herself into a tight ball and rested her head on the sofa cushions. My hand darted towards the cat's fur and found a lazy rhythm in the cadence of my fingers. Lucía reached out her hand towards her feet, her eyes still closed. The movement seemed natural, practiced, almost automatic, like the only likely response to her cat sitting on her was to touch it.

"Luli." My words were barely a whisper over the sounds of the rain hitting the terracotta tiles of the roof. Thunder rumbled far away, and the wind was blowing. Finally, there was a cool breeze coming into the house from the open windows. The curtain of water immediately took care of the heat, bringing much needed relief to this small town.

"Hmm." More of a statement than a question.

It was on the tip of my tongue, to ask her if she remembered. If she ever thought of me, of Jazmín. Of those times we sat quietly in the dark together, not saying anything but talking about a million things at the same time.

But what if I hadn't been memorable to her? Just another patient's relative, and Jazmín just another patient. Just blips in her timeline, barely perceptible in the dark of that room. Fleeting moments that I was lucky to have for myself, but that she didn't even cherish.

I moved slowly, my hand stretching a bit over the long cat hairs, my fingers itching to touch her. Our fingertips grazed the cat's fur simultaneously, and a jolt surged through me, an electric current that ignited every nerve ending in my body. It had happened that one time back in the hospital, also in the dark.

Her eyes opened, the blue shining bright like the brightest mountain day I'd ever seen, the day we walked to Lighthouse Point. She angled her head at me and stared, the silence loud between us. My breath hitched, and I found myself unable to break away from her mesmerizing gaze. Dizzy with her attention.

I heard her breathing, erratic and the complete opposite of moments ago, when she was lying peacefully next to me, her lashes shading her cheeks. In that brief moment, the world around us faded into the background, the sounds of the storm no longer audible to me. I reached out my hand and curled it behind her neck, leaning towards her.

Lucía's lips parted, and I could see her move closer to me, her blue eyes searching my face. It was dim, but her features were almost highlighted. I took a deep breath and looked at her mouth, closer and closer.

Without a second thought, but also incredibly aware of what I was doing, I leaned in, closing the millimetric gap between us. Her breath mingled with mine, a delicate dance of warmth and anticipation.

We were kissing. And it was tender and rough at the same time. Urgent but trivial.

And it felt so good to be so close to her after all this time.

Because the moment I pressed my mouth to Lucía's, I was done for. Unraveled. Everything drifted away until it was only us, our panting breaths loud over the sounds of the storm, the purring cat somewhere else, having jumped off the couch with the clumsy movements. She was close, so close that her knees were touching my thighs, and the only thing I had to do was reach for her thigh so she was straddling me. Our bodies created the most delicious friction, her hands draped around my shoulders and the lightest of touches making my skin light up.

"There," I said in between pecks. The corner of her mouth, her chin, the column of her neck. She was on my lap, tight against my body.

"Okay," she whispered back, almost like the word left her mouth automatically, a response to the stimuli. "Like this?" She rocked her hips once, settling on that one spot that had me clenching my jaw at the sensation. She let out a gasp, her movement small and deliberate, one of her hands on my hair, tugging at my scalp with need.

My hands lowered down to her waist, holding on for dear life because if I let her go, even for a moment, she might slip away, like she did once already.

So here we were, fused to each other, hands moving all around with reckless abandon.

It was so serious, our movements in the shadows, like we were hiding from something, maybe from the light of day, from moments when our relationship was so different than how it was in the darkness. But then, Lucía smiled.

I felt it with my mouth and with my body because her movements became relaxed, as if she was melting into me. And honestly, I was melting into her too. So I smiled back, trying with all that I could to show her how long I'd been waiting for this.

But even if I could tell her, if words formed and came out of my mouth, she didn't remember me. So we could pretend for a little bit longer while she was sitting on my lap, rocking her hips and making those little sounds—

Lucía shifted slightly, her hands loosening on my hair and sliding down to my shirt, down my torso and under the fabric. Her fingers moved shyly on my skin, like they were slowly committing every inch of me to memory. I grunted at the sensation, and Lucía took the opportunity to slide down to the side of the couch, taking me with her, her soft body under mine.

And it felt like a fantasy. Like this was supposed to have happened in the past and my memory was tricking me. Her smell enveloping us, her smile all over me. The smooth skin of her neck was almost addicting, like I could just stay there, my tongue rolling over that long column forever.

She sighed, and I wanted to reciprocate the feeling.

Finally, I thought. And like she read my mind, she whispered, "Yes," then smiled into our kiss again. Her teeth knocked into mine, and a small giggle came out of her throat. It felt like we were tangled up with each other for hours, the sounds and the lights of the storm long gone.

Then the lights came on.

And we were both startled into normality.

19

LUCÍA

Crap.

Shit. *Oh my god, what did you do?*

My eyes shot open, and my body stilled, the lights blinding me for a fraction of a second until I could get my bearings. Francisco was hovering over my body, his whole weight resting on his forearms by my head, his eyes hooded and a lazy smile on his face. I closed my lids for a second because I needed the darkness to think.

Shit.

He froze over me in... surprise? Shock? Remorse? Who even knew, but I had to get out of that situation immediately.

He was my patient's brother. And he didn't remember me, so no.

No, thank you.

"Stop thinking so loud," he said, his mouth right over

my ear. His voice was raspy, sounding like I would think he sounded when he woke up first thing in the morning, in a warm bed with me next to him.

"Oh god," I whispered, my eyes still closed, trying to avoid him at all costs. Maybe if I just lay there, he would eventually get the memo and leave? Wishful thinking for sure. "I'm so sorry."

"For what?" His mouth trailed down my neck towards my bare shoulder, the strap of my tank top having ridden down at some point. It was the weirdest thing. My brain was telling me I needed to shut this down immediately, but my body was not responding, just like that time at the hospital when he hugged me so tightly, I thought my heart was going to burst out of my chest from the emotion. "For this?"

He was kissing me, his movements soft and his mouth back on mine. Our tongues searched for each other, finding the other one in the middle and dancing together for a moment. I was plastered to the couch. I couldn't move my body, but I needed to do something. Anything. Because the temperature inside my body was worse than anything I'd ever felt in those long blackout moments. The interminable days that dragged on and on.

"Uh-huh," I replied, my hands moving gently about his body, up and down his toned back. I could feel his gaze on me, but I didn't dare open my eyelids, my skin flushing with embarrassment at the mere thought. "The power came back."

I wanted to facepalm myself at the obvious remark. I was never this awkward, and this man just—

He chuckled lightly, his body moving off of me and pulling me with him to place us side by side on the couch. He was smiling blindingly, more than the lights overhead. So bright, I had to look away because it was painful. The reminder of his sister and of what we had once *almost* been. Maybe? Maybe I was remembering wrong, and I was fictionalizing and romanticizing the patient-doctor relationship we had. He was a nice man, charming, and so confident.

"Yeah, I know."

What did he know? I was losing my train of thought, so concerned with whatever just happened, and he was so relaxed, so calm next to me, smiling and chuckling along to *this.*

I stood from the couch and walked to the fridge, looking for a way out of this. I didn't even remember the last time I kissed someone, let alone how to behave after. *It's a freaking kiss!*

I opened the fridge, then closed it again. It had remained closed for the whole day—a lesson drilled into my brain by my father no less than five hundred times throughout my life—and even closed, I knew there was nothing inside for me to eat or drink. So instead, I grabbed a glass from the cabinet and poured some water from the tap.

"What are you doing?" he asked. He was still sitting on the couch. His head was tilted back on the cushions, eyes closed against the harsh lighting, so bright in what had been a completely blacked-out evening. The candles were still flickering, slowly losing their flame as time passed.

"Just getting some water." I flinched because he knew I was avoiding him. "Would you like some?"

"No," he drawled. He stood up, slowly stretching his body to its full upright position. He bent over the coffee table, blowing out every single candle with the utmost dedication, like he was dragging his feet, trying not to leave. "Thank you."

"Uh-huh," I said, pouring the remainder of the water down the drain, not even thirsty anymore. I stood there, frozen on the spot, just looking at him because for a fraction of a second, I couldn't believe what had just happened. Three years ago, this was all I wanted. But the circumstances had changed, and maybe now it was too late.

He spun on his heel and took a few steps towards me. My mouth opened and closed multiple times. His hand reached out and grabbed my waist, pulling me hard against his body. He took a deep breath, and I closed my eyes in anticipation, goosebumps erupting all over my skin, weakening my knees.

"Stop freaking out," he whispered in my ear.

And then his lips moved down my neck, slowly and surely.

Kiss.

By my jaw, an intimate peck.

Kiss.

My temple. The corner of my eyes, where they crinkled when I laughed.

Kiss.

Our noses bumped, and then his forehead rested on mine, and he took one more deep breath.

I blinked, stunned into silence. Planted on the floor. Not being able to move an inch. Something hung in the air between us. Like this time, maybe it could be different.

"I'll see you later." He smiled. "Have a good night, *linda*."

———

My alarm clock was blinking next to me in the dark. There was no point in setting the time again if the power was going to go out eventually. Whenever the storm season passed, I would take the time to get it back to its regular programming. But for the time being, it stood there on standby.

It was the early hours of the morning, and there was a light breeze coming into the room. The A/C wasn't running, so the fresh air was a welcome respite from all the heat. But the strong smell of the flowers was keeping me up at night. And I could still feel his lips on mine. And the reminder of his gaze on me still burned my skin hot.

I jumped out of bed without even glancing at my phone. I wouldn't get any sleep, so might as well be productive, get anything done. Whatever needed to be done.

Being up so early reminded me of the first few years of

my residency. Getting used to unpredictable schedules, covering for colleagues and friends, and just trying to learn on the go took a toll on a lot of us. By the time we were close to finishing, only three of the original five residents remained, so it was a tight group. A lot of the cases we saw at the hospital were long-term, so it was also a close group of patients and their families. Very similar to what I experienced in Tres Fuegos, but the nature of the diagnostics was different. Here, in this town, people knew me, knew my family. There was a sense of intimacy that came with the small town.

At the hospital, we had built our relationships over time.

A scratch echoed through the big house, snapping me from my thoughts. The cat was at my bedroom door, asking to be let in. And so I quickly changed and left for the practice.

The light in Dr. Martín's living room was on, and I could see movement inside, two bodies going back and forth to what I knew was the kitchen. I walked into my office and dropped my things on the reception desk without a second glance. I scanned the waiting room, seeing two books out of place in the corner, in the small play area that children used while waiting for their appointments.

My hands were itching to do something. My brain was fired up.

"*Linda.*" His voice was husky and laced with intimacy. *Dios mío, estoy al horno.*

There was a loud knock on the door, and I blinked out of my trance.

"Lucía?" a soft voice called. Dr. Martín moved to the window by the door, his hair disheveled and not in his usual combed-back style. He smiled as soon as he saw me inside, then disappeared from view. He lived across the street, so I knew he had eyes on the office on a regular basis. But since his retirement, he had never bugged me, even giving me the courtesy of calling ahead if he needed something or letting Valentina know he would be stopping by.

"Good morning?" I said as I opened the door, the statement coming out more like a question given the confusion. It was way too early for any sort of visit from anyone. "What's wrong?" I asked, looking over at him from head to toe. I hadn't stopped to visit since before Valentina left. I felt pain in the back of my throat, guilt immediately taking over.

"*Nada*," he said, walking towards the waiting room and taking a seat in the farthest chair, where he had a view out the big window. "Why are you here so early?"

"Couldn't sleep."

"Is it the text messages?" he asked, a coy smile on his lips, like he knew. Because he did. He had been the only doctor in this town for decades before I came along. "People in this town are... *¿cómo se dice?*... Extra."

I laughed. "Partially the text messages. Did you send Gladys over to me the other night?"

His eyes widened, and he smiled big. "Maybe?" He made a funny face, sticking his tongue out and surprising me with his demeanor. "I told her I was retired. Perhaps she assumed you were available."

"Has it always been this terrible?"

"*Si les das la mano, te toman el codo.*" Give them an inch, and they take a mile. "You have to set firm boundaries."

I smiled at him and sat down on the nearest chair. The sun was slowly rising, a few rays coming in through the window. "You sound like Charlie."

"Smart man," he said with a chuckle. "But all joking aside, how's it going?"

Awful, I wanted to say. *It's awful and I'm confused and I hate it here. It's not where I saw myself at all.* "It's good," I told him with a smile on my face. I reached for my hair and pulled it from its ponytail, looking for something to do while his eyes were on me. "I love it here."

Liar. Liar.

"Alright," he said, his voice laced with doubt. "Let's go get coffee."

And he stood up slowly, his right hand tucked inside his pocket and a small smile on his face.

20
LUCÍA

THE RAIN WAS COMING DOWN HARD, and I could see the reflection of lightning on the glass, even though it was miles away. Thunder rumbled a few seconds later, making the cat lift her head and look around, disturbing her deep slumber.

It had been a lazy day, just sitting around the house and patiently waiting for the power to come back on. It was gray and gloomy, partially due to the weather, but mostly because we had lost power the night before. The grid was just not taking it anymore.

"Lucía?" I heard from the front of the house, followed by a few clapping noises right out the entry window. The doors to the house were solid wood, so the knocking had to be pretty hard and intense for me to hear it at the back, even when it wasn't thundering out. "Dr. Williams?" the voice repeated.

I stood, sighing slightly at the interruption. I had been

deep in thoughts about... well. Who even knew. I had nothing to distract myself except my memories. My phone was dead, so I couldn't scroll mindlessly on social media. And I refused to walk to Santiago's house, even though the plants were probably in desperate need of some watering. Nope. I had no business being there, hovering around Francisco, especially after what had happened two days before.

No, thank you.

Was I avoiding him? Definitely. But he was also avoiding me, so case closed.

I walked to the front, slapping on my best smile because I knew exactly what would happen once I got there. I opened the door and peeked my head out, using my legs to block the cat from getting out of the house. She was obsessed with exploring the yard, and I normally allowed it, but I was not willing to go out in the dark of the night to look for her once she couldn't find her way back inside.

"Ah, *doctora*," the elderly neighbor said. She was wearing a bright yellow raincoat reaching all the way to the middle of her calves. Her boots matched her coat, and on her head, she had one of those plastic bonnets to keep her hair dry. I squinted my eyes, taking a closer look at her head covered in small green rollers in a neat and orderly pattern. I smiled at her and stepped outside, but the moment I opened the door, the cat darted out onto the porch and to the side of the house, her fur grazing the stucco in a way that made it so she wouldn't get wet.

"*Mierda*," I muttered under my breath, looking in the

direction of the cat for a split second, then returning my gaze to the older woman in front of me.

"I'm so glad you are here," she said, a small smile on her lips. "The gal at the pharmacy said you hadn't taken a vacation."

I wanted to roll my eyes at Gladys for sending people to my home. And at myself for opening the door. Because I could have easily pretended that I wasn't home, and both my cat and I would be inside, dry as a bone in the comfort of my parents' family room.

"How can I help you, Carmen?" I asked as the woman started removing the yellow monstrosity covering her lithe body. "Did you walk here on your own?"

"Oh no, dear, my grandson is waiting in the car. See?" She pointed in the direction of a waiting car at the end of the driveway, where a young man was scrolling on his phone, the white light of the device reflecting on his face. "Can I come in?"

She shook her raincoat and then took a step towards me, crowding me against the door frame.

"I guess so?" I phrased it as a question even though I was reluctant to walk inside the house. She lived down the block. Her house sat on the corner of the street, a few doors down from Santiago's house. "How can I help you?"

She walked in the door, her bonnet dripping water in the foyer. She blinked a few times, then put her hand inside the coat's pocket and took out a small white paper that looked like a page from a prescription pad. I cocked my head, waiting to see what she would say, but instead, she dropped her coat and opened the note, shoving it in front of my face like the pharmacist had done weeks earlier. She lifted her eyebrows and then returned her eyes to the note, explaining without words that I needed to look at whatever was written on there. She started tapping her foot on the marble, impatient for a response.

"How can I help you?" I repeated calmly. My brain wanted to scream at her, but I just couldn't do it. She looked so tiny in the large entry, all of her outerwear drenched in water.

"What does this say?" No explanation of why she needed me to read some other doctor's handwriting. "We can't figure it out."

"Did Gladys send you over?" I asked, the smile back on my face despite my anger. It was on me, this... thing that I'd created for myself. Allowing people to take advantage of me. My brother was right. Francisco was right. Dr. Martín was right. "I won't be able to read it in the darkness. Why don't you call your doctor's office in the morning and ask them?"

"Lucía," she said in a stern voice.

"Carmen, I won't be able to help you. I apologize for making you come all the way here, but I can't help you." I walked to the door and opened it wider, then took a step back and gestured with my hand to invite her to leave.

"*Chiquita*," she said, her tone contemptuous. "I made my grandson drive me all the way here, and I even left the house with my rollers on."

"I understand, but I can't really see what it says and it's not my prescription, so even in daylight, I wouldn't be able to figure that out for you. Again, I apologize."

"Well, maybe you can write a new one for me?" she asked, her gaze almost pleading with me. "Do you have your pad here with you?"

I did have my pad with me; I always did. But that was beyond the point. "Carmen," I said, a little bit stern, but honestly, fed up. "You need to go see your doctor in the morning." I sighed. "Or, you know what? Gladys can call his office and ask for clarification."

"Lucía," she warned. "Where are your manners?"

I flinched. *What?*

She took a few steps to the front door, then abruptly grabbed her coat from the floor and hummed.

"Have a good night."

I didn't even wait for her to be off the porch before closing the door on her. I would hear about it the next day. Granny would probably call me to tell me that *someone* said I was rude to Carmen. But to be honest, I couldn't care less. I was on vacation, damn it. And everyone in town knew it. Just because I was home didn't mean I was available.

I dropped my forehead on the back of the door, my heart beating fast because I just disrespected an elderly woman. But, despite the guilt, it felt a little freeing. Like I was finally living for myself and setting my boundaries. Even if that meant hurting a fragile lady in the process.

I took a deep breath, then opened the door to go out in

search of the cat. I needed to find her before the storm. Judging by the previous days, she should have quickly realized it would rain too hard for her little body and instead would have stayed huddled under one of the bushes by the side of the house, her expedition being cut short by the storm that had kept the lights out since the previous day. The rain had stopped slightly since Carmen had left, so I walked around the house in the direction I'd seen the cat. Trees were still dripping, which made it impossible for me to hear anything but that and my steps on the wet grass.

I squinted, trying to see if I could figure out where that cat was hiding. It was hard to see. The dark of the night, combined with the power outage, made it almost impossible to make out the details of the small animal I was looking for. Maybe I could see the pair of bright eyes hiding under the bushes, the leaves covering her from the water.

"Lucía? What are you doing?" I heard from behind me. I stopped, squatting next to one of the planters, and then turned, looking up at Francisco. He was, once again, dripping wet and looking so much like a lost puppy that I had to contain a smile, even in the sour mood that neighbor lady had put me in. "What's wrong?" he added, cocking his head and taking a step forward. He squinted, adjusting to the darkness of the night.

I shook my head and closed my eyes. Everything felt so raw, so close to hitting me. The raindrops hot on my skin, the walls of the big house above threatening to cave in around me. Like my senses were heightened by the small act of rebellion I had committed. I was a helper; I helped. Until I reached this boiling point. No turning back now. I breathed in and out, looking at the scene surrounding me. My heart lodged in my ribs in panic.

"Lucía!" he roared above the sounds of thunder, his voice a little bit hoarse and washed out, tinged in something that I couldn't quite figure out.

"*¿Qué?*" I exploded, my arms lifting to the sides, hands almost pulling at my drenched hair. "What does everyone want? Just leave me alone!"

His head reared back in surprise, his eyes widening at my outburst. But then he softened and took a step towards me, one hand reaching for my body.

"What do you want? What?" I was suffocating. My lungs couldn't seem to catch a single drop of air, and his gaze was so intent on me, studying me like I was an animal at a zoo exhibit. Except we were outside in the pitch dark, soaking wet, and the storm was ringing loudly around us.

He opened his mouth to say something, then immediately shut it.

"What? Just say it." I stood, then followed his gaze and resigned myself. "The cat." I sighed. "Someone was at the door, and she slithered away when I was talking to them, and it's so dark, I can't seem to find her, and everyone thinks I'm available all the time for their own personal use and—"

Fuck. "Arghhhhhhhhhhhh!" I screamed into the night, large drops falling on my tipped face, my cheeks so hot with anger and embarrassment that the cool water was a nice respite.

"Okay," he said, taking a few steps, then putting his hand in mine. He squeezed once and tugged me towards him. "Let's look for her."

With our hands clasped, he walked me around the side of the house and towards the back of the lot. The wind of the previous days had done a number on the outdoors, branches and leaves and a few flowers littering the neatly cut grass and covering the pool. I was able to stack the outdoor furniture cushions and put them in the garage to avoid them getting lost, but that was the extent of what I'd done, despite my parents calling me multiple times to remind me.

Maybe I was rebelling against them too. They would never know anyway.

One of the lanterns was tilted to its side, the glass cracked in a million different directions. The first casualty.

Francisco stilled, his arm pulling me to his side, closer to his warm body. Despite being drenched, he was burning up, and upon closer inspection, his eyes seemed sunken and irritated. I tilted my head and looked closer, but I couldn't quite figure anything out in the dark.

Qué tarada, Lucía. I had been a real bitch to him, using him as my punching bag, and he looked like shit.

"Are you feeling okay?" I asked as he inspected the large yard, turning his body in every direction, squinting into the dark corners.

He grunted in response, his hand tightening in my grip. I

moved closer and lifted my free hand, going immediately to the back of his neck and squeezing gently there. It was hot to the touch, despite the water and the relatively low temperature that the storm had brought with it.

"You're sick," I said with a gasp, grabbing him by the arm and tugging him into the house.

"No," he rasped and closed his eyes, an expression of pain on his face. "No, I'm fine."

"Nuh-uh, we're going inside."

"The cat," he rasped, stopping in the middle of the yard and planting his feet there.

"The cat will be fine," I replied, looking one last time and finding her curled up under the couch, like a storm wasn't raging around her. "See?" I pointed, his gaze following my fingers and his shoulders relaxing immediately. "I'll come get her later. You need to be in bed."

"I'm fine," he said and then winced immediately.

"Nuh-uh. Inside."

We walked in through the back door and stopped in the laundry room to leave our wet clothes. The towels from previous nights were still there, draped on the mudroom hooks, waiting to be folded. I grabbed one and turned my body, offering it to him. He moved in slow motion, shivers running through his body and his hands shaking with the effort.

"Clothes off," I said, a little bit bossier than I would have liked, especially after what happened two nights ago. "Wrap yourself up in a towel, and I'll see you by the stairs."

21

FRANCISCO

Jesus, she was bossy. I shouldn't have been thinking about that in such a state, but it was inevitable. She was wonderful and even better than I remembered.

"Okay," she drawled softly, walking to me slowly and surely, almost delicately. Not like I was a grown man in my early thirties with a cold. Well, maybe the flu. "Let's go upstairs."

I focused on Lucía. Her hair was down, drenched from standing for however long under the rain, looking for that damned cat. The lights in the house were off, the darkness creeping in at a snail's pace. We hadn't had a break in the rain yet, ever since two nights ago. I had left her house almost with my tail between my legs after her small panic, but I was resolved to go back and talk about it. But the next day, I woke up and everything hurt, even my hair. I didn't have the energy to make the short walk to her, instead staying in bed all day, shivering inside the covers.

"What hurts?" She turned swiftly, her palm going to my forehead and pushing my hair back. Her blue eyes were darker than normal, full of concern. She transformed instantly into my doctor, and I was now her patient and not her... Who even knew.

"Everything," I said, trying to laugh at the ridiculousness of it all. I was wrapped in a towel like a little kid, the fabric draped over my shoulders and tucked tightly against my chest, both my hands holding it there. My legs were still dripping water, and the drops that were tracing down my skin were making me shiver. Yesterday had been bad, but today was worse. "I think I have a fever." My lids closed at the strain of just standing there.

"Yeah, no shit, Sherlock." She was smiling, but there was concern in her features. She stood behind me and placed her hands on my shoulders, pushing me slightly in the direction of the stairs, taking slow steps towards what I assumed was a bedroom. Once we made it to the top, she turned my body and led me to an open door towards the front of the house.

It was darker up here. The blinds in the room were rolled down, but the windows were open, likely to counteract the stuffiness of the hot summer days and the lack of power.

"Bed," she said, walking towards a door across from where we were standing. Everything in here screamed Lucía. It was so calm, the light-colored walls soothing. Feminine yet grown-up, despite it being what I assumed was her childhood bedroom. She walked into the bathroom and opened a few cabinet doors, then closed them swiftly and turned on the tap for a few seconds. She came back with a wet washcloth and a glass of water, a bottle of something under her arm. "*Dale.*" C'mon.

Bossy.

I dropped the towel and got under the covers, her smell all around me. The sheets were burning me, scraping lightly on my sensitive skin. She took a few steps towards me, eyeing me warily. She looked concerned. I was sure this was only a cold, but she was treating it like it was life-or-death.

"Why are you so concerned?" I croaked, my voice raspy and my throat on fire. "It's just a cold."

"Yeah, well..." she replied while setting everything down on the side table by the bed.

She pushed lightly on my shoulder, the movement making me lie flat on my back, my eyes closed towards the ceiling. The mattress dipped to my side, and a second later there was a cold feeling on my forehead. The relief was immediate.

"You are burning up," she added, her soft fingers roaming my face, touching my neck, then the top of my head, pulling lightly on my hair. I groaned from the sensation, the sound obscener than what I intended. I could feel her attention on me, so I turned slightly to look at her. Her hair was up in that tight ponytail now. Her doctor hair.

"In all these years, I never thought I would become your patient," I blurted. Clearly an idiotic, fever-induced comment. She scrunched her eyebrows in question but later relaxed her face. She stretched towards the nightstand and grabbed the glass of water and the medicine, then handed me a few capsules to take.

After I was done with the water, I settled back down on the bed, the washcloth now hot to the touch. She grabbed it and walked to the bathroom again, running it under the tap for a few seconds. My eyes were heavy, but I could still track her movements across the room. She looked tense, her shoulders tight and her body stiff, those loose limbs from the summer days gone.

"Come over here," I said, barely audible over the rush of my blood. Everything hurt, and I could hear the sound of my heartbeat in my ears. "I need you close."

There was a small sound from her direction, and then I heard her steps. She lay down on the other side of me, draping the washcloth over my forehead again, her hand caressing down to the back of my neck.

"That feels so good." I was drowsy, a small smile forming on my lips despite how fucking awful I felt. I closed my eyes, then said, "You feel so good." All of this was clearly fever-induced. I was loose with my tongue, saying things I would never say to her because she didn't remember me. She wasn't saying anything back, just idling there next to me, concern all over her face.

The mattress dipped again, and I felt her skin next to mine under the covers, her cold hand reaching out for mine, fingers linking together. Then my world went dark, the fever finally taking over and making me fall asleep, holding on to her tightly.

The door to Jazmín's room had been left ajar that night. Usually when doctors or nurses were in with her, they would close the door behind them, giving them privacy with the patient. I could hear murmuring coming from inside, the dim light of the bedside lamp spilling out into the hallway.

"Yes." Lucía laughed. I leaned on the door frame, looking into the room but hiding in the shadows. I was confident that they weren't able to see me from where I stood. "That's right."

I squished my eyebrows together, wondering what they were talking about.

"So med school is six years," she continued, lifting her hand and using her fingers to count. Jazmín's eyes were rapt with attention, looking at her like she hung the moon. Like she was her idol. "And then pediatrics is four."

"What?" my sister squealed. She moved under the covers, pulling her legs towards her body and sitting cross-legged on the bed. She leaned her torso and placed her elbows on her thighs, hanging on to every word the doctor was saying. "That's a ton of time."

Lucía snorted, and the sound was followed by a deep-chested laugh, airy and carefree around the edges. "Yeah." She scrunched her nose. "But I really like it."

"And what made you want to be a doctor?"

"Oh, it's not one single thing," she dismissed, almost like she was slightly hesitant about telling Jazmín the full story.

"But my whole family are lawyers. I always knew that was definitely not for me. So boring." She rolled her eyes, and Jaz giggled in return, leaning back against the pillows. Lucía reached behind my sister and wiggled one of them, making sure her head was resting comfortably.

"Yeah, but, like, there has to be a specific moment, no?"

Lucía smiled at her and gave her a little side eye, then said, "Alright, lady, time to go to sleep."

"No, *pluh-easeeeeee*, stay with me until my brother gets here."

I chuckled from my spot. That was such a Jazmín thing to say. She was desperate to be around people, as her days were long and boring. She never got along with other kids but favored grown-ups instead, so I understood where this affinity was coming from. She was curious about this kind woman. Hell, I was curious too.

"Okay," Lucía whispered and stood from the bed, tucking the covers under Jazmín's chin and smiling wide at her. She walked the few steps to the chair on the side and sat back down, tucking her legs under her and turning to face my sister. She blinked a few times, the silence stretching in the room, but her smile followed, and Jazmín's face lit up. Expectant.

"When I was about your age, I had a friend that got sick," she started, looking down at her nails and then back up at my sister. Her voice was even, like she'd practiced this multiple times. Her official narrative. What she told everyone about her journey to becoming a doctor. "And she died before even having a chance to get treatment."

Jazmín's gaze snapped to hers, and they looked at each other for a beat. I couldn't see my sister's face well enough from my angle, but I was sure she was even more curious now. Curious to know if it had been at all like her. Pediatric leukemia wreaking havoc on her body.

"And I was still young, but it really made me wonder how those things happened, you know?" Lucía added, tugging at the stethoscope that was draped around her neck. "And it got a tad obsessive, but here I am."

She winked and smiled, making a little joke of what had to have been a stressful moment. Or maybe not. She lifted her head and looked towards the door, and our gazes met. There was something behind her eyes, something I couldn't quite place. Maybe concern, maybe familiarity or intimacy. But the lighthearted woman I was just listening to disappeared in a flash of a second. Her chin dipped, and she smiled, then turned to my sister and sighed.

"He's here." She spoke quietly, her movements cautious around her patient. Those words she uttered got lodged in my throat, stuck behind my heart for me to treasure. I was there; of course I was.

I startled awake, shaking those memories away. I was draped around Lucía, her body flush against mine in the bed. It was still dark outside, so I tightened my hold on her and went back to sleep, relishing in the moment.

22

LUCÍA

THE COMBINATION of smells was the first thing I noticed when I woke up. It was a mixture of the scent of the summer flowers and the earth after a rainfall wafting in through the open window. The blinds were down, but I could see daylight peeking through, a ray of sunshine illuminating the closet doors opposite the window.

"Hi," Francisco rasped in my ear. His voice was all gravel and seduction, rough around the edges. Sleep was still lingering around it, and his breathing was even and steady. I stiffened because I couldn't remember anything from the night before. I had lain in bed with him, watching over to make sure he was okay, but eventually sleep took over. It was obvious we were drawn to each other, our bodies orbiting the other consistently, taking us to this moment, flush against each other, his chest moving behind me. "Good morning."

I smiled into the pillow and then tried to turn around to look at him, to feel his forehead and confirm the fever was gone, but he pulled me into his body instead, putting us incredibly closer to each other. His right hand was circling my stomach, his fingers sneaking under my shirt and giving me goosebumps. I closed my eyes, enjoying it for a moment and letting go. I knew I couldn't do much more than this because we needed to talk first. "Francisco," I said, but no more words came out. Instead, I moaned softly at the feeling of his body, hard against the curve of my ass.

"Yeah?" he mumbled, his mouth against my hair, giving small kisses down the column of my neck and to my shoulder. My hand reached for his, linking our fingers together and moving with his, up and down the soft skin of my stomach. I couldn't help myself. I needed more. My body was aching. "*Linda?*" he encouraged, almost desperately.

I was ready to melt into the mattress. Pretty. When had we turned into *this?*

He grunted and rocked his hips forward, his hand moving down to the waistline of my shorts and slipping under the stretchy waist, pausing for a second at my hip and tightening his hold there. I sighed, and my hand started moving his down, down, down to the sweet spot between my thighs where all of my energy was. I could feel his erratic breathing behind me, his body warm but nothing like the night before.

"Lucía." The gruff voice could only belong to one person, and that was Charlie. "Lucía," he repeated from downstairs, louder this time. He sounded exasperated, like maybe something had happened, and he needed help. Although that was completely out of character for him because he never needed anything from anyone. My eyes shot open, and I tried to say something, and then Francisco chuckled, his forehead resting on my shoulder. He was shaking with laughter, and I could feel the smile on his face on my skin.

"Yeah," I croaked, the sound bumpy against my pillow. "*¡Ya voy!*"

I sat up, my face heating with embarrassment. Francisco was still laughing, his eyes burning a hole through me. He moved under the covers and then draped a forearm on his face, his laughter still booming in the room.

"What is wrong with you?" I asked with a smile on my lips. How pathetic were we? Thirty-some-year-olds being interrupted by my older brother.

I stood from the bed and rushed to the bathroom, taking a moment to compose myself and put myself together before going downstairs to see what Charlie needed. Francisco was still on the bed, lying there casually and scrolling through his phone with a frown on his face.

"I'll be right back," I said, looking over my shoulder before leaving the room. He looked up and smiled, but there was a slight edge of concern in his eyes, his eyebrows scrunched slightly. "I'm going to see what he needs."

I fixed my hair on the way down the stairs, opting instead for a messy bun that looked more put together than whatever had resulted from whatever that was with Francisco. There were noises coming from the kitchen, cabinet doors slamming shut and the tap turning on and off.

"What is wrong with you?" I asked, walking towards the island. Charlie was standing by the stove, his hand holding the kettle hovering over the burner, frozen in mid-air. He turned slowly, blinking almost in slow motion and then cocking his head to the side.

"Oh, you're here."

I raised an eyebrow in question, wondering why he was surprised that I was, in fact, here. "Duh," I said and smiled wide to see if I could manage even the tiniest smile from him. "I live here."

He blinked a few times, then turned towards the stove, turning on the gas burner with a match and setting down the kettle.

"I let the cat in." He shrugged.

"What time is it?" I turned to look at the microwave, but the numbers were flashing.

"A little past seven."

"Seven? What is wrong with you? Why are you here so early?" Now I was concerned. Yes, he was an early riser, but he had his whole routine. Probably worked out and then headed for coffee or breakfast at Santiago's hotel. He stopped by every day to see if anyone needed anything now that our brother was out of town.

He grunted, then turned back to the stove, opening the kettle to see if the water was boiling yet. "I couldn't sleep."

"Are you sick?" I walked towards him, lifting my hand

towards his forehead, but he slapped it away with a glare that only made me smile wider.

"I'm going to the city today for a few days," he said, averting his eyes. "I'm meeting with a bunch of friends from law school."

"Okay," I drawled. "But I'm confused—"

"Lucía," he deadpanned, impatiently looking inside the kettle again. Slow footsteps came down the stairs, the fourth step creaking under Francisco's weight. The cat came into the kitchen first, trotting elegantly to her food bowl and sitting in front of it, waiting patiently for me to refill it with her morning snack.

Francisco followed her in, face glued to his phone and his free hand running through his mussed hair. Charlie turned towards me and widened his eyes, then pursed his lips. He blinked a few times, maybe trying to say something to me without any words.

"Shit," Francisco mumbled into his phone. "*Linda,*" he said absentmindedly, still looking at the screen on his hand. He ran his fingers through his hair once more, then looked up.

Charlie was frozen next to me, his eyes fixed on the man before me wearing nothing but a pair of running shorts. He had sleep all over his face, his hair tousled as if he had gone to bed with it wet. Francisco smiled widely and tucked his phone into his pocket, taking a few steps towards us behind the kitchen island.

"Hey, man," he said, extending a hand to my brother.

Charlie blinked, then looked at me, waiting for something, anything. Finally, after what felt like a lifetime, my brother lifted his hand and shook Francisco's, mumbling something unintelligible under his breath.

The kettle whistled at that moment, and Charlie turned back to shut off the stove, grabbing the appliance and moving towards the side, where a thermos was set up.

"Lu," Francisco said, startling me from the awkward moment. "I'm going to head out, but I'll see you later?" he asked, his head cocked to the side. He took a step forward, kissed my temple, and squeezed my bicep, then walked into the laundry room and grabbed the rest of his clothes.

On his way out, he crouched next to the cat and ran a hand through her soft fur, whispering, "I'll see you later too, sweet girl," like it was the easiest compliment ever, even for the non-cat person he claimed to be.

Charlie made a sound, and when I turned to look at him, he was holding a fist against his mouth, containing either a smile or a big, big laugh.

Once Francisco was out of the house through the back door, Charlie turned to me, giving me a look that was full of mirth. "Oh shit," he said, a smile growing on his face, the corners of his eyes crinkling with amusement just like Santiago's did when he was being annoying.

"*Callate*," I said, but I couldn't hide my smile. "It's not funny."

"It's a little funny," he replied, using those words from a few days ago back on me.

"When do you leave?" I asked, changing the subject abruptly, even though I knew that Charlie wouldn't say anything to me. He didn't ask a ton of questions because he expected us to leave him alone. Boundaries, he said.

"In an hour or so," he replied, turning back and preparing his *mate*. His Stanley thermal bottle was covered in a sticky residue—the direct result of Jacinto covering it with decals just to annoy him. Anytime he would leave that thing unattended, our youngest brother would somehow find out and plaster it with stickers, then hide it back in their office somewhere with a sly grin on his face.

The cat was still perched at her spot beside her food plates, waiting for her morning ration. I walked to her and ran a hand through her fur just like Francisco had done minutes earlier. "Do you want to eat, sweet girl?" She purred in response, nudging my hand with her wet nose and rubbing her face against my palm. "Maybe you need a name."

She blinked at me a few times, then looked at where her food was stashed. I shook my head and smiled. The impatience was contagious in my family, apparently.

23

FRANCISCO

It was probably time for the other shoe to drop. Because things couldn't be good for me, ever. Jazmín's mom, Florencia, had texted me earlier to tell me to call her. I knew there was something wrong the moment she answered, her voice filled with tears and her sentences quick and choppy.

"You need to come back," she said, her breathing erratic. I heard her pacing in the background, a door opening and closing behind her, and then the quiet sound of what must have been a hallway since there was a slight echo to her steps. "This is quite the shit show."

"Wait, slow down," I said, confused, because I couldn't find anything on the news earlier when she had texted. I had looked online and called a few of my acquaintances in the city to see if anyone had any leads, but nothing had come up. It wasn't out of the ordinary for her to text or call —we'd kept each other apprised of our lives since Jazmín's death, but this seemed urgent. "I don't know what's going on."

"Did your father call you?" she asked in a rush, trying to get all the words out of her mouth in one breath. "Oh my god!" she sobbed.

I still had a headache from whatever was lingering in my system. I felt much better than the previous day, but my throat was on fire, and my heart beat loudly in my ears. The sun was shining, and there was a nice breeze running through town, the trees moving slowly and carefully against the bright blue backdrop.

I walked from Lucía's house towards the town square to grab coffee, stopping at Santiago's stoop to put on my shirt and shoes. I had hightailed it out of that house the second I saw Charlie staring at me, a scowl on his face. I would come back later and finally talk to her about everything. The town square was buzzing with energy, and the line for coffee wrapped around the building. It was the first time I was seeing it like this, but it made sense—Santiago had mentioned that January was a busy month for the town, getting tons of tourists from all over the place.

I had to talk to Lucía.

"Yes, a few days ago," I said, frowning, because it had, indeed, been a while. If something was about to break, especially this, his dirty little secret, there would have been a stronger sense of urgency. "But he hasn't said anything."

"They know," she whispered into the phone, a wail coming out of her mouth. The sound made me gasp out loud in panic, my heart beating faster than it already was. "Someone leaked it."

"Okay," I whispered, trying to keep my composure. Florencia and I had become close in the years since Jazmín had been diagnosed with cancer. It was awkward at first because I was in my late teens when I met them. And she was wary of my intentions. "It's going to be okay."

"No, *no entendés,*" she cried. "Where are you?"

"I'm in Córdoba," I replied, trying to think of what I could do to solve this. Or not even solve it, but maybe help in any way.

"There's one reporter that has been calling me nonstop," she said. Her voice was elevating in pitch and volume, almost screaming on the other end of the line. "I was able to get away, but it's a matter of time until they find me again."

"*Bueno*, let me figure some things out and I'll call you back, okay?"

This had the potential of being a disaster for Florencia. My father had gone to the ends of the earth to keep his daughter a secret because it could potentially be career-ending for him. That was why he had forbidden me from seeing her.

I took a breath and looked around, trying to figure out what to do next. Maybe I needed to go back to the city, if only temporarily. Talk to someone, anyone. But the moment I stepped foot anywhere close to my home, my father would know that I was there. Because that man had eyes everywhere.

"*¡Eugenio!*" my mother had screamed that night when I was in my early teens. There was a loud bang—the front door, I assumed. I was perched on the edge of the couch, a game console beeping in my hands. The sound startled me, and the game flashed *Game Over* on the screen. I heard her footsteps go up the stairs, and then a door opened with force.

"What the *fuck* did you do?" she yelled. She wasn't a screamer at all. She was a stern talker, her words cutting like a knife. It was a big difference to how my father operated both in and out of the house, where screaming was his norm. Indiscriminately. Another bang that made me jump on my seat.

I stood, walking over to the staircase to see if I could make out what they were talking about, but all I could hear were faint mumblings behind closed doors. I tiptoed my way to the second floor, standing close enough to their bedroom door so that I could hear but far away enough so that I could scurry into my room quickly in case they came out.

"She is *pregnant!*" my mother roared. I heard a noise, followed by what sounded like the back of a chair hitting the hardwood floor. "What the fuck?"

"Graciela," he said, the name coming tersely out of his mouth. His voice was raspy, like he had just lit one of those disgusting cigarettes and taken a drag, the smoke leaving with his words.

"I can't believe you." Another bang, something crashing

against the floor. Maybe one of those chinoiserie vases they collected that were probably worth more than a month's salary for any of the help. I flinched at the violence behind the door. "She's the fucking help."

Who were they talking about? What was happening?

I knew my parents weren't happy. It was so obvious to me. I didn't have a point of comparison because I was hardly allowed to go to any of my classmates' houses. It was to and from school exclusively. And the breaks were long and lonely.

"The fucking help!" she shrieked. "You couldn't fucking keep your dick in your pants."

My eyes widened. *Oh no.* I wasn't supposed to be listening in on this conversation. This was exclusively an adult conversation; I knew as much.

I turned on my heel to head towards my room, but the floorboard creaked under my foot, making a loud, echoey noise in the big upstairs hallway. I froze, hoping my hasty movements hadn't elicited any of their attention. Instead I heard another vase crashing to the floor, and one of the tiny pieces slid under the door and into the hallway where I was standing.

This fight was much more violent than any of the other ones they'd had. I usually stayed in my room, far away enough from their room that I couldn't work out any of what they were fighting about. Usually it had something to do with my father's antics or behavior, but never like this.

I panicked, not knowing where to go. "*¡Graciela!*" my

father roared, and a small whimper came from my mother in response.

"*No me toques*," she cried. I could hear a faint grunt coming from their room. "Stop it," she said. I blinked, trying to think what to do.

There were footsteps coming from behind the door, but my body wasn't reacting. The knob moved slowly, the door opening in slow motion in front of me. I spun on my heel and went inside the hallway closet, shoving my body against the old coats that were hanging there. It was stuffy, and it smelled faintly of mothballs.

"Eugenio, come back here," my mother yelled in return, steps retreating into the room. The door remained open by the sounds of it because I could hear much more clearly than before.

"What the fuck is your problem, Graciela?" he drawled, his voice loud and commanding. "You don't even give a fuck about this."

What was *this?* I squinted, trying to rack my brain and figure out what was happening. Then there was a loud bang that made me flinch in the dark.

"You don't even care about your son. Why would you care about someone else's baby?"

Me? *Oh no.*

"Biggest mistake of our lives," he spouted. His jaw was clenched. It was obvious to me, even without being able to see him, because his voice sounded different, strained. But he said it with conviction. Like this was a conversation they'd had hundreds of times before.

As the weight of his words hung in the air, I felt a sudden tightness in my chest, like an invisible fist was constricting my lungs. The familiar cadence of his voice now carried an ominous tone, a warning sign of the impending storm that was about to engulf me. The walls of the closet started caving in, my breathing erratic and heat rushing up my body. I knew they didn't care much about me, their political careers their priority. But the biggest mistake?

My pulse quickened, a rapid drumbeat echoing in my ears, drowning out the sounds from outside the closet. It was a visceral response, my body's reaction to the sudden shift in the conversation—the confession hitting me like a train straight through my chest. The air around me felt thick, sticky around the edges and unable to get into my body, laden with unspoken truths and the burden of this—apparently—well-known secret.

I started breathing erratically, a desperate attempt to draw in air that seemed to elude me. The temperature in the closet soared, a surge of heat coursing through my veins like molten lava mixed with frozen icicles. Beads of sweat formed on my forehead, and my vision blurred, the boundaries of the small space distorting and warping before my eyes.

The room was swallowing me whole.

"Oh no," I whispered, the words escaping my trembling lips and darkness finally engulfing me.

"Fran?" A soft voice made me jump. Lucía was standing in front of me, one of her hands squeezing my bicep in that intimate way. "What's going on?"

I stumbled into her, my arms wrapping around her body instantly. She relaxed, one of her hands rubbing up and down my back in soothing motions. I could feel tears forming in my eyes, so I closed them to keep them there, hoping, praying she wouldn't see me panicking. She had seen it before, but nothing like what had just happened in broad daylight in the middle of the town square.

"Let's go home," she whispered in my ear, her body moving me slightly, pushing me towards the house. I let her go, undoing my hold on her. She took a step back, linking her fingers through mine. She crouched and grabbed my phone from the ground, tucking it in the back pocket of her jeans.

We walked slowly towards the big house, a few curious folks looking in our direction. She wasn't paying them any attention. Instead, she kept her eyes on me the whole way, occasionally lifting her free hand and squeezing my bicep.

24
LUCÍA

Francisco was shaking next to me, his fists still clenched even after sitting on the back porch for thirty minutes. His gaze was lost, looking out into the mountain. The cat kept going back and forth between the house and the backyard, looking at us with concern on her little face. No one was moving a single inch.

The wind was picking up, but there weren't any storm clouds on the horizon. It was a bright day, the sun high above in the sky. The birds were chirping loudly, like they were yelling secrets at each other.

"What's going on?" I asked for maybe the tenth time. He grunted and moved closer to me, one of his hands draping over my thigh. He moved his thumb absentmindedly, his eyes still stuck to the back of the yard where the trees met the hills.

"I think I have to go back to the city," he said, still not

looking at me. He had a pained look on his face, like his brain was moving a million miles an hour in different directions and he couldn't decide which one to take. "There's a family crisis."

The word "crisis" made me perk up. Technically, I knew about his family because I'd been his sister's doctor, but in this moment, in this situation, I was supposed to be oblivious.

"Okay," I said warily. "Is there something I can do?"

"No, thank you." He lifted his lips a fraction, a small, sad smile on his lips. His eyes were now focused on his thumb moving in slow circles on my inner thigh. He turned the top half of his body and faced me, his brown eyes bloodshot and sunken.

"Are you going to tell me about it?"

"No, thank you." He smiled now, big and reaching his eyes. Maybe the panic was over, maybe not. But he was definitely ready to change the subject. He was still wearing the same clothes as last night, probably still damp from the rain. "Let's get in the pool," he said, eyeing the large body of water in front of us. There were a few leaves floating lazily on the surface, the wind playing with them without any care in the world.

"*Dale*," I drawled, still eyeing him suspiciously. I stood from the loveseat, reaching for the hem of my shirt and pulling it up and over my shoulders. After Francisco and Charlie had left that morning, I took a long shower and put on my bathing suit, expecting the temperature to get high enough for a dip in the water. There was no rain in the forecast, but I was expecting another blackout. I unbuttoned my shorts and let them drop, stepping out of them and grabbing them from the ground.

I turned to set my clothes on the seat, and Francisco caught sight of my ribcage. His eyes widened at my small tattoo, like he was completely surprised about the fact that I had a single line of permanent ink on my body.

"You have a tattoo?" he asked, the obvious answer in front of him. He grabbed my hip and turned me towards him, his gaze fixed on the outline of that one special flower. "It's a jasmine," he whispered, his eyes shining with something. Tears, maybe. My throat caught in response. I couldn't read his expression, his eyes moving all over my body, searching for more. Going back and forth between my face and my ribcage, like this was just a weird coincidence and it had been there the whole time, ever since we met that first day in her hospital room but hiding under my loose scrubs.

"Yeah," I said, swallowing hard in response. The knot was still sitting in my throat, making it hard for me to breathe.

"Why?"

"Why do you think?"

"You remember?" he asked. His lids pinched tight, and he rested his forehead on my stomach. He looked so small, so vulnerable there, his body shaking slightly. My heart was beating fast, and the only sound I could hear was it pounding against my chest. I rubbed my forehead and ran my fingers through my hair, buying some time before I had to answer. He looked up, those brown eyes intently set on me.

"Of course I remember," I answered, looking away from his face for a moment. He reached for me, tugging at my waist and draping me over his lap, my legs sideways on the couch. "Why would I not?"

The world stopped moving. We were both frozen in silence. He sucked in some air, then let it go, a tear falling down his cheek.

"Why?" he croaked.

I shrugged and draped one arm around his shoulder, pulling him closer to me. "She was—is—so special to me, still."

He nodded, leaning his head on my shoulder, my heartbeat going faster at the movement, but I couldn't catch my breath. Because he did remember.

Of course he remembered.

Tears were rolling freely down his cheeks, his body shaking slightly under the covered patio.

"You left," he said.

There it was. The moment I'd been waiting for since the second I had laid eyes on him in my brother's house. He did remember; of course he did. Probably every single detail of it all.

"You did too," I blurted out in response. It came out defensively.

"My sister died!" he roared and stood abruptly, depositing me in front of him and taking a step to the side. I flinched at the sound because it was so out of character for him, for the man I knew then and the man I knew now. I couldn't catch my breath, the air in my lungs not quite doing what it was supposed to do.

"Do you have any idea what it felt like?" I asked, the question coming out as a sob. I hadn't realized I was crying, the tears streaming nonstop down my cheeks. He was wiping his with the back of both hands, rubbing at his eyes to make them stop.

"Do *you?*" he asked, but he flinched as soon as the words were out. I wrapped my arms around my body, hugging myself and hiding that stupid permanent reminder of her. Maybe this way, this would stop. "She died, and you weren't there, Lucía."

"I know!" I was bawling now, trying to catch my breath as the tears kept coming down. I couldn't see him clearly, my vision too blurry with too many tears to even see his reaction. "I've replayed that moment in my head for years."

Jazmín had been discharged from the hospital after that last infection, her labs looking good enough for her to go home, where she would be more comfortable. She still needed to take care of herself, avoiding many visitors and strenuous activity. But at least she could sleep in her own bed and shower in her own bathroom. Only a few days later, and seemingly with no explanation, she developed a fever that had her back in the hospital, a little more severe than her previous stay. And I wasn't there because I was visiting my family in this freaking small town.

"Me too," he responded, taking a step closer. He reached out for my hand, and I let him. It felt a little selfish, holding on to him while he was like this, remembering what was probably the worst time for his family in recent years. But my body needed him, my brain needed him, and my heart kept thumping in search of his, looking for the rhythm it was missing. "And you weren't there."

He dragged me towards his body, wrapping one arm around my shoulders and the other hand cupping my head. I rested my head on his shoulder, my tears making his shirt wet at the contact. I couldn't catch my breath. My sobs were way too loud and uncontrollable.

It was the first time I was talking to anyone about this. Not even Valentina knew.

"I am so sorry," I said in between breaths. His chest moved up and down against mine, his tears falling on my bare shoulder. "I am so, so sorry." I kept repeating it like a chant because I felt responsible for what had happened. I should have caught it. I should have been there instead of being in this town, celebrating the new year with my family and laughing at Jacinto's shenanigans. Because maybe, just maybe, if I had been there, the outcome would have been different and Jazmín would be here today.

He took a step back and searched my face.

"Sorry for what?" he asked, looking straight into me. He was both curious but serious at the same time, like it had never even crossed his mind that I could be partially responsible for what had happened.

Another sob, this time deeper, stronger, more painful. I could hear it, the pain coming out of my body. A wail. It was like an out-of-body experience. I didn't recognize it.

"I couldn't save her," I said, covering my face with my hands. My chest heaved spasmodically.

"Oh," he said. He blinked, then blinked again. There was a long silence, the sound deafening and overtaking all my senses. It was obvious in his response that he blamed me for this. He didn't want to see me again, so why was he still here? Standing in front of me and holding me like this?

25

FRANCISCO

"I couldn't save her."

"Oh."

Oh.

"Is that what you think, Lucía?" My eyes filled with tears, the back of my throat tight again. It was the first moment since Jazmín died that I had felt like this. Like finally I could talk about it with someone who would understand the pain. The ache. The anger. It was a lonely time for me, a moment where I realized that grief was a solitary stage. Where a person was alone with their thoughts, trying to navigate the giant waves of hurt, the what-ifs, the blaming, and the anger. All inside one's heart.

"Why didn't you come back to me?" she asked, her hands going to her face and covering her eyes once more. I moved, pulling her hands away and twisting my fingers through hers, dragging her back to the loveseat. Her tears had all but stopped, though evidence of them still remained in her blue eyes and her dark lashes lumped together in tiny groupings.

"No, *linda,*" I whispered, running my fingers through her hair. "That's not it at all."

That night I had walked into the hallway in the pediatrics wing and could hear the commotion coming from the opposite side of the hall. There were nurses coming in and out of a room, hurried steps and hushed tones. It wasn't yet dark outside, the summer day stretching to its fullest and still hanging on by a thread. The sky was a dark pinkish purple, and the last of the sun was peeking through the tops of the trees outside of the hospital window. Jazmín had been hospitalized just that morning, and I hadn't had time to visit her.

Being in the hospital was a strange thing, really. It was like everyone was living in their own parallel universes. Some parents and patients were happy, their bodies showing all that joy that getting good news meant. And others, somber in and out of the rooms, holding on to whatever hope they still had. I had been one of the former just days before, when that pretty doctor had uttered the happiest string of words anyone could ever say to me.

But now, there was a fog and a pressure in my chest that could only mean one thing. I raised my hand and rubbed it, hoping that it would pass.

Ahead of me, staff exited a room in a single file, their heads down.

No. I mean, it could mean anything, right? Maybe it wasn't Jazmín's room. Maybe they were just running a drill. Was that even a thing?

I rushed my steps, very aware that I had multiple eyes on me. I wasn't supposed to be there, but the staff had stopped paying attention to me months ago, the moment they had realized I was a constant in my sister's life. That if it weren't for me coming there, then she would be all alone, spending so many nights lying in her hospital bed, looking tiny and fragile, without a single person there to support her.

"Francisco." Sonia's stern voice came from behind me. Her gaze was soft, looking at me with something that I could only describe as pity. She shook her head.

That only meant one thing, I was sure.

She was gone.

"No," I whispered. My nose tingled, and tears filled my eyes. "No, no, no. I didn't—" I didn't even say goodbye to her. "I was running late. My meeting ran late."

She took a step forward and grabbed my forearm, tugging me towards her small frame. Her arms went around my back, and she squeezed hard.

"*Cuánto lo lamento,*" Sonia whispered in my ear, her voice laced with apology. "The doctor will be back shortly to talk to you."

"I—" My mouth opened, but no words came out. "My meeting ran late."

My breaths came in jagged gasps, each inhale a struggle

against the weight that had settled in my chest. I stumbled forward, my mind swirling with every single image of my sister—it all threatened to drown me. The hospital corridors, once familiar, now felt like a maze, voices and sounds so foreign to me. Sonia's touch lingered on my forearm, possibly an attempt to anchor me down to this new reality. I wanted to shake off her grasp, to run into Jazmín's room and discover this was all a sick joke they were playing on me, but my limbs were heavy with the burden of regret and grief.

"Francisco." A voice sounded next to Sonia. I looked at the man standing before me, but I couldn't focus on him. Guilt clawed at the edges of my consciousness, tearing through any semblance of composure. I hadn't said good-bye. This couldn't be happening.

I pressed my trembling hands against my face, attempting to stifle the sobs that threatened to escape. The doctor's whispered condolences echoed in my ears, a mumble of words put together in an explanation I couldn't quite grasp. I took a step towards the wall and melted into it, my body sliding down to the floor. The silence was deafening, broken only by the loud wail leaving my mouth.

Lucía's sobs broke me away from the memory, from that horrible night that had been playing on repeat in my brain. She was standing in front of me, my arms tight around her shoulders. She was perfect, even like this, with her guard down, shaking in my hold. I kissed the top of her head, her tears streaming down her face straight to my shirt. "I'm so sorry," she kept repeating, her words barely discernible above her loud weeping.

"No," I said, shaking my head at the same time to get the point across. "No, Lucía, that's not it at all."

"But I wasn't there," she said, sniffing hard and wiping at her tears. "I couldn't save her."

"Lucía, *please*," I begged. I needed her to stop crying so that she could hear what I had to say. "Please stop crying, *linda*, I beg you."

She turned her head to look at me, tears streaming still down her face, but her breathing started to even out. She wiped the back of her hand on her eyes and then grabbed her shirt from the seat beside us, using it on her face and dabbing it all around.

"I am so sorry," I said, being completely honest and open with her. I needed her to understand that this had nothing to do with her and everything to do with my screwed-up family. "I'm sorry I never came back to you." Tears started to fall down my cheeks again at the confession. "It had nothing to do with you and everything to do with me."

She nodded and licked her lips, keeping her mouth slightly open as she listened to what I had to say.

"I think you know about my father," I started, taking a deep breath after the words spilled out. "He's a powerful man. He was more powerful then than what he is today, especially over me. When I was in my teens, he got one of his aides pregnant. I found out because my parents had a huge, violent fight at the house, and I heard every single word of it. It was awful."

She nodded, looking in between my eyes with attention.

"You also might know that he runs on a 'family values' platform." I used air quotes because he was very far away from actually living and believing in those traditional morals. "So when his aide got pregnant, he hid her away, giving her a ton of hush money and trying with all his might to keep everyone away from each other.

"When I was in law school, I had a contact of mine at the registrar try to find her name and address—completely illegal, by the way—but I was desperate because if my suspicions were correct and my father was being my father, they weren't doing well. I later learned he never sent any child support to help out with Jazmín, so it had been tight for them for years. And that's when I met her and her mother, Florencia.

"And the rest you know because you saw me with her. She is the best thing that ever happened to me. She showed up at the exact moment I needed her, even if I only met her when she was in first grade. So her death was rough."

I was quote-unquote lucky that a few days after Jazmín's death, I had scheduled time off of work. Because I didn't know how I would have handled it if I had to go to work and also hide from my family at the same time. Even though my father knew I had been to the hospital to see her, he never made me aware of the extent of the information he had. Maybe he knew less about my relationship with Jazmín and

Florencia than what I thought he did, but that didn't matter.

"I pretended I had no idea of her existence in front of my parents for years, until she was hospitalized."

She sucked in a breath, her eyes closing and her forehead resting on mine. She was breathing calmly, one of her hands holding on to my arm steadily, like an anchor. "Oh my god," Lucía whispered. "That sounds awful."

I nodded. "But by that time, it didn't matter anymore because I had separated a little from him and from his public persona. I was doing my own thing in family law, far away from politics. I think that is what pissed my father off the most," I said, lifting my hand and stroking her bare back up and down, up and down in a steady cadence. "That I didn't follow in his footsteps in politics."

"Mm-hmm," she mumbled, her forehead still on mine. Her free hand had moved to my hair, stroking my scalp with the tips of her nails and giving me goosebumps.

"So now, apparently," I added, not even stopping for a second, wanting everything out in the open once and for all, "someone leaked it to the press that he has a daughter out of wedlock and as a result of an affair, so Florencia is freaking out, and I'm guessing he is too. He might lose his biggest supporter."

"Oh shit," she said, and I didn't miss the small smile on her lips. I smiled in return, pressing my mouth against her in a chaste kiss. I loved that response because she knew exactly what that meant.

"Yeah." I ran my hands over her arms, from her shoulders to the tips of her fingers, linking mine with hers. "I'm driving back for a few days to see how I can help," I added, my eyes searching her for a reaction. She smiled and nodded, her face still splotchy from all the crying.

"When are you leaving?"

"Tomorrow?" It came out as a question, even though it was a fact. I had already called the head of PR at our firm to see what we could do, and they were all looking into it as a small favor to me. "Early tomorrow."

She sighed, then, with a big smile on her face, said, "I guess I'll have to water the plants, then."

26

LUCÍA

THE DIM SUNLIGHT filtered through the front windows in Santiago's house. The room was stuffy with the early morning heat and the fact that they had been closed for almost a full day since Francisco had left earlier that morning. I made my way to the back of the house, grabbing the watering can from the back patio and filling it up at the kitchen sink. It took me seven refills to finish all the plants, even watering the few succulents in Santiago and Victoria's bedroom that I hadn't done the time before.

I slid the back door closed and made sure to lock it and turned on my heel, walking briskly out of the house and in the direction of my parents'. I had been mid-laundry when the power went out, and I was hoping that it would come back soon so I could finish washing my bedsheets.

The sun was already starting to set, the birds starting to quiet for the evening. I turned into the driveway, and he was standing there, his arms loose against the sides of his body like a man without a single care in the world. The top button of his dress shirt was loose, and his hair looked disheveled, probably because he kept playing with a few strands like when he was concentrating on his work. I'd watched him the night before, perched over his laptop, scowling at the screen because he was supposed to be on vacation, but his sister's mother was more important.

"What are you doing here?" I stopped. The door to his car was still open, an alert beeping inside. He took a few steps closer to me, and I squirmed. He wasn't supposed to be here; he was supposed to be back in the city, fixing his thing. I was supposed to be doing my thing here too. Watering plants and vegging on the couch with the still-unnamed cat.

"I forgot to give you something," he said, frozen in place. He smiled softly, and that made me smile, the absurdity of it all. My entire body tingled in response. I watched him move like my life depended on it, his gaze lit with something hot. Sizzling.

"Okay," I drawled, tilting my head in confusion. "Is it another tongue depressor? Because I already told you those are disposable." I laughed at my comment, and he stalked towards me, his gaze fixed on mine.

He shrugged. "Yeah, actually." He took a few steps towards the sidewalk where I was and grabbed something out of his pocket, producing a still-wrapped wooden stick he probably bought at the pharmacy. Not at all like the one he had taken from my house that first night.

The feeling of seeing him again was overwhelming me. The air was thick with humidity, and I could feel beads of sweat forming on the back of my neck, getting warmer and warmer as he approached. He had to be stifling hot under that shirt of his. And why was he wearing dress pants if he was going to drive ten hours to get back home? It was ridiculous.

But intoxicating. The heat, the smell, Francisco, everything.

I closed my eyes and inhaled deeply, allowing the scent of the summer flowers to fill my lungs. When I opened them, he was standing there, looking at me with a heated gaze, his lips centimeters from mine.

I looked up, my heart racing as he leaned in closer. His hand cupped my cheek, his thumb brushing over my bottom lip. I closed my eyes again, my breath catching in my throat as he leaned in and pressed his lips to mine.

Time stood still, and we were the only two people in the world. The outside world faded away as we lost ourselves in each other, and nothing else mattered. The only thing I could hear was my heart beating against my chest. Francisco's hand came up to tangle in my hair as he pulled me closer, and I wrapped my arms around his neck, pulling him even closer to me.

Every cell of my body was lighting up, and I couldn't get enough of him. His lips were soft and warm against mine.

Our bodies were pressed together, and I could feel the heat between us growing with each passing moment. This was different, more intentional. Our first real, intimate kiss since the conversation we'd had.

"Hi," he said as he smiled into my mouth. "I missed you."

I laughed out loud, looking straight into him. "I just saw you last night!"

He shrugged, not a single fuck given. "So?"

I beamed. "Is that what you forgot to give me?" I pointed at the tongue depressor still in his hand.

Francisco laughed in response, hooking his arm around my shoulders and bringing me into his side. He kissed the top of my head and pulled me towards the house. The cat was lounging on the stoop, and she lifted one brow as soon as she heard our steps getting closer.

I skipped ahead hurriedly, unlocking the door and dragging him into the house by his hand. The cat scurried inside, and I jumped at the sound of the door closing behind him.

I turned abruptly, hitting his hard chest. His hands immediately went to my waist, holding me close to his body while keeping me upright. "What are you doing here, really?" I asked, searching his face for answers. He was not supposed to be here. Family came first, always. I couldn't catch my breath, his body pressed against mine, pushing me hard into the front door.

"Doesn't matter," he said, his mouth going to my neck and moving up and down, delivering small kisses all over, frantic. His hands were everywhere—one moment by my head, the next tugging at my dress, the straps sliding down my shoulders.

"Slow down," I tried to say in between breaths, but the man was not having it at all, pulling my hair out of its knot and tugging at the length, tilting my head back. He looked feral, his eyes dark with want. My stomach bottomed out, my hands going to his hair and sinking into his scalp. He growled in response, the indecent sound going straight to my center. "Oh my god, okay," I rasped, my toes curling in my shoes.

One of Francisco's hands was on my thigh, the hem of my dress bunched up at my waist. "What?" he retorted, mouth still on my skin, dragging down, down, down.

"Nothing. I just—nothing." *Jesus.* "Keep going." Desire thundered through my whole body, making me light up just like the night sky lit up with those wonderful summer storms. But this time, instead, it was Francisco's doing. A long time coming, if anyone asked.

He crouched, setting both his hands under the curve of my ass and lifting me to his body, my legs wrapping around his waist automatically. Practiced, like this had happened for years before this moment. I smiled into his mouth at the same moment thunder rattled the house, the windows shaking with the intensity of the phenomenon. The cat meowed and scurried past and then tucked her lithe body into the small nook under the stairs.

"Where?" There was an edge to his voice, a sense of urgency I'd never heard from him before.

"Bedroom." I lifted my head and found his eyes crinkled up in a smile so wide, my heart stuttered for a few beats. He turned us, his grip tightening on my body, my legs squeezing harder around him in response. His steps were light up the stairs. Seventeen. That was how many there were. And within a few seconds, we were at my bedroom door. Francisco kicked it open in a messy, fevered move.

"Where are the sheets?" he asked, his mouth still on me, burning my skin from the inside out. I wasn't sure how he'd noticed it since his attention was rapt on me.

"Oh fuck." I laughed at the absurdity of this.

"Why is this so cursed?" he groaned, resting his forehead on my collarbone. He was still holding me tight, his fingers sneaking below my underwear, caressing my ass with soft movements. I barked a laugh, kissing his temple for a moment and tapping him on the shoulder.

He turned us again, scanning the room and shifting the weight from one foot to another. He took a few steps forward and out the door, and then he kicked open the one across from mine, straight to Jacinto's bedroom.

"This will do," he said, giving zero fucks about the fact that he was about to fuck me on my brother's bed.

"Yeah," I drawled, my eyes wide with amusement. He dropped me on the covers and started unbuttoning his dress shirt, toeing off his shoes while looking at me panting in front of him, my weight on my elbows. He was delicious.

"Strip."

I blushed. A woman in her thirties blushing at this. I was pathetic. But so, so turned on.

I sat up, kneeling and sliding my dress down, the straps falling easily down my arms and getting stuck at my bent elbows. Francisco sucked in a breath and took a step closer to me, his hand reaching for my bare shoulder. His face was glowing. "Oh god." I shuddered, making quick work of my dress.

"Jesus fuck," he said, slowly moving his hands down my legs and grabbing my ankles from under me, dragging me towards the edge. He was almost naked except for his boxers. I extended my hand and placed it at his waist, my thumb sliding under the elastic for a beat. A deep breath rattled out of him, his chest rising and falling in fast, erratic movements.

I let my feet touch the floor and opened my legs, pulling him towards me with my hand. He leaned down between my open legs and pressed his mouth against my collarbone, making a needy sound, almost like a whimper escaping from his lips before he could hold it back. He started moving down. My nipples were tight and demanding attention. I squirmed under his hot breath, then said, "Fran, *please*."

He made another sound, more like a grunt meeting a moan, and that went straight to my core. "Light," he said. Monosyllabic. That was what I was doing to him. Turning him into a blubbering, monosyllabic mess. "I can't see you."

"Okay," I whispered, leaning on my elbows on the bed.

He walked to the window and lifted the roller blind just a few centimeters, the last light of the evening shining in a diagonal line on the hardwood floor. His eyes snapped to mine, lighting me up. I stared at his body, his lean muscles from all the running on full display. I had seen him shirtless many times by now, but this was so much better. Because this was all for me. Only for me.

He pulled his underwear down, his thick length bouncing up against his toned stomach. I closed my eyes and prayed, begged, for something. Anything. Patience? Peace?

I shifted on the covers, goosebumps running up my legs as his hands went up to my underwear. He tugged down hard and dropped the pair on the floor next to him.

"I think I'm about to die," he said, his face serious as he contemplated me lying on the bed, body splayed and completely bare in front of him. He fisted his shaft once, twice, and closed his eyes. He looked so good, standing naked there. Completely mine.

Finally.

27

FRANCISCO

My heart was going to leave my body, I had no doubt about that. *Any minute now.*

"*Dios mío,*" Lucía said again, covering her eyes with her forearm. She was lying on the covers, her hair fanned out around her. Her whole body was flushed, her breathing rapid and erratic. "*Fran.*"

Just a tiny whisper in between her panting, barely audible above the beating of my own heart. I bent over her, dragging the tip of my cock through her opening. She shuddered and flushed even more, her chest getting all sorts of splotchy and cute. "Fuck," I rasped. It felt so good. She felt so good. Everything felt so good when I was with her.

"*Decime,*" I said, closing my eyes because I couldn't hold off for much longer. I was so hard, my whole body aching for her. "Please, tell me."

"Tell you what?" She moved her arm from her face,

lifting one eyebrow in question. Then it clicked, and her face transformed. "Yes, god, yes. *Please.*"

That was all I needed, so I thrust forward into her, the sudden warmth making me shiver in arousal. My spine tingled, but I held on, thrusting in and out for a few beats before moving again.

"Condom?"

"Motherfuck," she said, a big smile on her face. "Maybe this is, in fact, cursed." She laughed. Laughed! At the whole absurdity of it all. Maybe this was Jazmín's doing, shooting me daggers from beyond the grave because she never got to see us together when she was alive.

I sighed against her shoulder, one of my hands moving up and down her side, the other one holding her hip tightly. It would leave a mark for sure.

"I'm covered," she said with a small giggle, her eyes shining with glee. She looked so relaxed, so happy, like I'd never seen her before. This was completely new, and it felt so, so right. "I'm fine with it if you are too."

"Yeah, *linda*," I rasped, thrusting back into her hard.

"Baby," she gasped, her back arching off the bed and her eyes closing at the feeling. "God, you feel so good."

I groaned and dropped my mouth to her neck, kissing down the long column and towards her soft shoulder. I stopped at her collarbone, resting there for a minute before moving again. She was panting, her lashes lowered and her lips slightly parted, all swollen and red from all the kissing.

"Move a little," she said, one leg wrapping around my

ass and pulling me into her, deeper and deeper until I was fully seated. "Please, move," she whimpered.

I slammed back in hard and fast, filling her completely. Her pussy fluttered, slightly squeezing my cock in response. She cried out, chanting my name and enjoying this with me.

"You feel so good."

Her eyes drifted shut in ecstasy, her chin tipping back and mouth parting in a small O. She released a long, charged breath, the feeling spreading across her features. Her legs went limp around my body, but her hands reached into my hair and tugged, then scratched my scalp. The move sent shivers down my spine. And I couldn't hold it in.

I collapsed next to her, trying to catch my breath while staring at her perfect profile. She looked drowsy, a sleepy smile on her face. I kissed her cheek, then dragged her into my body in the tightest hold I could manage.

And then we both fell asleep.

———

When I woke up, the room was dark and quiet, but the panic never set in. I heard faint mumbling coming from downstairs, probably Lucía talking to the cat about something or other. Her steps faded, followed by the opening and closing of a sliding door.

I found my clothes lying on the floor, the slacks completely scrunched up by the window. Once I was dressed, I went down the stairs, leaving my shirt untucked because I wanted to see her more than I wanted to be dressed at all. Maybe I could convince her to go back up to bed with me.

"What are you doing?" I asked. She startled at my words and stumbled from the counter, landing on her feet right in front of the cabinet she was trying to reach. Her delicate hands went up to her neck, probably as a reaction to hearing me behind her.

"Jesus," she said. "What are you doing here?"

I smiled and waited for her to turn her body to face me. "You left," I replied, using the same accusatory words I'd spouted just a day earlier when we finally discussed the inevitable. Her eyes shone with something, but it was gone a moment later, just a flash of lightning in her dark blue irises and a small blush rising up her cheeks.

She was wearing the dark blue sundress she had on earlier that left her back completely exposed, and her feet were bare, her toenails painted a barely-there pink. Her hair was up in a messy thing on the top of her head that bounced every time she moved even a centimeter. I grabbed her by the waist and moved her to the side, then stretched up to the tall shelf she was attempting to reach.

"Is this what you needed?" I asked, cocking my head to the side. "What is it for?"

She smiled and took the vase from my hand, then set it on the kitchen island and immediately put a candle inside. "I thought we could go sit outside for a bit, since it's a little cooler." She shrugged like that was just a casual idea, her bun following her movements. "It's really hot inside today. Not sure why." She lit the candle, then turned towards the back of the house, walking in small steps like she'd done dozens of times already, waiting for me to catch up and follow. She saw me coming this time, and she was prepared.

We sat in silence on the small loveseat by the back door, the wind moving the branches and the crickets chirping in the pitch black of the powerless night. The light of the candle flickered weakly between us, and it reminded me so much of those nights in the past, where the only light that would shine on us came from the hallway and through a small window on the hospital room's door. It was harsher than this candlelight, making her look washed out and tired. Tonight, she looked warmer, happier, healthier than back then.

I'd gone back one night to find her, probably three weeks after Jazmín died, fueled by anger or desperation or a need for closure. I couldn't put my finger on it, but I had been desperate for answers, and I didn't know where to find them. It was dark, darker than I would have preferred, because she was only working nights, and I needed to catch her during one of her breaks. I waited in my car in the parking lot long after everyone was gone, visiting hours well over by then.

I couldn't drum up the courage to go upstairs and talk to her, so I just waited. I'd practiced a speech; I just wanted to know what had happened.

Lucía wasn't there and my sister died, or maybe my sister died and Lucía wasn't there.

And someone had to explain that to me like I was a five-year-old boy trying to understand death for the first time in his sad, pathetic life.

After three hours of scrolling on my phone to keep me distracted, I saw her come out the automatic doors, her steps hurried and her mouth pinched in what looked like pain. Her stethoscope was draped around her neck, one side longer than the other, and she looked... disheveled. Disheveled was the word, yes. Like she'd rushed through everything and was just trying to be done with it all.

I empathized. I hadn't shaved in weeks. My hair was longer than I'd ever had it, and I was then on my last clean T-shirt, all my dirty laundry piled up in the corner of my bedroom.

I followed her movements from the inside of my car, only a few meters away from the entrance to the emergency room. Her arm grazed the side of the building, and she bumped her shoulder, the move making her stop in her tracks and close her eyes. It all happened in slow motion.

One second, she was walking along the perimeter of the building, and the next she was bent over and wailing, her screams of pain discernible even from where I was, all windows shut and doors closed. She couldn't catch her breath, and my own caught in my throat. And the need to run to her, to find her in the dark, was overwhelming. Because Jazmín had died, and she hadn't been there. Not because she was her doctor, but because I needed her with me.

Tears immediately flooded my eyes. My nose started running, and then I lost sight of her. I couldn't figure out which direction she'd gone in, either back inside or deeper into the shadows. All the questions I had about my sister's death vanished in a second, and instead they were replaced with feeling so painful, the only thing I could do was leave that place—and Lucía—behind.

The sudden nudge to my knee shook me from my memories. It felt like time had passed so quickly, but it had been years since the last time I saw her. And now she was sitting here, her lithe body stuck to mine, my mind escaping to thoughts of her consistently. I had avoided doing that like the plague since my sister died, but now the proximity made it impossible. A second chance.

"*¿Qué estás pensando?*" she asked, facing forward, one of her hands playing mindlessly with a lock of hair on the back of her head and her eyes closed. Her skin was flushed, no doubt from the heat of the day, a sheen of sweat covering the nape of her neck.

"Nothing," I whispered back. But I wanted to scream at her. Because she'd been missing from my life for years, and I never knew she was what I needed. And now I was here and she was maybe mine, and we fit so perfectly and I had to leave her again.

She moved to lean her body to the side of the loveseat, her waist barely touching the arm of the seat. She looked so delicate, her eyes still closed, enjoying the breeze that was enveloping us in the large yard.

"Did you know that if you look close enough, you can see Lighthouse Point from here?" She turned to look at me, then back to the mountainside, squinting her eyes so much they were barely visible. She lifted a finger and pointed to a peak, a bright star just touching it, exactly like a lighthouse on the shore.

"Huh," I said, looking at her with a big smile on my face. "That's so…" And at that moment, it clicked. This whole metaphor of my time in Tres Fuegos. I was here with her, my lighthouse, after so many moments of darkness. *Her.*

And now it didn't seem so heavy, weathering this darkness. I moved the candle closer to us so I could see her better, the day getting darker by the second. It was the exact moment when you needed light, but sometimes, light was not enough to show you what you had to see. What you had in front of you. The light flickered, and I flinched, almost like an automatic response to the potential darkness. Lucía froze next to me, waiting for more, for a reaction.

"Oh my god," she gasped, her eyes wide open. "You're afraid of the dark." Her features softened.

"No, I'm not," I said childishly, trying to laugh it off. I had no idea how she got to that conclusion from just this interaction.

"Yes, you are!"

I smiled, trying to alleviate some of the concern I saw on her face. It was the first time I would say this out loud to anyone. "It's not that I'm afraid of the dark, it's just…" I shrugged, like this really wasn't a big deal to me. "Creepy." I ran my fingers through my hair, the sound of the action making me shiver. "I don't know the town and its noises, so it's—whatever."

"It's okay, baby," Lucía whispered. She moved closer and reached out her hand to me, linking our fingers together. "The creepiest thing in this town is probably Jacinto," she said with a laugh. *Baby.*

I pulled her towards me, my heart racing at the ease in which she came towards my body, like I was lifting a bag of feathers.

My eyes found her lips, and she licked them, no doubt an involuntary response to everything, anything going on with us. I leaned forward, giving her a small peck and pulling her towards me, her soft body flush with mine and our hearts beating to the same drum.

I love her.

28

LUCÍA

It was a weird thing, going from being practically strangers to being this.

Whatever *this* meant.

Domestic was the word.

We went from an awkward hello a few weeks ago to unloading groceries and putting things away in my parents' kitchen. To circling each other in the space like we'd done this thousands of times, over and over again for years.

But instead, we were two strangers who were joined by one obscure thing that happened to both of them, drifting apart with time and no excuse to talk to each other. To see each other outside of that one setting that pulled us together.

"Where does this go?" he asked, his head cocked to the side in question. "Why did you even buy this flavor of ice cream?" Francisco scrunched his nose, and the only thing running through my mind was how adorable and kissable that face was. But I didn't want to push my luck; it all still felt like a dream. Like I was about to wake up from a heat-induced nap that lasted for weeks. A dream in which I suddenly found myself doing all the things I had wanted for a while. With the one I wanted for a longer while.

"What?" I turned to face away from him and smiled at the image of him standing there looking like an innocent boy, his hair tousled and all his clothes wrinkled from his failed drive back to the city. "I like it."

He laughed, bending at the waist and setting the container on the counter, his chest vibrating with amusement.

"*Linda.*" Pretty. Gosh, this man. I would let him do anything to me. "Only old people buy this flavor." His smile reached his eyes, crinkling them at the corner. It was the first time I'd seen this smile since back then. At the pralines and cream ice cream that was definitely melting.

I smiled and turned towards the sink, huffing at his comment. "I do live with my parents, you know."

He chuckled in response, then walked over to me by the sink, his arm grazing my shoulder delicately, making me shiver. It was accidental, maybe, but I liked it a lot.

I couldn't catch my breath every time he was around me.

"What do you want for dinner?" I asked, my back still turned to him, setting the tomatoes on the counter. My parents had a weekly grocery delivery—a mix of refrigerated and shelf items to withstand the power failures—from the different businesses around town, which came in particularly handy during these times because I didn't have to drag myself out in the heat and figure out what to get. This way, it was almost like the meals were planned for me. Excessive? Maybe, and sometimes it made me feel like a child, but today, it was perfect.

Because I could spend more time with him. Before he went back to the city—for real this time.

"You."

I blushed. Immediately. "Oh my god," I gasped. He was standing behind me, his hands caging me in against the countertop. He dragged his nose up the back of my neck and took a deep breath, the sound of it giving me goosebumps. "Fran."

"Uh-uh," he said, his lips on my neck, small, intimate pecks. "*Baby.*"

I turned to face him, his hard body leaning against me. My hands went to the back of his neck, tugging him towards me. "You like that?"

He shuddered, then kissed me. It was a different kiss. Slower, deeper. With no angst or regret or rush. Like he was here with me, forever. Like he wanted to be here with me, forever. And like I was enough for him. Not just his sister's doctor. But *his.*

"It's way too hot," he said, taking a step back and grabbing the carton of ice cream. He went into the mudroom and put it inside the chest freezer, the only appliance that could handle the consistent blackouts. It wouldn't last past the evening, but at least we had a little treat for later. Maybe we could sit outside and share it on the patio.

"So," he said once he was back from the pantry, having grabbed a few other things and tucked them away without asking any questions. "I think I'll go tomorrow, if that's okay with you?"

I cocked my head. "Why wouldn't it be?"

He smiled, one of those sly ones that reached his eyes but crept up on him. Slow, slow, slow. Then he took a huge step towards me and wrapped his arms around my body, tugging me up into him and nuzzling into my hair, not a single care in the world. "I don't want you to be alone, *linda*."

Swoon. Was this what I was missing? This man sweet-talking in my ear all these years? If things had been different, maybe. "That was the plan all along," I responded nonchalantly. "Are you coming back at all?" My heart caught in my throat, dreading one of the potential answers. I would be devastated. But we were nothing, just two people who enjoyed each other's company.

"Fuck yes," he blurted, walking me backward towards the couch. The cat meowed from somewhere around our feet, scurrying out of the way. He turned and plopped us, pressing my body on top of his. He looked into my eyes and smiled, then kissed my nose and sighed.

"What's that about?"

"Nothing," he said, closing his eyelids. I let it hang in the air between us, the nostalgia, maybe. The longing.

I wanted to ask him so desperately, to finally have all the answers I needed. Because right now, we were both in limbo, living in this bubble where everything was great. I took a deep breath, my heart breaking in a million pieces at even the thought of him disappearing again.

"You never came to find me," I whispered, my eyes tightly closed, avoiding his glance at all costs. My heart was beating wildly inside me. The sound of those six words snapped him out of his cloud, whatever he must have been thinking about, with that soft smile and those long lashes resting on his cheeks. Maybe it was longing. It sure was for me. He reared, trying to get his head deeper and deeper into the couch, an impossible feat given the way our bodies lay there, joined together in all the right places.

"Lucía." He sighed, defeat on his face. My nose tingled with sadness.

"Just tell me." I wanted to know. No, I *needed* to know. It was life-or-death at this point. Because I had already turned around and found a new path after Jazmín. I couldn't let it happen again, let it rip me apart at the seams completely. "Tell me why."

"We talked about it." He winced, his hold on me going limp, allowing me to sit up and crawl to the opposite corner of the couch, putting some distance between us. He looked at me, studying my movements. My heart picked up its pace, already out of control from the adrenaline of this. What was he trying to say? I couldn't read him—his face was stoic, almost like I was annoying him. Impatient. But we hadn't talked about it!

"No." I shook my head, tears now falling down my cheeks at the embarrassment. Embarrassment of not being enough for him or for my career. Having to be here in this town, being coddled like a child and almost harassed by my patients.

"Why are you even saying no?" he whispered, reaching for my hand.

"I don't know!" I pulled my arm away from him and stood abruptly. His mouth opened and closed a few times, like he wanted to say something, but it wasn't coming out. Or he was holding back.

"*Decilo*," he said. Say it.

"You left me," I said, words pointed directly at his heart. "And you didn't come back for me after she died."

"I did." His eyes were shiny with tears, his breathing level. He ran one hand through his hair and squeezed at the nape of his neck. "I sat in my car for three hours, building up the courage to come find you, even to see you for a second. I had so many questions, and I wanted answers. And then you strolled out of those hospital doors and started wailing outside that fucking death trap of a building, and I lost it. I couldn't do it."

My eyes were wide with surprise. "What?" I gasped, my hand going to my mouth, trying to muffle a sob. "Why?"

"I—I'm..." he replied, the sentence dying on his tongue before coming out. There was pain on his face, all over his features, his body all stiff sitting on that couch in that huge house. "I couldn't do it. I don't know how to explain it."

"No," I whispered again, not able to stomach those words. "No, no, this can't be happening." Just moments ago, we were fooling around in this kitchen, laughing and kissing and being. Together. And now, the moment slipped away, leaving dread in its wake.

"Lucía," he said, his brow furrowed and his hands closed into fists on his lap. "It was an awful time for me. I just couldn't deal with it all, with my sister's death and what it meant for my family, and what it meant for us." He lifted a hand in the air and gestured around both of us, ping-ponging from my body to his.

"It was too much," he added, the last word dying on his lips.

My insecurities surfaced immediately at that sentence.

Too much, yet again. But not enough, once more. Not enough doctor to save her, not enough ambition to keep going, not enough woman to make him stay. Just like it had happened before, where my career was too demanding and too much, but at the same time I wasn't giving enough. I couldn't win.

"I've been moving aimlessly for years, thinking I wasn't enough." A sob wracked my throat, and I turned around, wiping furiously at my tears. I heard him moving behind me, one of the springs of the sofa screeching under his weight. There were steps, and then I felt his warm body behind me. A hand on my bicep. A squeeze. "I left my career after that. Quit."

"Lucía." He sounded resigned, but I didn't dare turn to look at him. I was a weak woman; I knew that. Desperate to help everyone and save everyone. But no one saved me, ever. Nobody ever considered *me*.

"Do you know what it felt like? Do you?" I was yelling, my voice hoarse with the volume.

He blinked. Frozen.

"Of course I know," he whispered, his voice barely audible above the storm outside.

"No. No." I wiped my tears once more and spun around. Lightning flashed somewhere outside, followed by a deep rumble of thunder that shook the whole house, rattling the windows in their frames. There was a loud bang of a door somewhere upstairs, probably the result of a breeze coming in through one of the open windows. I was too distracted by the sounds of the storm to notice Francisco had moved, his arms wrapping around me tightly. I could hear his breaths, and his body started shaking with mine, tears soaking my bare shoulder.

We stood there for what seemed like an eternity. Tangled in the dark of the night, with occasional flashes of light illuminating our shapes. The cat roamed, swirling in between our legs, rubbing her soft fur on both of us. It felt like stolen time. Like this should have happened years ago when Jazmín was still alive, then ended the moment she was discharged. A fleeting spark, just like the lightning during the storm. This was what was supposed to happen before the storm.

Not now, not during it.

"I think you need to leave," I said, my voice weak, a sob right on its heels. He recoiled, surprise in his eyes. I needed the space and to figure this out for myself. "Yeah, you need to leave."

I was resolved.

Finally.

29

I WAS STUNNED. Too stunned to move. She was standing in front of me, the flashes of light from the storm highlighting her sweet profile, tears streaming down her face.

"Lucía," I rasped, a knot forming in my throat immediately. I wasn't going to lose her again, but I needed to respect her wishes. "Please."

"Why didn't you fight for me?" she yelled, her voice echoing around the house, louder than the boom of thunder outside. "I get it, Francisco. I understand why. But three years? Three years, and you still never showed up?"

"What would you have wanted me to do, huh? Just show up at the hospital and say hi?" I asked, not expecting an answer. The first year had been so bad, I was barely above water. But then the waves of grief started slowing down and life had gotten a little bit easier to navigate, day after day.

"Yes," she whispered. "I would have talked to you in a heartbeat if I could."

Oh god.

"I can't do this anymore," she said in between sobs. It was heartbreaking.

I blinked, watching her come undone only a few steps away from me. Her hands were shaking so bad, she clenched her fists and crossed her arms, tucking them against her body.

"Please," I begged, feeling the sudden urge to get on my knees and fucking plead for this. Plead for her to have me. "I'm coming back, I swear."

A spine-shuddering sob escaped her throat. The sound was completely heartbreaking and made me weak at the knees. "Leave."

"Lucía."

Blink. Blink, blink.

Blink.

She spun on her heel and ran up the stairs, the cat following behind her footsteps. She slammed the door to her room, then another one. And suddenly, the world was deathly quiet.

I walked back to Santiago's house in the complete dark. Lightning flashed in the sky occasionally, giving it a purple glow. But it wasn't like the other times when I dreaded the walk, Lucía the light at the end of my black tunnel. Instead, I was walking away from my beacon, leaving her again. For a second time, even after life had given us a second chance. I stood at the edge of the driveway, the jasmine bushes taunting me with their smell and the softness of their flowers. And the deep, dark color of their leaves. That was the first thing I had noticed on the day of the wedding. How strong the smell was compared to what we were used to back in the city. It was almost like everything was enhanced in this town—the colors, the smells, the emotions. Even the cats had softer fur somehow.

My phone started buzzing in my pocket, ping after ping after ping in an interminable succession of annoyance.

> EUGENIO
>
> we have a problem
>
> answer the phone
>
> right now
>
> Francisco, goddamnit

I groaned and kept walking, the keys to my friend's house in my hand. My car was still parked haphazardly up the driveway, the urge to see her earlier much stronger than any attempt at obeying any sort of traffic laws.

> FLORENCIA
>
> are you on your way?

. . .

"*¿Qué querés?*" I asked into the phone, clenching my jaw because this was now getting out of control. I had been able to speak to the head of PR at my firm, and they were looking into what was happening, trying to figure out where the leak was coming from and exactly what had been leaked.

"Oh, sorry," Florencia squeaked from the other end of the line. My tone startled her, for sure. But her call caught me off guard, and I hadn't checked who it was before answering.

I rubbed my forehead. "*Perdón.*" Fuck. This was going to do me in. "What's wrong?"

"Someone from your office called me yesterday," she said, her voice much calmer than it had been a few days ago. I had told her I was going to figure something out, and I would. It still wasn't clear why this was happening now, especially since my sister had been dead for years. "They are coming here tomorrow. Do you think you can join me?"

"Yeah," I said. "I'll be there."

"Thank you." She sighed. "You have no idea how relieved I am."

"That's what family is for," I blurted.

"Francisco," she said. I could picture her face, sad eyes, and a heavy expression. We were not family, not anymore.

"I'll see you tomorrow."

I walked into the house and stood in the middle of the living room. The window was open, and the blinds were slightly up, so I walked over to close them, a slight breeze coming through.

"You are not supposed to be here," my father had said that night. His voice was all raspy and terse, the edges wrapped in tension. I was visiting Jazmín at the hospital, and I had brought a small bouquet of jasmines for her. So she could have something to keep her happy. It had been the only time he ever caught me in person and was a definite turning point in our relationship. Because it was obvious that I was blatantly defying his orders. "*¿Cuántas veces te lo tengo que decir?*"

How many times do I have to tell you?

"Eugenio," I said. I had been instructed at an early age that I should call him by his name in public. Never *papá* like a normal child. "What are you doing here?"

I wanted to scream at him, warn him that he was going to get caught. But I wouldn't do it because that would give him a leg up, and he was getting sloppy. We were standing outside her hospital room, the lights dim and the faint sounds of machines far away, tucked tightly behind closed doors.

"*Cuidado*," he warned, his gaze scanning our surroundings. I was clutching the flowers like my life depended on it, the tight hold making my knuckles white and the cellophane wrapper crinkle with the tension. From the corner of my eye, I had seen Sonia leaving one of the patient rooms and heading towards the large nurses' station in the center of the pediatrics wing. The first time I visited, she had eyed me defiantly, definitely doing her job. Neither of us knew if we could trust the other, and that had been okay. And slowly, just like everything Jazmín did, she captivated them with her charm—a trait she inherited from our father—and they let me in, welcoming me as if I were actually a part of their tiny, fragile family.

Sonia raised an eyebrow at the scene, turning her body slightly so she was facing us, one of her hands on the hand-held phone they carried around with them, sometimes in their scrubs, sometimes in their palms. I shook my head slightly, letting her know everything was okay.

"You brought her flowers?" he sneered, his yellow teeth bared at me, like the action disgusted him. "Such a cliché, jasmine."

I took a deep breath, trying to calm my nerves. It had always been explosive in our house, the fights getting out of control many, many times. But I tried so hard to keep my temper even for the sake of my sister and for my own sake. And I owed him no explanations. He was just my father; that was it.

"Well." I walked past him, bumping my shoulder against his, eliciting a snarl from him. His tie was draped on his forearm, and the movement made it slide down to the floor. "Fuck off, will you?"

I looked at him for a second, his face red with agitation. "Look what you did!" he boomed. In a hospital, with sick children around. Because his tie fell on the floor.

It was at that exact moment that Lucía opened the door

to the room, eyeing us with a warning on her face, her jaw tight, like we pissed her off. She excused herself, then walked out, a team of other doctors trailing behind her towards the nurses' station a few meters away. I followed her with my eyes, and she looked back at me, a question right on the tip of her tongue. Sonia had caught up with her and said something in her ear, making her glance at me one more time.

I turned and went inside the room, smiling at my sister. She was scowling in the bed, a magazine on her lap and her gaze lost in the pages. I closed the door softly, but she didn't hear me come in, instead flipping the pages mindlessly as she bit her bottom lip.

"What's the latest gossip?" I asked, trying to inject cheer into the air. She was on her third round of chemo, the days long while the treatment ran through her blood on an endless drip. Florencia had called me earlier to tell me she wasn't able to visit her that day, so I had decided to stop by instead. We did that a lot, took turns visiting and spending time with her.

"I know he's out there," she said with a scowl and without looking up from the pages of the tabloids. "I can smell him from here."

I barked out a laugh, and the corner of her mouth ticked up just a smidge, her face finally tipping up and glancing at me. She sighed dramatically, closing her magazine abruptly and pulling off the covers.

"Jaz." I sighed. She slid her legs off the bed and arranged

her IV line, grabbing the tall rolling pole from behind the bed. She put on her slippers, then pulled at the thing, dragging it behind her and walking towards the door. "Not worth it."

"I am freaking tired of him coming in here and telling everyone what to do and never even showing me his face. I don't want him here. Now or ever. *Movete.*" She glared, her cheeks flushed from the exertion of getting out of bed in her state. Sometimes, chemo would amp her up, but she was now on day four of six, so the high was wearing off fast. "Francisco."

I moved to the side, setting the small arrangement of flowers on a low table by the window. It was the companion's table, right next to the reclining chair, where I'd slept many a night during these hospital visits. Uncomfortable but worth it to see her face, even for a few hours.

She threw open the door, the knob slamming against the wall behind it, leaving a small indentation on the material there.

"Eugenio!" she yelled out into the hallway, totally out of breath. She was holding on to the IV pole, her forearm wrapped around it and her petite body leaning on it. Dread covered my face. He would chew her up and spit her out, but she didn't care. "Where the fuck are you?"

He wasn't outside the room or at least anywhere visible from where we stood. Lucía was standing with another doctor by a desk on the other side of the hallway, across from the nurses' station. She turned to look at me, a question in her eyes. I lifted and dropped my shoulders because I legitimately did not know what was about to happen. Jazmín had a mind of her own—feisty. And I loved her so much because of that. I had never been able to stand up to him, not even then, already in my thirties.

"Just to make this very fucking crystal clear for everyone," she said, short of breath, cheeks flushed. "That man that calls himself my father is anything but. He's an abusive asshole that doesn't deserve a second of your attention."

Lucía's eyes found mine, wide and surprised. The corner of her lips ticked up, but she composed herself quickly, blinking away the amusement. There was absolute silence in the hospital wing. "If you need anything, you talk to my mother or my brother. Or else."

I beamed behind her, a cackle rising from my chest and leaving my mouth. Lucía snorted, turning her back to Jazmín so she wouldn't be caught. Sonia walked swiftly towards my sister and whispered soothing words in her ear, running her soft hand through her hair and pushing her towards the room. Within a minute, she was back in bed, her eyelids drifting shut.

The sound of a door shutting in the distance jolted me from my daze. I was still standing in Santiago's living room, the house completely dark.

30

LUCÍA

It had to be me, the problem. I couldn't make anyone stay. In and out of my life like I was one of those fucking tongue depressors. Disposable.

The view out the window was complete darkness. Power was out in every single corner of this town, not even the stars illuminating the sky.

"Shit!" I screamed into my pillow. The cat hopped on the bed, her small head nudging my ear, purring steadily there. Maybe she was telling me I was being too dramatic. Maybe she empathized. I hoped she knew how heartbreaking this was.

I tossed and turned all night in Jacinto's bed, the sheets still smelling faintly of Francisco. I was torturing myself, I knew that, but my bed was still unmade, the unwashed bedding long forgotten in the washing machine.

I tugged on the first set of scrubs I could find and tied

my hair up in a ponytail. I needed to get out of that house, where every corner reminded me of him. And being outside was torture because the smell only reminded me of her. Of what could have been.

The walk to the office dragged for longer than it should have, dawn making it hard for me to see where I was going. I avoided Santiago's house in case he was up and looking out the window like he'd been weeks ago, that day we went up to Lighthouse Point. But my curiosity got the better of me. The curtains were drawn, windows closed, and not a single light was on inside.

The keys for the front door to the office were loud against the quiet morning. The birds weren't even chirping yet, a sign that I was up before anyone else in this town. It was common that I would be the first one up, at least in that big house. But this morning, the contrast was jarring.

It was musty in the practice—I hadn't been in for weeks at this point, so I walked to the window to crack it open. I turned on the ceiling fan so that the air could circulate, the smell of summer leaving through the small opening.

I heard the snick of the latch behind me. Dr. Martín's head poked inside the office.

"*Querida*," he said. "Why are you here?" He looked so much older than the last time I'd seen him. His hair was combed back, the salt and pepper much more salt than pepper. He was wearing a pair of brown slacks and a light blue, short-sleeve shirt, the buttons closed at the top.

I smiled at him, at how much he reminded me of my

own grandparents. I sighed. "I couldn't sleep," I replied. He looked worried, his bushy eyebrows wrinkling. "It's been a wild few weeks."

"Ah," he said, walking in and locking the door behind him. He walked slowly but firmly, his energy put into each of his steps. Dr. Martín sat in one of the waiting room chairs, then patted the seat next to him, inviting me to take a seat. "Indulge me for a minute."

I scrunched my nose in question, uncertainty surely coloring my features. I hesitated for a moment, and he raised an eyebrow, so I sat across the way, giving us a little more space.

"Are you okay?" I asked.

He looked healthy. He looked great, in fact. Somewhat frail, but he had a hint of summer coloring in his cheeks, and his green eyes were shining with something. He nodded in response, linking his fingers and placing them on his lap. He stretched his legs out in front of him and crossed them at the ankles, the long limbs almost at my seat. "What is going on?"

I blinked, taken aback by the question. I knew he was observant, but he hadn't seen me in weeks at this point. And I'd been holed up at that big house with Francisco.

He eyed me cautiously, and I felt like a bomb exploded in my stomach. "You can tell me. I won't judge."

A sob got caught in my throat. Heartrending.

The exact words I needed. Three years too late, probably.

"A patient died a few years ago, and I can't get o—"

"I have one of those," he interrupted so nonchalantly that I couldn't believe my ears. "Early in my career, I made a mistake, and he died."

I gulped. We'd never talked about this. He was always so calm with patients, always so level-headed and exhaustive, even when there was reason for concern, for urgency. We didn't get many of those but maybe once a year. They would have to be driven to the closest hospital an hour away. But then they would be treated there, and it would have nothing to do with us. Handing them over. Exactly like I planned after Jazmín's death.

"It was rough, yeah," he said after a long silence.

"Only one?"

"It takes only one, Lucía, to realize you can't save them all." Tears were falling down my cheeks. I wanted to save them all, damn it. "But we do our damn best, and we try, don't we?"

"Uh-huh."

A fractured mosaic of feelings. Going from heartbroken to happy to sad to joyful in the span of a moment. Of a single life touched by our profession.

"Why didn't you tell me?" he asked. He moved his linked hands to the back of his head, elbows out, looking so relaxed, like this was a normal conversation. The skin of his hands looked so soft, like my grandmother's, wrinkled with age but softened as the years passed.

"I'm embarrassed," I admitted. "No one in the hospital reacted that way, and I feel like a failure."

Three or so weeks after Jazmín had died, I had walked into the attending's office and told him I was quitting. That I would be done with my residency, and I would, under no circumstances, be seeking out the fellowship spot for pediatric oncology. I couldn't do it. It just wasn't for me.

"Sit down," he had said, walking over to the door to close it. It was the middle of our twelve-hour shift, and we were slammed. But he still took the time to speak to me, measuring his words. "You are a talented, empathetic doctor, Lucía." He spoke quietly, a sad smile on his face. "Don't let this one patient take that away from you. We need more doctors like you here."

I shook my head at him, a lone tear falling down my cheek. My stethoscope was on my lap, and I wrapped the tubing around my finger in one direction, then the other one. Over and over again. He cleared his throat, then said, "Please don't make a rash decision about this."

I nodded then and stood up, draping my stethoscope around my neck. I left the office and walked swiftly towards the stairs, running down the steps towards the emergency department and out the ambulance bay. I couldn't walk fast enough, the panic rising in my chest until I couldn't hold it in any longer. A wail sounded among the shadows of the building that had given me so much but had taken so much too.

"Grief is a unique thing," Dr. Martín said, pulling me back from the memories of that time, drowned by the loneliness and the singularity of my situation. "There is no timeline for it."

And I agreed that grief was a weird thing. Because I could be completely fine for weeks and then, *bam*, it hit like a truck with no brakes.

He cocked his head, the silence burning between us. "It's okay, honey," he said. And at those words, I was gasping for air, looking for a way out of the depths of this horrible puddle, where the more I fought to get out, the deeper I sank. I bent at my waist, placing my forehead on my knees and crying loudly into my scrubs. So reminiscent of the night I gave everything up.

I felt his warm hand on my back, small, soothing motions on my skin.

"And that boy?" *Oh fuck*. That hurt. "He is good for you."

"He's her brother," I said in between sobs, my breath catching after each word.

"Oh, honey." I heard the pity in his voice first, and then Dr. Martín stood up. "I want to show you something." I followed him with my eyes, his slow steps heading towards what had once been his office. "Come over here," he said over his shoulder.

I stood up, wiping my tears with the back of my hands and grabbing a few tissues from Valentina's desk. He was opening and closing the file cabinet drawers, running the tip of his finger over the manila folders, the names of our patients scribbled on the tabs in his clunky handwriting. "Right here." He pulled out a file we hadn't gotten to yet. It was in the bottom drawer, tucked halfway into the stack.

He moved some things around the tabletop and laid the folder flat, sitting on my chair while he scanned the patient form. I turned towards him, looping around to where he was behind my desk. I looked at the paper. It was an old form, yellowed at the edges and created using a typewriter, the font recognizable even to me. At the top, the name of a patient I didn't recognize, and just below, scribbled by hand, the name of Dr. Martín's wife.

"What?" My eyes flooded with tears again at the realization. How did I never know? This had to be town lore by now.

"My son." His voice caught, and he licked his lips, his eyes going back and forth between my face and the form. "Appendicitis," he said. "I didn't catch it in time."

"How?" I asked. It was one of the first things we learned how to recognize in residency, and those diagnoses were the majority of the cases we saw in the hospital, especially during our surgery rotations. Cut and dry—symptoms were always textbook with pediatric patients.

"The symptoms didn't present until it ruptured." He blinked.

"Oh my god." My lower lip trembled. How did he even survive that?

"You learn to live with grief"—he stood up, smoothing

out his slacks and tucking his hands in his pockets—"instead of letting it consume you, honey."

He stared at me for a bit, then smiled, the wrinkles around his eyes on full display. "We can't save them all, but the ones we can make this profession so, so worth it."

31

LUCÍA

THE FIRST THING I did the next morning was call my parents to tell them that I was heading to the city to spend a few days with Valentina. Dr. Martín and his wife agreed to take care of the cat for a few days until I figured everything out, and then I would make arrangements to bring her to me, depending on what I was able to work out at the hospital.

I paced my room, waiting for it to be light out. I'd had a second night of restless sleep, but this night was because adrenaline was coursing through my veins. My phone was on the bed, the other end of the line ringing. It was early, yes, but Valentina would answer my call.

"Hey," she whispered, her voice filled with sleep, but there was a smile on her lips. I could tell from where I was standing. "Is everything okay?"

"Yeah," I said, suddenly shy about what I was about to say. "Any chance I can stay with you for a few days?" I blurted. I wasn't ready to tell her what I would be doing in the city, but I would no doubt fill her in as soon as I saw her later that day.

"Umm, not su—"

"Who is it?" a soft voice croaked in the background. I heard a hushed sound from the other end of the line, a groan. Some shuffling. And then the unmistakable sound of a door closing.

"Valentina." I dragged her name, my voice loud above my movements. I had tugged a suitcase from the attic, the sweltering heat making my hands sweaty and my movements clumsy. The luggage rolled down the stairs, the sound making the cat dart across the room directly under the bed. "What the fuck!"

"Oh my god," she said, her voice muffled, probably because she was covering her face with her hands. She was hardly embarrassed at anything—she let go of things with such ease. Nothing fazed her. "*Qué vergüenza.*"

"You do you, baby." I snickered, even though I was confused about it all. I thought there had been something going on between her and Charlie. "Who is it? Do I know him?"

"Just some guy," she whispered. "Alright, enough about this. When are you getting here?" She sighed on the other end of the line. "I'll make sure he's out of the house by the time you get here."

"Text me the address again. I'm leaving in an hour or so."

"Wait, I'm confused," she said, the door opening again. The hinges screamed at the action. I winced.

"I'll tell you later. I have to finish packing."

"Love you."

I moved back and forth from my bedroom to the downstairs for the next hour, tidying up the house and finding all my loose items. There was a different pair of scrubs in the laundry room, the set folded on the countertop and smelling nice and fresh. That was probably my mother's doing before she left, even when she knew I wouldn't need them for a while. The thought made me smile, and I suddenly felt relieved after coming to the decision that I did.

After the conversation with Dr. Martín, I had returned to the house, still heartbroken about what he'd shared with me but determined to understand what it meant for me. So I hatched a plan. I recruited Sonia, who was still the night nurse at the hospital, and had her do some sleuthing for me. Then I had called the head of the pediatrics service and asked him for a meeting. He was happy to hear from me but a little bit surprised since I'd cut out all communications with everyone I knew from the hospital.

I shoved my hand in between the cushions in the sofa, trying to find the remote to turn the TV off. It happened every time there was a blackout—the damn thing wouldn't stay off. I felt around the tight space and came up with three still-wrapped tongue depressors. I barked out a laugh. It was absolutely ridiculous. Had he taken these to have an excuse to see me?

I love him.

The realization hit me hard, and suddenly there was more impetus to my actions, propelling me forward to the next step.

———

A drive that would usually take eight to nine hours took me less than seven. Not because I was being reckless, but because everything was coming up Lucía. I hit all the green lights, all of the toll booths were free of cars, there were no trucks on the roads, and all the gas stations and rest stops were empty, allowing me to speed through anything that I needed to do to get to my future. It was like the universe was telling me to get out of Tres Fuegos, and then it delivered. Handed me that big city on a nice, shiny platter.

Valentina's family home was inside a big gated community in the suburbs a few miles outside the city, so different from our small town but somehow very similar. All the houses were large, sprawling buildings with manicured lawns. The security guard at the gate eyed me curiously, calling in my arrival and cross-checking it with a list on a document to confirm I was, in fact, welcome there.

I pulled up to the house. The large building was somewhat in disrepair on the outside, which didn't surprise me, since not a lot of people used this home on a regular basis. Her sister, Francisca, had an apartment in the city center, and her father was incarcerated. For over a decade now. Her family had been the first one to live in this neighborhood back when it was just a large piece of land, so they were practically royalty—the home sat on a double lot with a golf course behind it, right in the middle of the community.

I parked the car on the circular driveway and got out, the door immediately opening to my left. The house was beautiful, even in its current state, ivy growing on the sides and over the windows. The roof tiles were covered in moss, and it was evident that no one had lived here in years. And to top that, it was eerily quiet out on the street. There were no sounds of leaves being ruffled by the wind or birds chirping in the trees.

It immediately felt different than Tres Fuegos. Contrasting. Despite being in a small community that had its fair share of similarities with my hometown, it felt like part of a city. In the way any city was different from any small town, with its city things I craved the most, even if my town was home.

Valentina walked outside, my brother Charlie trailing behind her, concern in his eyes.

"What are you doing here?" I asked, tugging at the collar of my shirt. His face went somber at the comment. Valentina turned to look at him for a second, and then her eyes were on me.

"I called him," she said, almost nonchalantly. "Just to make sure he was aware you were coming here."

"How did you know he was here?" I cocked my head.

"I didn't," she squeaked. "Just a weird coincidence."

"I'll get your suitcase," Charlie said, avoiding my gaze and heading towards the back of the car. He unlocked the trunk and slid the piece of luggage out with ease. He looked good. Relaxed. A second later, he was right next to me, sliding his arm around my shoulder and kissing the top of my head. He didn't look like the uptight attorney that greeted people with formal words like "good evening" or scowled at passersby on his way to work.

We walked into the house and back towards the kitchen, where I set my things and sat at the small table by the window. I looked up, and both of them were staring at me, eyes intently on mine, waiting for answers.

I sighed. "I…" I looked around, trying to come up with a coherent order to my words. "I think I'm ready to move back."

Charlie cocked his head, and Valentina smiled, her face lighting up with excitement. My eyes watered a little, the tears threatening to fall. All because of her reaction.

"About damn time," she said, extending her hand over to Charlie. He grunted and took out his wallet, placing a large bill in her hand. She was giddy like I'd never seen her before.

"You bet on it?" I squeaked, my mouth falling open. "When?"

"Duh," she said, twirling a lock of hair around her finger. It'd been a few weeks since I'd last seen her do this, a few days before the wedding. It seemed like a lifetime ago. "I've been on to you for months now."

I stood abruptly, then lunged towards her and wrapped

my arms around her. Her chest was vibrating with laughter, the sound muffled against my shoulder. "Why didn't you say anything?"

She shook her head, and I pulled back. There was something else there. If I didn't know her as well as I did, I would say it was pity. But maybe it wasn't. Maybe it was true, genuine concern.

"Mom and Dad have also been on our case for months. Why do you think they've been so extra?" Charlie asked.

"They are always extra, Charlie."

"Yeah, but probably since July, they've been more worried."

"I thought it was just the wedding jitters." How had I been so oblivious to their concern? Was it so obvious that I was walking on eggshells around my family, trying to get away with my grief while helping out? I had always been a helper—I loved it. And it was partially the reason why I was a doctor. I wanted to help. It was my calling. "Oh my god."

"Did you talk to them?" Charlie asked, leaning against the island counter. Valentina was focused on me, probably trying to absorb every single moment of my reaction.

"Yeah, briefly. But I owe them an explanation."

He grunted.

"Okay," Valentina said. "What next?"

What next?

"An interview. Tomorrow."

32
LUCÍA

The hospital smelled and sounded the same as the last time I'd been here three years ago. The constant beeping of the machines was front and center, yet so far removed from me because I hadn't touched one in as long. The hustle and bustle of the pediatrics wing was so familiar to me. It was not the pace we had at the practice back in Tres Fuegos, which had once been a welcome breath of fresh air but had slowly turned musty.

I recognized a few faces, especially at the nurses' station, but a lot of the doctors were unfamiliar to me. New residents and new attendings, for sure. I wondered who the patients were, if I knew any of them still. Because Jazmín had been in and out of this hospital for years, it was a very likely possibility.

Sonia was standing in the middle of the nurses' station in her street clothes. She had been, ever since I started, at least, in charge of the night shift, so she looked out of place in plain daylight, out of her scrubs with her hair down and relaxed by her shoulders. She was talking to one of the nurses I didn't recognize, but she turned her face towards me and winked, a bright smile on her face.

"Dr. Williams," someone said from behind me. Dr. Varela was standing right outside a hospital room, wearing the pediatrics pink scrubs and his white coat over them. He looked older, deep lines across his forehead and hair thinning. Once upon a time, he had been a great teacher, and I was sure it was still the case for the incoming residents. "It's nice to see you again," he said with a big smile, walking a few steps towards me and wrapping one arm around my shoulders. His smile crinkled his eyes, his gaze studying my face closely.

"Hello, Doctor." I smiled back at him. My heart was beating inside my chest from the nerves, but I couldn't help feeling joy. Being back here, even just for a visit, gave me a rush of adrenaline.

"Pft, none of that." He draped his stethoscope around his neck and tucked his notepad in one of his coat pockets, a move that I'd most likely learned from him. He always took notes while seeing patients, making it easier to chart later, when the shift was quiet and the kids were asleep. "I'm not much older than you are," he said with a laugh.

He spun on his heel and walked the opposite way, and I rushed to catch up to him. His steps were light, his sneakers squeaking on the linoleum floors of the hallway, one of many shoes that announced a presence in the space. The attending's office was located in the far corner of the pediatrics wing, tucked away between two on-call rooms. It was shared among all the attendings, so there was always someone inside. As residents, we could also use the computers there if we needed to chart and if the ones by the nurses' stations were being used. It was familiar being here. The smell, over everything, was something that reminded me so much of those interminable nights, when we would spend so many hours together, talking through complicated cases or even catching each other up on our lives. I hadn't had that in years, and I missed it terribly.

"So," he said, taking a seat at one of the desks, swiveling his chair towards me. The office was rectangular in shape, and desks lined either side. I sat on a chair close to the door and crossed my legs, then uncrossed them. "What have you been up to?"

"Well." I pursed my lips, suddenly embarrassed. "After I finished pediatrics here, I moved back to my town and worked at the practice there. I've been head of that practice for over a year now."

He nodded, paying close attention to what I was saying, studying my face closely. His hands were linked on his lap, his legs crossed at the ankles and stretched in front of him, just like Dr. Martín had done a few days prior. "Mmmm," he mumbled, twirling his thumbs. I couldn't get a read on him —never could, not even back then, when I saw him almost daily.

"Lucía," he said, his voice level and calm, his gaze fixed on mine. "Things have changed around here." He cocked his head.

"Okay," I drawled, not quite grasping what he was trying to tell me.

"We have new policies in place." He sat up and crossed one ankle over a knee and draped one arm on the back of his chair. I swiveled in my seat, the rolling chair not helping my nerves. I was squirming under his gaze. "To avoid what happened to you from happening again."

My shoulders sagged. I had gotten too close to that family, and that had hurt my career. *Fuck.*

"Therapy is now mandatory for all our doctors," he said, counting off on his fingers. "We provide that resource for you." He flashed two fingers in front of me. "Staff are now expected to take two weeks off every three months." He looked at me with a steady gaze. "Does this make sense?"

"Dr. Varela," I said softly, a slight blush creeping up my cheeks. "I'm so sorry about how it all went do—"

He stopped me, raising his palm at me. "Lucía, it happens. More than you think it does." His voice sounded reassuring, but I couldn't read him at all. "You don't need to explain yourself, not to me."

I sagged again. I wasn't sure what he was telling me. If he was trying to give me a second chance or if he was absolutely turning me down. I came here with the intention of asking for a job, maybe the only spot this year or next at the pediatric oncology fellowship that started in the winter.

"You know that feeling of wanting something so much that every step you take towards it feels like two forward and one back?"

He nodded and smiled.

"This is how I've been living for three years," I said. My eyes flooded with tears, and I tried to blink them away, but instead one of them fell down my cheek, followed by another one. "It's all I've ever wanted for so long that it just didn't seem possible, and then things exploded with Jazmín here, and I couldn't take it." I took a deep breath, waiting patiently for his response.

"We all have that one patient that makes us doubt ourselves." He smiled. "Ask around. Every doctor and nurse here will tell you theirs."

I sobbed, covering my mouth with my hand, my chest shaking with the pain.

"I can offer you an attending role for the time being," he said, extending one of his hands and placing it on my shoulder, a reassuring pat, pat, pat. "When the time comes, if you want to go for the fellowship, I will support your candidacy. But you have to go to therapy." He pressed his lips together in determination. "That is a non-negotiable for anyone on my service."

That was it? All I had to do was have a few candid conversations about my experience, and that was that? It surely couldn't be as easy as that.

"Of course that's it," he said. My eyes widened because I had said that out loud, and he smiled. "This is a hard job,

Lucía, and you are a talented doctor. We were sad to see you go."

I let out a wet laugh, tears streaming down my face freely. "Oh my god, I'm so embarrassed." I wiped my tears away and looked around, taking in the office. My new office.

Nothing had changed, but so many things did, in fact, change.

"Nonsense," he said, standing and smoothing his scrubs down with his hands. He extended his palm to help me get up and then shook it. "When can you start?"

I left the office beaming because I was one step closer to those goals I had set for myself years ago, and one step closer to getting back to him.

Sonia was standing at the edge of the hallway, the hand-held phone up by her ear despite not being on call, but she was nodding and jotting down notes precariously against the wall. She saw me walking towards her and nodded a few times, speaking rapidly into the phone, then hanging up. She quirked a smile, not one of her big, friendly ones. But one that was reserved for Francisco on those evenings he snuck into the hospital, carrying something or other in his hand or backpack. *Contrabando*, she would call it, rolling her eyes but smiling wide, like she was one hundred percent in on it.

"Ready, girl?" she asked, cocking her hip to the side in the most playful way. I'd never seen her like this, but many things had changed since. "I just need my purse from the office."

33

FRANCISCO

"We can't figure it out," Lorena said, all tense and stressed. Her shirt was untucked on one side, the sleeves rolled up carelessly on her forearms. She headed the external comms department of our firm, which took on its fair share of celebrity cases—mostly high-profile divorces and custody battles—and she was a motherfucking beast at her job. A sleuth like no other. But neither her team nor any of her contacts had come up with the source.

Somehow, one particularly ruthless reporter had gotten wind that my father had a second child out of wedlock. It was still whispers, but it was going to go wide soon. We were just waiting at this point. For the cameras to arrive. For the calls to start.

But it was squeaky clean. Looked like a professional job. Like a master plan designed to hurt. And the source was nowhere to be found.

We were on hour eleven of this meeting, the sky already dark outside despite the long summer night. It was quiet here, the middle-class neighborhood where Florencia had lived all these years since Jazmín was born.

"It's impossible," I argued back, my shoulders sagging in resignation. "There has to be a paper tr—" I froze. "Unless it's him."

Florencia gasped, and Lorena snapped her fingers, pointing at me. "That's an idea," she said, sitting back down at her computer and typing furiously, her eyes moving across the screen rapidly with every hit of her keyboard.

"I don't know," Florencia said quietly. She was curled up on the couch, looking out the window. "Why would he?"

My father had lost his seat in the house a few months earlier to a more libertarian candidate, but he was still hell-bent on running for the presidency eventually. I didn't know many details, but I had heard that he was keeping his ears to the ground and hoping that the incoming government would select him for a cabinet role. Despite his loss in the governor race, maybe his political party would still take him in. This would, allegedly, position him favorably with the press, and then he would eventually run for president. It was a long game. A game he was an expert at playing. So I saw Florencia's point.

"Because this is career-ending for him," she said absent-mindedly. She picked up her glass of water, her eyes still looking out the window.

She was smart, and she would have done great in politics, but then my father happened, and he wreaked havoc on her life.

There was a loud boom from outside the house, followed by the distinct slamming of three car doors. "*¿Qué te escondes, cagón?*" Coward. He was calling me a coward.

Florencia's gaze snapped to me, and she scurried away from the window towards the back of the house so that she wasn't visible from the outside. It was Eugenio's unmistakable voice, yelling from the street, right outside the living room window. I could hear someone else talking to him, asking him to calm down.

"*¿Vas a salir, o no?*" Are you coming outside? he asked, fury in his voice.

Florencia looked at me, then looked to the front door, waiting for the knock. Lorena was focused on her research on the computer, barely acknowledging what was happening outside. A few minutes later, there was a flurry of activity, and a bright light shone into the house.

"What the fuck?" I asked, walking to the window to understand what was going on. The press was standing outside, lights and cameras blaring. "Shit," I said under my breath, but Florencia had noticed. She stood still, not moving a single muscle, her eyes blinking rapidly with incredulity.

"He's not the leak," she said. And I nodded. His ego wouldn't let him throw away his career like that, and if he were, he wouldn't be out for blood. Did he assume it had been me?

"I'm going outside."

"Francisco." Lorena perked up, straightening her back and squaring her shoulders. "I advise against that. We need to prepare a statement."

"Okay," I said to her, looking straight at her. "You do that, and I will see what he wants."

She cocked her head in defeat but smiled nonetheless, her eyes shining still. Maybe an idea popped into her brain. I opened the door, and he was standing there, swaying a little in his spot. His eyes were glazed over, and his breathing was irregular, like the screaming match he had against the house took it out of him completely. He startled as soon as he saw me and leaned into my body, his breath reeking of alcohol.

"Why are you doing this to me?" he slurred. He was blinking in slow motion, almost like he was trying exceptionally hard to focus on me. I opened my mouth and then shut it again, thinking about my next words.

Play coy. "What are you talking about?" I cocked my head for maximum impact, but there was a prickle of wariness raising the hairs on the back of my neck. The sound of my voice seemed to snap him from his drunken stupor, and he lunged for me, trying to get a punch in. We were tucked under the house's awning, the cameras set up a few meters away, right in front of the window, but no one was getting close to us. Maybe my father's security detail was holding them off, possibly bribing them to deter them for a few more minutes. "Calm down, old man. You are going to hurt yourself." I couldn't help but smile at his reaction, his nostrils flaring at my words. His personal security guard was standing to the side, his back to me and facing the street. I could see the slight shake in his head, like he disapproved of this too.

"Leave before you embarrass yourself."

"You are ruining your mother's life. Is that what you want?"

"Oh, please, Eugenio. Like I don't know I'm the biggest mistake she ever made." At that, he sobered up. "But honestly, I don't know what you are talking about. I'm not the leak," I added calmly.

"It's that whore! She's been out for revenge ever since that child died."

"What did you just say?" My voice sounded incredulous to me, taking a high pitch I didn't recognize from myself. "Eugenio, I swear to god." I sighed, trying to control my temper. It was about to get explosive here, just like one of the many fights I'd witnessed as a child. I clenched my fists, tucking my hands into my pockets.

It was a weird feeling, this heavy, sinking thing in my body. Like this was the absolute end of this relationship. There was no saving it, not for my benefit or for the benefit of anyone else. He was ruthless, and he didn't care who went down with him.

"She is the closest thing to a mother I've had. Don't you dare talk about her like that," I said through clenched teeth, my heart beating fast inside my chest. I wanted to punch him square in the face, to see that motherfucker lying on the ground, wailing in pain. But the press was here, and I had to protect Florencia, so I brushed past him.

As soon as my arm brushed his shoulder, his hand closed around my wrist, tugging me back into him, his breath on my face, the stench nauseating. "This is how you speak to me after all I've done for you, boy?"

I closed my eyes, then snapped them to his, so similar to mine. "I never asked for anything from you. I just wanted to be normal, and you paraded me around like I was a little prop," I spat. "Please, Eugenio, don't be delusional thinking that who I am today has anything to do with you." I tugged my arm, trying to get rid of his hold, but he tightened his grip. For an older man who was significantly impaired, he was strong. He wasn't above physical violence. I had witnessed it many times. "The only thing you ever did right for me was Jazmín."

And at those words, he threw a punch, barely missing my face and stumbling towards me. I used the momentum to push him back, and he grunted as soon as his back hit the brick of the house, his face transforming with pain and surprise when his head bounced off of the wall.

The press seemed to pick that exact moment to finally break through, and the cameras flashed brighter, capturing the dramatic scene. My forearm was pressed against his throat to keep him in place, my face mere inches from his. His jaw was pulsing with fury, but he was too stunned to speak. Reporters shouted questions, trying to make sense of the unfolding drama.

"Francisco," someone said behind me, a soft hand tugging at the back of my shirt. "He's not worth it." Florencia was looking between me and my father, a pained expression on her face.

I blinked, suddenly realizing the scene we were causing. I took a step back, attempting to create some distance between us. Maybe the cameras hadn't caught all of it and we could still figure it out, although I was certain this was the final nail in the coffin.

Pain throbbed through my face. "You just ruined any chance you had left," he sneered, his eyes full of pity towards me, like he had been doing me favors all these years. I let my father go, and he took a deep breath. He turned on his heel, looking down towards the ground and walking to his car. The reporters continued their barrage of questions, capturing every nuance of the broken relationship playing out before them.

"I'm done with you, Eugenio," I said, my voice cutting through the chaos. "I will not hold back if you ever come near me again."

"Francisco," Lorena said from inside the house. She was clutching her closed laptop with both hands, and her long hair was up at the crown of her head, held by a pen. "Your mother just filed for divorce."

"She's the leak," I said. The realization finally hit me.

34

LUCÍA

THE NEWS of Francisco's family's downfall hit me like a train straight into the chest. I was sitting at the kitchen table in Valentina's house when my phone started buzzing with a few text messages from the staff at the hospital. Of course they knew who that family was. We were intimately familiar with their dynamics, toxic as they had been.

The headlines screamed of scandal. It was bigger than the most recent celebrity hookup, a famous *fútbol* player and a pop princess who had *hard launched* their relationship by climbing into a convertible and driving away into the sunset.

"What is it?" my mother asked, her face full of concern. They had arrived in the city a few days after I had, claiming that they wanted to visit with some friends. But I knew it was Charlie who had tattled, and really, they were here because they wanted to talk to me. They were walking on eggshells around me. She leaned her body towards my phone, her eyes scrolling the screen. "Is that that boy from New Year's?"

"Mm-hmm, sure is," I replied, following the thread with a little more interest now. Francisco's mother had put out a statement to the press saying she was filing for divorce due to irreconcilable differences, but the press was catching on quick—her husband had lost his power in politics, and she wanted out. And I believed it.

And Francisco had been on repeat on the news cycles.

The images of the fight with his father outside of that home; the look of disgust on Francisco's face. The constant barrage of videos and photos of his political campaigns, his wife and son standing next to him. Clips of old press conferences or interviews with the media. It was on at all hours of the day, the hottest scandal of the year.

"What a weird coincidence," she said, her gaze bouncing from my phone to her crossword puzzle, her lips pinched in concentration. "Did you know he used to work with Santiago?"

"He is the brother of one of my patients," I said, looking into her eyes and studying her closely. She placed the crossword puzzle on the table and set both her hands on it softly. My father was sitting next to her, glasses perched on the tip of his nose and his eyes scanning the small font of the newspaper. Not the front pages but the classifieds, just for the fun of it. To see what types of things people were selling.

"Really?" Her shoulders sagged slightly, but not in

defeat. It was more like amazement. The gossip was coming out of her, and I smiled at her reaction because you could take the girl away from the small town but never take the small town away from the girl.

"Yeah, my last year of residency."

"*No te puedo creer.*" She really did sound incredulous. Like this was a charming twist of fate. And it was, partially, but it was also full of darkness and grief. A whole lot of drowning.

"Her death is the reason why I went back home."

There. My mother's shoulders sagged in defeat. My father looked up, newspaper discarded on the table. All four eyes were on me.

"Honey—" he said, his voice laced with anguish.

"No, you know what? It's fine," I said. "I'm fine now."

"Why didn't you tell us?" she asked, her tone full of concern. She did this thing when she was worried about us —her hand would automatically go to our faces, cupping our cheeks like when we were children and we scraped our knees while playing outside. I was in my thirties now, and this didn't get old. It did work to soothe the pain. "We've been so worried about you."

"I was embarrassed," I said, nose tingling and tears threatening to fall. "I fought so hard to be a doctor, and I couldn't hack it. But it's fine. I get it now."

"What do you get now?" She twisted her body on her chair, her knees bumping against mine, one hand still cupping my face, the other placed softly on her leg.

"Honey, you can't save them all," my dad added, cutthroat and straight to the point but logical. My mother turned to look at him for a second, and then her gaze was back on me.

My heart dropped. Had I been so transparent with my feelings yet so oblivious to what was going on around me that I hadn't seen it? Silent tears rolled down my cheeks, and I choked back a sob. My mother smiled sadly at me, her eyes shining too.

"I'm so sorry."

"No, please don't say that, *mi amor*," she continued. She looked heartbroken, like the words coming out of my mouth were wounding her. It was such a contrast to the last time I'd seen her, elated out of her mind back in town, her son marrying the love of his life. And in only a few days, I had hurt her so much. "You've been unhappy for such a long time. I wish you had felt you could talk to us."

I wiped away my tears and took a deep breath. "I didn't want to burden you. I thought I could handle it on my own."

She sighed, her thumb gently brushing away a tear that escaped the corner of my eye. "You're never a burden to us."

I nodded, grateful for their understanding. It felt so good, finally having said those words out loud. "Thank you."

"Lu." I turned my body towards the window. Sonia was peeking the upper half of her body from the door to the nurses' lounge, a wild smile on her face and her eyes doubled in size with mischief. "Come here."

I blinked at her, logging off of the computer and walking in her direction. I was sure I looked confused, my brow furrowed and my gaze narrowed in suspicion. If she was smiling like that, it couldn't be wholesome.

There were a few nurses and two doctors huddled around the lounge's TV, watching the screen like it was feeding their soul. I didn't blame them—long hours in the hospital and dealing with such complex cases made you cherish every drop of information from *real life*. It was the same in Tres Fuegos.

I'd started work the week after I spoke to Dr. Varela, easing into the job and only taking two twelve-hour shifts a week, with the intention of ramping up into a full-time position by the spring. I still had to figure out what to do with the practice back home, but Dr. Martín had agreed to open the office for me a few times a week, and I was going to start looking for a doctor to take over. Maybe a recent grad from the small towns surrounding Tres Fuegos.

"What's going on?" I asked, my teeth trapping my lower lip. Sonia tipped her head over in the direction of the TV, the image becoming clearer with every step I took. Francisco was on the screen, smiling sadly and having a conversation with someone I didn't recognize. I snapped my eyes to Sonia, and she nodded, stepping to the side so I could get closer. One of the nurses was shushing the rest of us, as if we were in a movie theater instead of a hospital lounge.

"He's doing a live interview," Sonia whispered, her excitement barely contained. "Just watch."

I focused on the screen, and Francisco's voice filled the room. The reporter was asking him about what had happened outside that house the other night. I'd seen the pictures—they were calling it the Gómez Downfall. His responses were measured, thoughtful, and surprisingly sincere.

"I understand that people are curious about my family's situation," Francisco said, his face conveying a mix of sadness and resilience. Or at least that was what I thought. Not exactly the man I thought I knew but the most recent iteration, the one dragged down by his own grief. Real, raw. My favorite version yet. "But I want to make it clear that this is a very personal matter. It's painful, and it's something we've been dealing with privately for over three years."

The nurses in the room exchanged glances, and Sonia nudged me, her eyes wide with admiration. Francisco's composure under the scrutiny of the public eye was impressive. It was that switch he turned on, the one that screamed politician. It was probably the same thing his father saw in him, grooming him to follow in his steps. The interview continued, with the reporter trying to dig deeper into the details of the scandal.

His jaw ticked. He looked annoyed at the million and one questions the woman was spewing, his eyes burning with a fire that I didn't recognize.

"Oh shit," she said. I had zoned out, focused more on the

sad man on the TV rather than on what he was saying. "She brought up Jazmín."

"How do they even know?" I asked. Sonia shrugged, then turned back to the TV. Someone found the remote and turned the volume up, his voice clear through the speakers.

"Yes, she was my sister." Confirmed. "But you'll have to discuss it with Eugenio because I obviously don't know the details," he continued. He swallowed, then glanced to his left, eyeing the reporter cautiously. "I ask that you respect me during this time, that's all."

"Oh my god," I whispered under my breath. The tension in the room escalated as Francisco's admission hung in the air. The nurses exchanged wide-eyed glances, their hushed whispers forming a background hum to the ongoing interview. Sonia gripped my arm, her excitement now replaced with a mix of shock and anticipation.

"The one thing I'm going to say is that he is not the man he claims he is. He's selfish and self-centered, and he used his children as pawns for his own personal gain. I'm glad my mother is able to get out of that relationship, and I wish her well," he added. The reporter opened her mouth but closed it quickly, her hand frozen on her lap, clutching her note-cards tightly.

"Anything else you'd like to add?" she asked, blinking rapidly in his direction.

"We can all agree his career is over."

Mierda.

"Lucía," Sonia whispered, her tight grip on my forearm. She wore a round-eyed expression, still staring at the TV. "*Dios mío,* poor kids."

35

LUCÍA

"Dr. Williams?" Sonia called from outside the attending's office. Her voice was soft and hushed. Patients were already sleeping right across from where I sat, looking at patient files. The bright screen was hurting my vision. It had been a grueling shift, dealing with two new intakes from the emergency department during the first few hours. We were finally settled, and everything was under control. "There's a Francisco Gómez Alcorta here to see you."

She waited for me to look away from my computer, then smiled and winked, moving to the side to let Francisco stand in the doorway. My heart threatened to jump out of my body at the sight of him.

Late last week, Sonia and I had scoured the patient files to see if we could find a note somewhere with Francisco's phone number. It was hidden deep in one of the doctor's notes from Jazmín's first chemotherapy session, probably when she was in her early teens. So Sonia texted him and asked him to come to the hospital. Maybe she had told him I was back or that we found some of Jazmín's personal effects, but whatever it was, it had worked. I'd been on the lookout for days to see if, ever, he would come back. Like he promised the last time I saw him.

I smiled at him, and his face softened in a way that made my whole body go warm, the color reaching my cheeks. I had never been so happy for the darkness.

"Were you expecting me?" His voice was laced with uncertainty, despite his body saying otherwise. His hands clenched. *Open, close. Open, close.* I stood from my seat, the chair rolling with the movement and hitting something behind me with a thud. He looked like shit, almost like that day he showed up in the pouring rain with a fever and helped me look for the cat. His eyes were sunken, deep purple rings around them. The scruff on his jaw was proof that the past few weeks had been a shitstorm for him and his family.

I took a deep breath and smiled, taking a tentative step towards him. My body was itching to touch him, to feel the beat of his heart against my ear once again.

"Hi." It came out shy, like the first time we'd met each other years ago in this same hospital. "How are you?"

There was apprehension all over that handsome face. He rapped the fingers on one hand against his thigh in a loose pattern. *Tap, tap tap, tap.* But then he smiled, one of those smiles he saved for me. The smile that had said *fuck yes* when he told me he would be coming back to Tres Fuegos after figuring his things out. The smile that made him look elated. Like nothing else mattered.

Because nothing else mattered.

"Thank you for coming," I said. Francisco tipped his head towards one side, then walked into the office, his hand curling around the edge of the door and leaning there. Stopping himself. He rocked slightly on his feet and tucked his free hand in his pocket.

"Sure," he replied, his gaze studying my face for a moment, then darting to the pager on the desk. "You need to get that?" he asked, scrunching his nose at the interruption.

"No, that's fine." It was probably the lab letting us know results were back and we could call them to confirm our diagnosis. "It's not urgent."

"Okay." He nodded, moving his head up and down a hundred times, it seemed, an endless stream of acknowledgement.

"I forg—"

"How have—"

We spoke at the same time, interrupting each other in a clumsy dance of words. I couldn't help but chuckle, breaking the tension that lingered in the room. Francisco's eyes lit up at the sound, and I saw a glimmer of the familiar warmth that we used to share. Before the storm.

"You go first," he said, a playful smile tugging at the corners of his lips.

"Okay." I took a deep breath and tucked my right hand

inside my coat pocket, rummaging to get out what I needed. "I forgot to give you something."

His face crinkled up in a smile so big that it blinded me in the dimly lit room. He rolled his lips, trying to contain his laughter. I took out the tongue depressor from my pocket and handed it to him. His hand stretched out towards me, and I placed it in the center of his palm.

He erupted in laughter, filling the room with a warmth that transcended the years we'd spent apart. It was such a simple moment, something that belonged uniquely to us, and it cracked my heart into a million pieces.

"Lucía," he finally said, the remainder of a smile still in his eyes. The weight of unspoken words hung in the air. My name on his lips punched a hole straight through my heart, and my first instinct was to reach for him. To pull him into my chest. To keep him there, tight against my body in a silent dance. "You are enough."

Francisco's words lingered in the room, and for a moment, time seemed to pause. No beeping machines, no buzzing pager, no murmuring staff. We stood there, facing each other, the silence saying everything that needed to be said. My words repeated back to me, cracking me wide open.

"You are more than enough," he continued. "You might be way too good for me," he said with a sad smile, his lids pinching tight at the confession.

"Three years," I said. "I need you to wait for me for three years."

"No." For a single second, I thought this conversation

might not go the way I needed it to go. But then he opened his eyes and looked at me, a storm raging on his face. "I'm not waiting."

"Okay."

He threw his body at me, wrapping his arms around my shoulders and using one of his hands to untuck my long ponytail from his hold. "I'm not waiting. Do you understand?" *We've lost enough time already*, I wanted his words to say.

And the tears started. My brain wasn't moving fast enough. It wasn't computing what he was saying. But the tears were real, streaming down my face in a mix of joy, relief, and a lingering sadness that this conversation had been three years in the making.

"Lucía," he whispered against my hair. "I love you." His fingers gently traced the lines of my back, and for a moment, the weight of the past lifted, leaving room for a future that was ours to shape. "*Linda.*" The edges of his voice were covered in desperation. "Say something."

"I love you too," I managed to choke out. A heart-wrenching sob wracked my chest and echoed around us in the small room. "I'm a mess."

"You're a mess that I want." He chuckled, but his amusement died quickly once he looked into my eyes. And at that moment, I wanted to kiss him. So badly, to make up for the lost time, for the moments I'd replayed in my head, for the what-ifs.

A second later, his mouth was on mine, splitting me at

the seams. My heart picked up its pace, thrashing around my chest wildly. Highly inappropriate for my workplace. And it was more than just a kiss; it was a promise.

"Why three years?" he asked against my mouth, a smile forming on my lips in response. He moved back, giving me soft, fleeting kisses on my cheeks, on my jaw, down my throat. His hold was still tight around my body, like if either of us let go for even a fraction of a second, we would evaporate into thin air.

The moment gone.

"I'm going to apply for the pediatric oncology fellowship," I said, a little bit of pride in my words. I had spent the past few weeks trying to play catch-up to the unique flow of the hospital and working with a team instead of by myself. But I was rusty and not confident enough. Therapy was helping, and even after a few sessions, I already felt like I had a better handle on everything. I felt lighter. "And it's a three-year program."

"You're not going back to Tres Fuegos?" He looked confused, his eyebrows scrunched and a wrinkle between them, smack dab in the middle of his forehead.

"No." I laughed. "That town was drowning me. This is a better fit."

He took me in for a moment, then rested his forehead on mine, taking a deep breath. "I'm so fucking proud of you," he added. Francisco's exhale was heavy, like a weight had been lifted off his shoulders too.

I grinned at him, feeling a surge of confidence. "I love you."

He chuckled, a low and soothing sound that resonated in the small office. "This is a better fit, I agree."

My hands found his hair, nails digging into his scalp and scratching lightly. He groaned, the sound so familiar to me.

"I want to be with you," he said, his voice sincere but tinged with a hint of uncertainty. I placed my palm over his heart, the pitter-patter vibrating against my skin. "I come with baggage. My family, especially."

"I know," I whispered. "I'm so sorry about what happened."

I cupped his face in my hands, my thumbs gently brushing away the worries etched on his forehead. He leaned into my touch, his eyes searching mine for reassurance. "And what do you want?"

"This," I said. "Baggage and all."

A warmth spread through his features, evident even in the dim room, the darkness no longer an issue. He pulled me against his body, and we stood there, wrapped in each other's arms until the world outside faded away.

And in the end, the things that we had were the things we needed the most.

An "I love you" said at the right time.

The silly, made-up excuses to see each other again.

Lasting silences that were not uncomfortable.

That smell that took you back to before.

The first kiss that said it all.

EPILOGUE
FRANCISCO

"Hɪ, ʙᴀʙʏ," I rasped at her ear and squeezed her bicep, that one silent signal we'd been using for years.

"Oh fuck," she said, placing her palm over her heart. "You scared me."

I chuckled. Her hair was down today, the blonde shining with the daylight streaming in through the big hospital windows. "You knew I was coming to get you." I smiled into her neck, placing a small kiss where it met her shoulder, right over her new bright white coat. She shivered at the contact, squeezing her eyes shut.

"What's wrong?" I asked immediately, my voice cracking towards the end of the question.

"Nothing." She sighed. "It was a long shift."

She was on the verge of finishing her fellowship. She had

spent the past three years roaming the hallways of this hospital, treating all sorts of patients. She was exhausted. But happy. Like I'd never seen her before, even back then, before Jazmín.

"Ready?" I asked, the small package crinkling in my hands behind my back. We were standing in the hallway, Lucía looking at a screen on a rolling cart, probably adding the last few things to her patients' charts before we took off for vacation.

She turned on her heel and eyed me suspiciously, the noise making her peek her head around my shoulder and straight to my hands. "Yeah." Lucía logged off her computer and opened the cabinet under the machine, grabbing her purse out and beaming at me. "Ready."

———

The familiar sights of Tres Fuegos passed by the car windows as we drove into town, heading directly to the big house. The sun dipped lower in the sky, casting a warm golden hue over the quaint houses and tree-lined streets. The comfort of familiarity clashed with the nervous anticipation building within me.

We hadn't been back to visit her family since the year before, instead opting to host her brothers and parents back in the city for the holidays. As we approached the familiar driveway, memories flooded back—of those rowdy family gatherings that had once made me feel so lonely, of the shared laughter and camaraderie between her siblings, of the strong smell of the flowers that wafted through the air. The big house stood tall, its windows gleaming against the setting sun.

Lucía's hand found its way to mine, fingers intertwining in a comforting gesture. I glanced at her, a mixture of excitement and nervousness on her face.

"Wait," I said, stopping halfway up the driveway. She turned to face me, a big smile on her face. She could read me perfectly, and I couldn't help but chuckle.

"Did you forget to give me something?" she asked, her lips flattening in amusement. She was biting her cheeks to hold in her laughter, but her eyes screamed joy. She took a step towards me and draped her arms around my shoulders, scratching the back of my neck. "I already told you those things are disposable," she whispered in my ear.

"No, that's not it at all." I shrugged. I blinked a few times and inhaled deeply, allowing the scent of those summer flowers to fill my lungs. When I focused back on her, Lucía was studying me curiously.

"Shit, are you okay?" she asked, concern lacing her voice. She took a step back, and her eyes roamed my body from head to toe, looking for something, anything wrong. I barked a laugh.

"No, *linda*, I'm fine." She visibly relaxed, her features going back to that joy she carried with her recently, like she was on top of the world. I took a moment to collect myself, the small package now hidden inside my pants pocket. "I'm more than okay," I said, a mischievous grin playing on my lips. "But I do have something for you."

She giggled. My favorite sound. And the way she was looking at me made my chest tighten. Her eyes were bright and pinched at the corners, the blue darker than normal.

"You said three years."

She nodded, and a smile stretched across her face. I pulled the tongue depressor from my pocket and laughed.

"I forgot to give you this," I said.

"*¡Qué tarado!*" she huffed and then rolled her eyes at me once more, tugging me against her body and kissing me deeply, intently. Like we'd done three years before that in that same spot. My hands found hers, and I pulled her towards the house. Her family was waiting for us inside, ready to celebrate her accomplishments.

"Wait," she whispered, her voice barely audible over the sounds of the birds and the wind. "*I forgot to give you something.*"

A chuckle rumbled from the base of my chest and vibrated with amusement. She reached into her bag, rummaging for a moment before taking out a small square of paper, a little wrinkled in the center and one of the edges curled up towards the middle.

I blinked, waiting for her words. One side of her mouth tipped up, a sly smile barely there.

"I'm pregnant."

I let go of her hands and took a step back, watching her

like my life depended on her. And if those words she just uttered were true, then it just might.

"*¿Qué?*" I heard her just fine. "How?" Nope, that wasn't the right question.

She laughed, a hearty laugh that was soft and wonderful and everything I ever wanted. Full of hope and excitement. Full of joy.

"When did you find out?" She was still holding out the ultrasound in my direction, but my hands were shaking so much, I couldn't even attempt moving them from their spot.

"Just this morning." Her eyes were shining with unshed tears, the smile on her face so big I could barely discern their blue color.

"Oh my god." I was crying. Tears streamed down my face. I kneeled in front of her and grabbed her by the waist, dragging her body to me and resting my forehead on her stomach. Mine. *Mine, mine, mine.* Finally mine.

Forever.

FIN

If you liked this book, please consider leaving a review. Support from readers like you really help indie authors like me get our work out in front of more readers, and it would mean the world.

ALSO BY MARIA RIGOU

ACKNOWLEDGMENTS

I've always believed that writing (or any creative process, really) was a very solitary endeavor because you spend a lot of time alone with your thoughts trying to bring words to paper. However, this time around it hasn't felt that way at all.

To my family: sorry I was checked out for a minute and thank you for giving me the space and time to write these stories. To my daughters: thank you for always being in awe of me. It sometimes does feel surreal to me, too, that I wrote two books!

Baddies: thank you for the late night texts and for being there, always. It feels like we've known each other for years but it's only been a few months.

Katie and Bobbi: thank you for your keen insight, invaluable feedback and endless patience. This story is much, much stronger because of you.

Paula: your presence and understanding have been a lifeline since I started writing this book. It really looks the way it does because of the endless conversations we've had. Almost ad nauseam, really.

Lau and Kari: even just asking about the book has encouraged me to keep going. Thank you.

Milagros: I asked you a million questions and you answered a million and one. Just know that I took some creative liberties... and I did it for the plot. And thank you, thank you, thank you.

To my beta readers: thank you for your time, enthusiasm and constructive criticism.

And to my readers and the online book community: thank you for embracing my stories and characters and for giving them a space in your hearts and minds.

Maria

ABOUT THE AUTHOR

Maria Rigou US-based author hailing from Argentina. She infuses her stories with the vibrant spirit of her heritage while exploring the complexities of love and relationships.

She lives in South Florida with her husband and two daughters and loves to read.

Before the Storm is her second book.

———

CONNECT ONLINE

www.mariarigou.com

@mariarigouauthor

9 798988 205715